"Xylo, watch your back. You've noticed, right?"

PATAUSCHE KIVIA

XYLO FORBARTZ

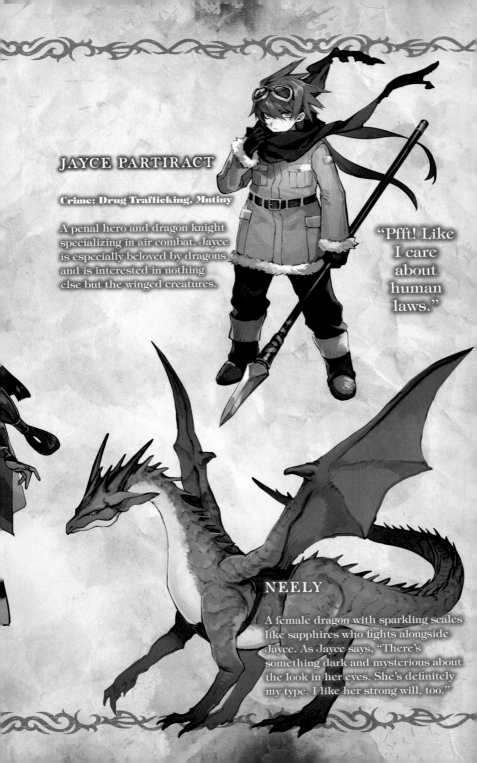

# JAYCE PARTIRACT

**Crime: Drug Trafficking, Mutiny**

A penal hero and dragon knight specializing in air combat. Jayce is especially beloved by dragons and is interested in nothing else but the winged creatures.

"Pfft! Like I care about human laws."

# NEELY

A female dragon with sparkling scales like sapphires who fights alongside Jayce. As Jayce says, "There's something dark and mysterious about the look in her eyes. She's definitely my type. I like her strong will, too."

"They had this ritual where they would kidnap children and offer them to the goddesses. Well, that one—"

TSAV

TEORITTA

I couldn't lock Teoritta away in the barracks like a sheltered princess, not this time. I had to uncover who was after her life and capture every last one of them. Those were our orders from Galtuile.

Although Kivia hadn't said it in so many words, Teoritta was being used as bait to lure the enemy out

> "Let us join hands and work together for the happiness of all mankind."

# RHYNO

**Crime: None**

An eccentric individual who committed no crimes but instead volunteered himself to become a penal hero. Although he speaks like a man of virtue, there is something fishy about him. He is also an extraordinarily skilled artilleryman and wears a suit of armor engraved with sacred seals into battle.

> "Do not do anything to jeopardize my work."

# FRENCI MASTIBOLT

Daughter of the leader of the Southern Night-Gaunts and Xylo's fiancée before he became a penal hero. She has a sharp tongue despite her blank, masklike expression, and she refuses to break off her engagement with Xylo.

# SENTENCED TO BE A HERO

## II

### The Prison Records of Penal Hero Unit 9004

**Rocket Shokai**

Illustration by MEPHISTO

YEN ON

NEW YORK

Rocket Shokai

Illustration by MEPHISTO

Translation by Matt Rutsohn
Cover art by MEPHISTO

YUSHAKEI NI SHOSU CHOBATSU YUSHA 9004TAI KEIMU KIROKU Vol.2
©Rocket Shokai 2022
First published in Japan in 2022 by KADOKAWA CORPORATION, Tokyo.
English translation rights arranged with KADOKAWA CORPORATION, Tokyo, through TUTTLE-MORI AGENCY, INC., Tokyo.

English translation © 2023 by Yen Press, LLC

Yen On
150 West 30th Street, 19th Floor
New York, NY 10001

Visit us at yenpress.com • facebook.com/yenpress • twitter.com/yenpress
yenpress.tumblr.com • instagram.com/yenpress

First Yen On Edition: December 2023
Edited by Yen On Editorial: Emma McClain
Designed by Yen Press Design: Eddy Mingki

Yen On is an imprint of Yen Press, LLC.
The Yen On name and logo are trademarks of Yen Press, LLC.

The publisher is not responsible for websites (or their content)
that are not owned by the publisher.

Library of Congress Cataloging-in-Publication Data
Names: Shokai, Rocket, author. | MEPHISTO (Illustrator), illustrator. | Rutsohn, Matt, translator.
Title: Sentenced to be a hero / Rocket Shokai ; illustration by MEPHISTO ; translated by Matthew Rutsohn.
Description: First Yen On edition. | New York : Yen On, 2023– | Contents: v. 1–2. The prison records of Penal Hero Unit 9004 —
Identifiers: LCCN 2023015000 | ISBN 9781975368265 (v. 1 ; trade paperback) | ISBN 9781975368289 (v. 2 ; trade paperback)
Subjects: LCGFT: Light novels.
Classification: LCC PZ7.1.S517814 Se 2023 | DDC [Fic]—dc23
LC record available at https://lccn.loc.gov/2023015000

ISBNs: 978-1-9753-6828-9 (paperback)
978-1-9753-6829-6 (ebook)

10 9 8 7 6 5 4 3 2 1

LSC-C

Printed in the United States of America

# CONTENTS

A faint stir rippled through the crowd the moment Dotta Luzulas appeared in court. The confessor and the judiciary committee on the other side of the thin veil were clearly taken aback. *Whatever*, thought Dotta. This was just a place to shame him publicly while proving to the world that he was an idiot.

*It does...kind of bother me, though.*

He unconsciously rubbed at the stub where his left arm used to be. The only thing that remained from the elbow down was the phantom pain that came with its loss. Right now, there was a dragon by his side, which only made it hurt worse. The dragon was a massive lizard-like creature with beautifully vivid green scales, wings, and four legs equipped with powerful claws. It looked no bigger than a horse while crouching, but if it were to stand up on its hind legs, it would be at least three times as tall as Dotta.

His mistake had been to believe the rumor that green dragons were more kindhearted than red ones. He'd learned his lesson. There was no such thing as a gentle dragon.

*I messed up.*

He was filled with regret. Not because he'd committed a crime. No, it was the poor execution and motive that bothered him. *I wasn't stealing for myself. That's why I failed. Why am I like this?* All these thoughts swam through his mind, and they all led to one conclusion.

He had a *fatal lack of patience.*

That was the core trait that had determined his whole life.

The problem was that his skills as a thief were extraordinary. Nobody could catch Dotta. Technically, he had been caught three times in the past, but he always managed to escape... Until now, that is. His luck had finally run out when he was captured a fourth time and locked away in a cell in the castle.

"Defendant Dotta Luzulas," the confessor announced solemnly. "You have been accused of over a thousand crimes."

*That's all?* thought Dotta. He'd stolen a lot more things than that.

"But you are only being charged with one of those today. After being arrested for multiple counts of theft, you escaped from your cell." The confessor paused for a moment before continuing. "And you stole that dragon from the stables."

Dotta was caught completely off guard by the accusation.

*...What?*

This was bizarre. Something didn't add up. Something important was missing. Dotta sat, chained to his chair, and cocked his head in confusion. The dragon was here—that was one piece of evidence. But the other key figure was nowhere to be found—the *real* evidence, what he'd really wanted to steal, was missing. The dragon was just a means of escape. So where was *he*?

"Defendant Dotta Luzulas, explain to me and the committee how you broke out of your cell."

"Oh, I..."

It was simple, really. Dotta had already been in possession of the key to his cell long before he was thrown into the castle prison. At the time, he hadn't had a real reason for stealing it. He figured he could, so he did. That was all there was to it. Dotta, however, was far more concerned with something else right now.

"Wait... Uh... B-before that..." Even he could tell that his voice was cracking. "Where's the child?"

"What are you talking about?"

"Isn't *he* the reason I'm here?"

Dotta spoke as loudly as he could. *That* was supposed to be the crime he'd been arrested for. His one and only failure. As far as Dotta was concerned, failure wasn't determined by method or result. The problem was his motive. Stealing should be done without much thought, for much stupider reasons. That was why he had failed.

"The crown prince!"

A stir swept the judiciary committee, giving Dotta a small sense of satisfaction, though it didn't mean anything.

"He asked me to save him! I'm telling the truth. The crown prince has been locked up in the castle and—"

"Defendant Dotta Luzulas, that is enough. All you need to do is answer the question." The confessor's dignified voice drowned out Dotta's. "And refrain from talking nonsense. The crown prince never said such a thing to you, and he never tried to run away."

"What?"

There was no way the confessor was telling the truth. Dotta most certainly ran into the crown prince while trying to escape from the castle.

From what Dotta had seen, the first prince of the Federated Kingdom had appeared to be around ten years old, and his eyes had been trembling with fear. It was probably the first time Dotta had ever seen someone more afraid than he was. The prince told him he had run away and that he wanted Dotta to save him. He was desperate. He was truly afraid of something, and he was going to do whatever it took to get away. He was even willing to ask an escaped prisoner for help—that was how desperate he was. Deciding to help the kid, however, was where Dotta had messed up.

*I'm such a softy.*

Although he was often misunderstood, Dotta believed that even he had a conscience. There just weren't a lot of people who could draw it out of him. Specifically, he had a soft spot for anyone weaker than he was. Those were the kind of people he would consider helping. He had no desire to do anything for the strong and powerful. The problem was that there were few people in the world weaker than Dotta. The prince had met that key requirement, if only barely.

*My motive was impure*, he thought. *It was a result of my own weakness.*

*But...being told it didn't happen really pisses me off. The prince needed help. It didn't have to be me who saved him, but someone had to do it.*

He was being ridiculous. How would saying any of this help? His rational side was telling him to keep quiet, that it was pointless to argue. But Dotta had never once let his rational side win, and this time would be no different.

"I...I'm telling the truth," he claimed, his voice hoarse. "It really happened. The prince said that there was something wrong with the royal family, and that he was living as a prisoner."

Dotta tried to stand up from his chair, but was immediately reminded of the chains holding him down.

"He said the king started acting weird a long time ago, and that surely the chancellor—"

"Silence, Dotta Luzulas."

"No! There's something really wrong going on! The royal family—!"

"Silence."

"B-b-but the prince was even willing to ask a guy like me for help! Can you believe that? Normally, someone like him would never come to a petty thief like m-me for help, especially when I'd just escaped from p-prison. I—"

All of a sudden, a guard covered Dotta's mouth from behind. A gag was pressed to his face.

"I-it doesn't have to be me! Send anyone! Just save the prince! Th-this is insane!"

But his words were muffled as the gag was stuffed into his mouth. The judiciary committee seemed taken aback, but once the confessor rang the bell in his hand, the room fell silent.

"It appears the trial cannot go on," he said.

Not a soul objected. That meant all of this had already been decided.

"The prosecutors are demanding the death penalty… However…"

The confessor seemed to hesitate. It was hard to see his face on the other side of the veil, but he appeared puzzled. He kept looking back at a scrap of paper in his hand.

"Confessor."

One of the members of the judiciary committee suddenly spoke. His voice was calm but carried strangely well.

"I believe the death penalty is reasonable. We cannot reduce his sentence, no matter what the circumstances may be."

"…Yes. But in the case of this defendant…I must impose an even harsher sentence."

"By whose orders?"

"This proposal was sent by the Central Noble Alliance and signed with the king's seal."

Dotta had no idea what was going on. All he could figure out was that he was to meet with a fate worse than death. All he could think about was how badly he had failed—it was almost physically painful. If only he could be given a second chance, he would surely manage to steal the prince as well. He'd have to be more casual, more detached. He couldn't let his excitement or his nerves get the better of him. Otherwise, he wouldn't have the patience.

*Dammit! That's right—I'm upset because I failed.*

He needed to do this for himself, not for the prince. No matter what happened, even if the prince refused to go, even if he died and Dotta had to take his corpse, he was going to steal the prince and get him out of that castle. It was all Dotta could think about.

"Dotta Luzulas, for the crime of trying to steal a dragon belonging to the royal family, in addition to the other thousand counts of theft and your fallacious slander directed at the royal family, I hereby sentence you to a fate far worse than death," declared the confessor.

"I hereby sentence you to be a hero."

I needed two full days to recover from the injuries I sustained during the battle at Mureed Fortress, but it gave me a lot of time to read. It was the first time I had gotten to relax in what felt like forever.

Altoyard Comette's poems were truly something. Despite him being hopelessly inebriated, the way he chose his words was always so graceful, and at times stirring. He was a master in the expressions and wordplay of the ancient kingdom.

Of course, things weren't always quiet while I was healing. Teoritta, for starters, brought a zigg board over *twice*. I could tell she really wanted to play, but she gave up once she realized I didn't even have the strength to sit.

"I suppose we will have to play some other time, my knight," she said, shaking her head with clear disappointment. "It is quite a shame, though. I figured you would be bored out of your mind, so I brought the game and pieces all the way here."

"Yeah, sorry about that."

"Hurry up and heal your body."

With that single merciful order, she settled down and spent most of the day reading by my side. She had a book of poems she must have borrowed from the military's recreation room. Perhaps she was simply copying me. Did she even understand the contents? I caught her frequently dozing off.

Teoritta seemed to be staying at the same hospital as me for protection…which meant that at least a few other members of my unit were likely here as well. Dotta, Tsav, and Jayce, the last of whom had been ordered back from the western front, each paid me a visit while I was awake.

Jayce Partiract was a dragon knight, and his job was exactly how it sounded. There were only about three hundred dragon knights in the Federated Kingdom, each operating as an independent unit. Their dragons were massive, winged, lizard-like creatures that could breathe fire. They fought bravely against the enemy, and were said to be just as intelligent as a horse, if not even smarter. For those reasons, dragons were raised by the military from a young age to be ridden in battle. As far back as you could imagine, people had been using animals other than horses in battle. From elephants to camels and cockatrices, man had tried them all before settling on the ultimate beast: the dragon.

"Heard you did some damage to the Blight, Xylo," said Jayce with a cold glare the instant he walked into the room. He stood out with his heavy winter clothing and bright blue scarf. Teoritta, book in hand, stared at him in surprise.

"Oh… You haven't met him yet, have you? That's Jayce," I explained to Teoritta. "I told you about him. Remember? Our unit's dragon knight."

He was a man of small stature with a similar build to Dotta's, but he was oddly intimidating. It was probably the fact he had a dragon, and his unique scent of fodder and herbs. Anyone nearby could smell him.

"Don't let it get to your head, though," continued Jayce, completely ignoring me and my introductions.

"You may have taken out three demon lords, but what happened at Couveunge Forest was eighty percent thanks to Dotta, and you had Norgalle and Tatsuya to help you in the tunnels."

I had a lot to say about the incident with Dotta, but I decided to swallow my pride, since arguing would just be a waste of time. I kept my mouth shut instead.

"Iblis—well, I guess I can give you that one. That's it, though."

Jayce then pointed at himself with his thumb.

"I killed two," he said with a little smirk. That was quite an accomplishment, to be honest. An extremely impressive achievement.

"Seriously?"

I found myself skeptical of his claim, though. Pointlessly showing off, bragging, and bluffing was common behavior between the two of us.

"Did Rhyno not do any work?"

"He ignored orders again, so he'll be locked up for a while."

"A penal hero in solitary confinement, huh. Wow."

It wasn't very common to throw a hero into a cell, since their punishment was supposed to be suffering on the battlefield, only to die and be resurrected to repeat the process. Being locked away in a private cell would give you a safe environment where you could enjoy some alone time. Plus, it was difficult for heroes to ignore orders in the first place, since we had sacred seals on our necks that limited what we could do.

"The guy's a weirdo, though, so I guess it's not surprising." That was the only reason I could come up with. "Anyway, so you're saying *you* took out those two demon lords, then? I better not find out you're lying later."

"Go check for yourself," Jayce said, snorting. "I win again, Xylo. Looks like you're not as hot as you thought you were."

"S-stop right there!" said an anxious voice.

Teoritta promptly got up and stood between Jayce and me, straightening her back proudly and meeting Jayce's sharp gaze.

"Xylo is my knight, and I will not allow you to look down on him!"

"Oh. So you're the goddess, huh?" He briefly glanced at Teoritta as if he wasn't interested, then shifted his gaze back to me. "I heard Dotta found her. Seems like she's really helping you out. It must be nice having a child protect you from all the big, scary monsters out there."

"Wh-what insolence!" Teoritta cried. "I have never felt such disrespect! Xylo, are you going to let him speak to us like this?!"

"Just drop it, Teoritta. Getting mad won't change anything."

I patted her on the shoulder and sat her back down before she exploded with rage. Getting angry was pointless when you were up against Jayce.

"Dotta didn't...find her. He stole her from the Holy Knights."

"Hardly makes a difference."

"It makes a huge difference. It's a serious crime."

"Pfft! Like I care about human laws."

This statement encapsulated everything you needed to know about Jayce.

He was assigned to the penal hero unit for drug trafficking and mutiny. His first crime, drug trafficking, was simple. From what I'd heard, he used to cultivate plants meant to promote health in dragons. It just so happened they could also be used as narcotics for humans.

The second crime he committed...was pretty simple, too. Apparently, he'd revolted against the military in an attempt to free its dragons. If any ordinary person had done this, it would've only amounted to a reckless stunt and would have ended in a matter of hours. Once the troops got there, the revolt would be immediately crushed.

However, there were two problems in Jayce's case. The first was that Jayce was a powerful noble. That made the incident an unbelievably huge deal. The second was how much dragons loved him. Every time he walked into the military's dragon stables, the creatures would start making a fuss. Jayce would get seriously pissed off if you said this to his face, but for whatever reason, he was especially popular among the female dragons. As a result, the revolt escalated further than anyone could have imagined. There were even records of him leading the dragons in a direct attack against the Second Capital. It was a rebellion for the history books. I wouldn't be surprised if they ended up calling it Jayce's Rebellion.

"Anyway, I won the bet." Jayce held out his hand. "I destroyed you

by sheer number of kills alone. Now, hand it over. I don't have all day...
Neely's gonna be upset if I keep her waiting."

Neely was the name of Jayce's dragon. She was an azure dragon with
sparkling scales like sapphires. "There's something dark and mysterious
about the look in her eyes. She's definitely my type," Jayce once told
me, adding "I like her strong will, too." Having a "type" of dragon didn't
make any sense to me, but whatever. A deal's a deal, as they say, and I'd
lost. I handed him a stack of military notes.

"Say hi to Neely for me," I said, knowing this would put Jayce in a
better mood.

The corners of his mouth curled into a smile, and he left the room.
Teoritta, on the other hand, didn't seem happy at all, but that didn't
matter. For whatever reason, Jayce's behavior didn't upset me. He may
not give a crap about humans, but he was pretty honest, all things
considered.

The guy I had issues with wasn't him—it was Venetim, who showed
up about the time I'd recovered. The pea-brain apparently thought I
was still injured and couldn't move, so when he found me out of bed
and stretching, he froze.

"Xylo, wait. Please." Those were the first words out of his mouth.
"Before you resort to violence, I want you to hear me out, okay?"

"Nope."

I stopped stretching and grabbed Venetim by the lapel. I was going
to give him an earful. He'd lied to me. I specifically told him not to ask
the Mastibolt family for reinforcements when we were defending Mureed
Fortress.

"I hope what you did was worth having your face rearranged!" I
began. Then I paused. "...Or, well..."

I hated to admit it, but Venetim had made the right call. The front
gate wouldn't have lasted as long as it did if the Mastibolt family hadn't
sent two thousand soldiers to our aid. Countless miners would have
surely perished. And that wasn't all Venetim had done, either. If he
hadn't negotiated that deal for us, we wouldn't have had the leeway to

SENTENCED TO BE A HERO, VOLUME II

implement a good plan. I would have been stuck inside the fortress. Venetim might be irritatingly useless once a battle was underway, but beforehand, he was a valuable asset. And that was why...

"Two punches, and we'll call it even. Sound good?"

I swiftly stood and introduced my fist to his stomach and then to his chin. He theatrically fell to the floor, pretending to be in intense pain, really hamming it up. You could see the absolute dread on Teoritta's face. She looked genuinely worried for him.

"Xylo, you mustn't resort to violence!" she said. "He is not only a fellow hero but our friend—"

"It's fine. Trust me. He's still hiding something from us." I grabbed Venetim by the lapel again and stood him up. "You thought I was bedridden, right? That's why you came."

"Wh-what? I have no idea what you're talking about."

Even I could tell he was lying.

"I'm not hiding anything," he continued. "Before you got back, I was approached and asked if I could arrange a meeting with you... I have been doing everything I can to evade and delay, but I don't know how much longer I can make them wait..."

I seriously doubted he was doing anything to help. I tightened my grip on his lapel, surprised by how much I'd recovered.

"Let me guess. The person who wants to see me is Frenci. Frenci Mastibolt."

"Yes, uh... That...is correct... She has been begging to see you. She told me she wouldn't leave until she did, and that if she had to wait another day, she was going to kill me."

"Really? Well, aren't you in luck? You can't die."

"Wait. Who's 'Frenci'?" Teoritta tugged at my sleeve, looking up at me curiously. "How does she know you?"

"She was my fiancée."

Teoritta made a face that I could only describe as *disturbed*. Her right eye opened wide while her left narrowed. Suspicion and surprise swirled together in her expression.

"What did you say? Y-y-your fiancée? My knight's fiancée...?!"

"That was a long time ago. We're not engaged anymore."

It was depressing to remember, even now. The Forbartz family had been decimated by the Demon Blight. I was the only surviving member, and the Mastibolt family had taken me in and raised me. For the survival of my family line, I'd had no choice but to agree to an engagement with Frenci Mastibolt. Her cold, empty glare flashed through my mind. I had a good idea of what she was going to say when she saw me.

"You're a mess, Xylo."

Those were the first words to come out of Frenci Mastibolt's mouth. I'd known she would say that, word for word, and I couldn't help but laugh. Laughing, however, only served to infuriate her further.

"Do you think this is a joke?"

She turned a cold, piercing gaze on me, her face stony. Her dark, bottomless black eyes were the trademark of her clan, the Southern Night-Gaunts.

"I see you haven't changed," she went on. "If anything, you're getting worse. I would have equated you to a fly last time, but now you're a caterpillar, at best. What a disaster."

Frenci looked exactly how you would imagine a woman from the Southern Night-Gaunts would look. She was tall with long limbs and smooth brown skin. Her long, well-kept hair was a dull gray—what people usually described as iron-colored. Legend held that the Night-Gaunts hid their horns under their iron-colored hair, but that was an utter lie. They didn't have horns.

The Night-Gaunts ruled over the southern ravine. Due to the nature of the terrain, their people were split into several smaller clans, which had led to a high degree of technological advancement in warfare. Supposedly, sacred seal technology owed much to their contributions.

But at the same time, their society had grown increasingly insular. Anyone who set foot in their ravine would either be erased from existence or, if they were lucky, be sent back without a limb as a warning to others. Apparently, that was how they came to be known as the Night-Gaunts.

"…What are you doing?" Frenci pointed at the couch on the other side of the room. "Hurry up and have a seat. You're making it look like I'm reprimanding you. Are you slow in the head, or just in the body? Whichever it is, I suppose I'll have to draw up some strategies for improvement."

We were in a room in the barracks set up for receiving visitors, so the furnishings were of rather high quality, especially the couch.

"…I'm not making it *look* like anything." I decided to speak up, since she could keep rambling on like this forever. "You *are* reprimanding me. So shouldn't I stay standing until you finish?"

"I'm doing no such thing," replied Frenci with her usual blank expression, making it impossible to tell whether she was joking or not.

"All I am saying is that as long as you are marrying into my family, then you must act presentable. If you cannot do that, then at the very least, I would like you to show me that you are working to improve yourself. So stop saying that I'm scolding you like some sort of overbearing wife."

"What would you call what you're doing right now, then?"

"I would call it giving you advice because I am expecting my husband to improve."

"I guess we have different definitions of the word, then."

"…I see." A few seconds of silence passed as Frenci seemed to think about this. "Then I will accommodate my husband's culture."

She easily changed her opinion as if it were nothing.

"I shall completely acknowledge your definition in addition to apologizing for my behavior."

She traced a sacred seal in the air with her right hand. It was an apologetic gesture, and she did it with a completely straight face. This was exactly why she was so hard to deal with.

"I made a mistake, and I am extremely sorry for upsetting you. That was not my intention."

"...Then could you stop comparing me to flies and caterpillars while you're at it?"

"Oh. Do the People of the Plains consider such expressions to be insults? I was simply trying to make things easier for you to understand, but it appears as though I have upset you. I will make sure to improve so that it does not happen again."

"In fact, all your advice sounds like you're insulting me. Do you think you could...?"

That was when it hit me. Did my own suggestions for improvement sound like insults, too? The thought alone was exhausting, so I just gave up.

"...Never mind."

"Are you sure? Well, if you say so." Frenci nodded without blinking.

Her expressions were very stiff, a trait common to the Night-Gaunts. It seemed altering one's facial expression was considered rude, and the higher your social rank, the more strictly you were taught to control them.

In addition, it was common for Night-Gaunts to criticize others—or at least that was how it sounded to me. Yet another cultural difference. They seemed to share the baffling opinion that "Good advice should make you uncomfortable, lest you forget it." As a result, even everyday exchanges could sting. I knew this from the years I'd spent growing up with them, but to an outsider, it only contributed to their terrifying reputation.

"...Now, Xylo. Sit." Frenci urged me to take a seat once more. "It's hard to talk when we're both standing."

I patted a dumbfounded Teoritta on the shoulder, then sat on the couch. I hadn't expected the goddess to ask to join us. I knew it wasn't going to be pleasant, and I'd said as much and tried to persuade her not to come, but she kept demanding to tag along and wouldn't take no for an answer. Thanks to that, I'd wound up in a room with a terrible mix of company. Nevertheless, it was probably better than meeting Frenci alone.

"…Interesting." Frenci nodded, observing Teoritta. "So this is the goddess I've been hearing about."

"Yeah. Now, stop glaring at her. You're scaring her."

"H-how rude of you, my knight," protested Teoritta, raising her eyebrows. "I am not afraid. I am a goddess!"

"She's right, and I wasn't glaring at her, either."

Despite what she'd said, Frenci kept her eyes fixed on Teoritta.

"'Frenci Mastibolt,' was it?" Teoritta said, as if to prove she wasn't afraid.

"Yes, Goddess. That is correct."

Frenci's expression didn't change, even when facing a goddess. It was as if she were wearing an expressionless mask while her gaze remained locked on Teoritta. It was hard to tell if she held any respect for the goddess at all. Teoritta hesitated for a moment before straightening up and asking:

"What is your relationship with my knight, Xylo?"

"I told you already," I cut in, exhausted. "She's my ex-fiancée."

"I am not your 'ex' anything," replied Frenci immediately. "Our oath has not been retracted. It remains even now, which means our engagement is still valid, Xylo."

"Stop being ridiculous," I said with a strained smile. "I'm a hero now. There's no way I can get married."

Obviously, heroes didn't have rights like that. Ending one's family line was part of the punishment. Legally, I wasn't even recognized as human anymore, much less a potential marriage partner.

"Exactly! 'Frenci,' was it? This man is both a hero and my knight," boasted Teoritta, puffing out her chest. "It is his duty to treat me with utmost care and shower me with praise for the rest of his life."

This was the first I was hearing of such a duty, but Teoritta sounded very sure of it.

"Therefore," she continued, "while I am sorry to disappoint you, he cannot get married to you any longer!"

"…Xylo, you sure attract the strangest creatures. I was just reminded of how much my father's long-eared armadillo used to love you."

"Oh yeah."

Long-eared armadillos were bizarre creatures that dwelled in the southern ravine. Frenci's father once brought one of the animals home, and it took a strange liking to me, often sneaking into my bed.

"I remember you always kept your distance, though," I said.

"That's because it was an extremely dangerous beast. It scratched me when I tried to pick it up."

"That's because you weren't doing it right. You reached over her head when you tried to pick her up and scared her. And you're always glaring."

"Preposterous. If you want to see a real glare, you ought to look in the mirror. Don't tell me you have already forgotten about that merchant from the West, who—"

"N-not so fast!" cried Teoritta, extending her arms and blocking my vision. "Reminiscing about old times is cheating! Stop being a coward and let me join the conversation! And how dare you blaspheme against a goddess by comparing me to some weird creature!"

"You are being unreasonable. What is so wrong about reminiscing with my fiancé, especially after not having seen him for so long?"

"He is not your fiancé! Holy Knights are not allowed to get married."

"There are Holy Knights who married even after forging a pact with a goddess," observed Frenci.

While it was extremely rare, such things did happen from time to time.

"And as Xylo and I have pledged an oath to each other," she continued, "it is our destiny to wed. This is the law of the Night-Gaunts, and my clan recognizes and accepts our marriage."

"Seriously?" I said.

"Of course. I persuaded them all."

"Are you sure all you did was *persuade* them?"

"Yes. What kind of husband doubts his wife? You must reflect on this shortcoming. You are more thick-skulled than the turtle in our backyard. I shall make a plan to help you improve your personality."

"First of all, you're not even my wife…"

"I will be soon enough," Frenci insisted. "Pay attention. I am working on your pardon, so do not do anything to jeopardize my work. It will take time for the Night-Gaunts to reach a unanimous agreement, so I need you to be on your best behavior until then."

*Sounds like she's up to something crazy.*

I didn't know she was like this until after my sentencing. Though I grew up in the Mastibolt household, I didn't see Frenci all that often, since it was customary for the men and women in the clan to live in separate dwellings. Back then, I only knew her as a little girl with a sharp tongue. I didn't really enjoy our meetings, either, since it took me a while to understand she was only giving "advice."

Regardless, I didn't have a choice—I *had* to break off our engagement. That was what had been decided at my trial. And more importantly, I didn't want to cause any trouble for Frenci's father. He had already done enough for me. He'd taken me in after I lost my family and my family's territory to the Demon Blight. Good people like him were rare. I could see why he served as the clan's peacemaker. That was why I didn't want to cause any trouble and jeopardize his position in the clan. That went for Frenci, as well. She shouldn't have sent those two thousand reinforcements to Mureed Fortress. Sending so many had been a dangerous move, politically. But perhaps Frenci's stubborn attitude regarding our engagement was yet another Night-Gaunt custom. Whatever the case, I didn't want her to put herself or her family at risk.

"Frenci. Listen, I—"

"Oh, I forgot to tell you. I will be stationed in this city for the time being. I will send back most of our forces, but I shall retain my own troops. Do not worry, though. I will come visit you from time to time so that you do not get lonely. At any rate…"

Frenci continued speaking over me, as if she had no interest whatsoever in what I had to say. But then she lowered her voice and uttered a phrase I couldn't ignore.

"…We must continue pursuing the Demon Blight."

"What?" I replied on reflex. Her words had taken me by surprise. "What do you mean?"

"I am not speaking in riddles, so stop asking me pointless questions. You are wasting our time. I am taking measures against the Demon Blight as a lord of the Night-Gaunt clan."

The Night-Gaunt clan was considered an ethnic minority within the Federated Kingdom, but they owned territory under the legal protection of the government, and had been granted positions as nobles. In other words, they were expected to defend their territory themselves.

"We have been facing off against an outbreak of the Demon Blight for the past month… But then, the demon lord suddenly disappeared along with its faeries."

"What do you mean they 'disappeared'?"

"Yet another meaningless question. Do I have to keep repeating myself?"

After ruthlessly reprimanding me, Frenci shifted her gaze toward Teoritta, who immediately tensed up.

"Again, this is not a riddle. They suddenly vanished while we were facing off near town. Demon Blight Number Fifty-Nine—Spriggan…" I could see what appeared to be disgust on her face. It was a rare sight. "It appears it can take the form of a human."

There were monsters with such abilities, but they were rare even among demon lords. Normally, such powerful creatures wouldn't have a reason to disguise themselves as humans, since taking on the guise of a weaker life-form would mean sacrificing their physical advantages in battle.

There were exceptions, though. If a demon lord was highly intelligent, they would understand that hiding among humans could be advantageous at times. Whenever that happened, there were bound to be a lot of civilian casualties.

"It is highly possible the enemy is already among us, so be careful," Frenci continued. "This demon lord has already destroyed a town in our territory."

"…An entire town?" I asked. "How many casualties?"

"Not a single survivor. Everyone either died or turned into a faerie. Spriggan most likely killed one of the townspeople and took their place. By the time anybody noticed, it was too late. We tried to stop it before things got out of hand, but that only led to more casualties. To make matters worse, Spriggan escaped. We must find it and kill it before it's too late."

Just what I needed—yet another depressing event to add to the list of garbage I had to worry about. Would it kill the people around me to bring some good news every once in a while?

"…Xylo," muttered Teoritta, trying her best to swallow her fear.

"Yeah, sounds like a tough one." I tried to sound as casual about it as possible. "But this town'll be fine. We're here after all."

Even I wanted to laugh at the words coming out of my mouth. I didn't know how a bunch of sociopathic, morally bankrupt heroes were going to help, but I decided to say it anyway.

I would have to solve our issues one at a time. I'd start with Tsav. There was something I needed to ask him.

"I suppose that brings our little meeting to an end." Frenci shifted her eyes toward the door. "By the way, who has been eavesdropping on our conversation over there? Am I being investigated for something?"

"…No, it's nothing like that."

The sound of Kivia's voice drifted over from the room's entrance.

"B-by law, it is my duty as supervisor…to make sure there isn't any suspicious activity when a penal hero under my command meets with a visitor," she continued.

So it was Kivia who had been hiding over there this whole time. She really took work seriously. She could have just had one of her men keep an eye on us.

"Very well." Frenci nodded blankly and stood. Her cold, piercing eyes were locked on Kivia. "Now, if you will excuse me… By the way, I suggest you think of a better excuse for next time."

The port city of Ioff was built on the east side of the massive Korio Bay, and developed as a strategic domain for commerce due to its residents' trade with the communities on the West side.

The town was vibrant and bustled with life—it was one of the most developed cities in the kingdom after the First and Second Capital. In the port was a structure known as Tui Jia—meaning Coral Tower— which resembled a red spear and was a keystone of sea defense. Countless colossal ships equipped with sacred seals were docked there and merchant carts went in and out of the area throughout the day.

The city was so important that it was not included in any noble's domain and was instead under the direct control of the Allied Administration Division.

As for tourist spots, its most famous was no doubt its main street, which split the west and east sides of the city right down the middle. Known as the Road of Steel and Salt, it served as a major thoroughfare for countless people and goods, from the era of the old kingdom right up into the present.

That was where Teoritta wanted to go first.

"We *have* to see it." She was very adamant. "Venetim and Dotta told me about it. They said there were street stalls in the west and north selling rare goods, and every day was like the Great Exchange, and you could eat whatever and as much as you wanted!"

"It's only an all-you-can-eat buffet if you're Dotta, and what he does is illegal." I rolled my eyes. "I better not see you grabbing anything you didn't pay for."

I couldn't lock Teoritta away in the barracks like a sheltered princess, not this time. I had to uncover who was after her life and capture every last one of them. Those were our orders from Galtuile.

Although Kivia hadn't said it in so many words, Teoritta was being used as bait to lure the enemy out. There were two reasons why Galtuile would take such a risk. The first was that when planning an attack, the side acting first could decide when and where they would strike, giving them a massive advantage. But if we used a decoy to lure them out, it would narrow down that window significantly. The second reason was it wasn't possible to stay on constant maximum alert. Humans didn't have the mental capacity, and we didn't have the numbers to make up for that deficiency. Ideally, we needed to take the initiative, uncover every last detail of their plan, and strike first.

...At least, that was what Galtuile had stated as their reasoning. I had a feeling about half of it was crap. This was another place where Teoritta's awkward position came into play.

*I'm relieved, though.*

This meant that the higher-ups still had no idea how we'd killed that demon lord. Venetim's painful excuse to cover up for the Holy Sword Teoritta had summoned seemed to have worked, including his explanation of how we'd defeated Iblis.

"There was actually a small core inside that demon lord," he'd said. "And we were able to destroy it with the sheer number of swords Goddess Teoritta summoned."

It was the kind of story a child might come up with. But to an outsider, it would have seemed the most logical explanation.

Galtuile's envoy had been ordered to take back whatever information he could to explain what had happened. With no knowledge of the Holy Sword, this was the only explanation he had. Venetim was good at this kind of thing—rattling off impromptu nonsense that nevertheless satisfied his target's goals and obligations.

As a result, the military now saw Teoritta as a useful resource in battle. Though nothing more…probably. I had a thing or two I wanted to say to the people back at Galtuile, but well, the situation wasn't as bad as it could be.

We had another advantage going for us too: We had gained the cooperation of the Thirteenth Order of the Holy Knights. They didn't seem that thrilled to be working with a bunch of penal heroes, but Kivia took her job seriously, and she seemed to have put a lot of thought into how to position the guards and allot their time. And when Teoritta and I headed out, she insisted on coming with us.

"I will join you on your excursion," she declared. *See? Talk about dedication.* "And should the time come, I will serve as the goddess's shield and sword. You can count on me."

"…Uh. I have Xylo, so I think I will be fine." Teoritta seemed bothered by her offer, however, and tried to turn it down. "My knight and the other heroes should be more than enough to guard me. Wouldn't you agree?"

"Goddess Teoritta, we need to take every precaution we can to keep you safe. Therefore, I will join you."

"…Then would you at least limit your activity to watching from afar?"

"I cannot, Goddess Teoritta. Xylo and I must walk on either side of you so you will not fall victim to an ambush. You may leave everything to us."

I could tell this back-and-forth would keep going unless I cut in, but I didn't have the right to refuse or oppose Kivia's wishes. The only thing I could do was offer her some tactical advice.

"If you're coming with us to town, then you're gonna have to do something about those clothes, Kivia."

I looked over her outfit from top to bottom—she was wearing her usual military uniform, modified for easier movement.

"Wh-what are you staring at?" she asked.

She was covering her chest, but that wasn't the issue here.

"At least wear something that shows you understand the mission. If you're in gauntlets and a breastplate, it's going to be obvious you're with the military. Don't wear your uniform, either, okay?"

"Hmm? O-oh..." Surprisingly, Kivia groaned as if she'd just now realized what the problem was. *'O-oh,' my ass. Get your act together*, I thought.

"...I knew that," she said after a moment. "It's obvious. Your advice was unnecessary."

At any rate, Kivia and her Holy Knights were coming with us. That much was fine. The problem was on our side—which penal heroes to choose for the mission.

There was no way Venetim could guard anyone. He'd just get in the way, and if he had to, he'd use the person we were supposed to protect as a shield. Meanwhile, Dotta couldn't be allowed to roam the streets without being handcuffed. And Norgalle? He wasn't cut out for battle at all. If anything, he'd probably think we were guarding *him*. Tatsuya, of course, was not someone we wanted walking freely around town. If a fight broke out, the thought of protecting civilians wouldn't even cross his mind.

That left Jayce, so I decided to stop by the dragon stables where he was staying.

To say I was taken aback by what I saw would be an understatement. Jayce had dragged Venetim all the way there and was making him help take care of the dragons. Most dragon knights were in the First or Second Capital, but there were apparently six stationed here in Ioff along with their dragons—seven if you included Jayce and Neely. It was a magnificent sight, to say the least.

"What a terrible environment. An absolute dump," said Jayce.

He was busily hammering away and measuring the dragons' heights while Venetim held up a giant wooden board for him.

"Like hell I'm gonna leave my darling Neely in a place like this. Assholes. Frankly, I'd like to rebuild these stables from the ground up.

But since I can't, the least I can do is give the dragons enough space for their tails and to spread their wings."

"Hey, uh...Jayce?" said Venetim. He was holding on to the board, panting and looking like he was about to die. "I can't hold this much longer. Plus, there's not a lot I can do here, and I need to resume my work as commander... So can I go back to my room now?"

"Shut up, conman," said Jayce. "'Commander'? Do you even do anything?"

"Of course I do. I update Galtuile on our situation, join unproductive meetings to discuss strategy—"

"You can do all that later. Hey, who's the strongest in this unit?"

"...You and Neely."

"Then you'd better make sure we're in tip-top condition." Jayce turned and started to rub Neely's chin. "Just a little longer, Neely. I'll have a nice bed ready for you in no time."

Neely, the beautiful azure dragon, softly cooed, and her vivid, sky-blue scales rippled like water. Jayce's lips curled in a faint smirk, as if he could tell what she was saying.

"Hmm? ...No. I was just measuring the other dragons," he said to her. "I wasn't peeking under any of their wings... I wasn't. I promise."

*This is going to take way longer than I have patience for*, I thought. Jayce was off in a world I couldn't comprehend, and there was nothing I could do to move him while he was taking care of the dragons, so I gave up immediately.

All of that happened the day before, and so Kivia and I wound up accompanying Teoritta without Jayce. In his place, however, someone else came along.

"They're seriously the worst."

It was Tsav...who had been rambling on and on ever since we left the barracks.

"They were always doing crazy stuff, too. They'd hold at least one human sacrifice a month. I mean, wow. A secret society of pure evil— that's what they are. Even I feel that way, and they *raised* me. They had this ritual where they would kidnap children and offer them to the goddesses. How much more diabolical can you get?! I mean, come on, right? Have you ever heard of the 'Holy Communion'? Well, that one—"

"Um, excuse me…," growled Kivia when Teoritta started to pale. "Do you never tire of talking?"

"Huh? Oh, don't worry. Just leave it to me! I can talk nonstop from dawn till dusk! I went through special training for it."

In the short time it took to move from the barracks to the main street, Tsav's nonstop, tiresome rambling had already begun to drive Teoritta and Kivia up the wall. I was actually impressed by how little time it had taken him. We'd had no choice but to bring him along, however, and Tsav was one of the best candidates for this particular job.

At any rate, that was how Tsav, Teoritta, Kivia, and I ended up walking down the Road of Steel and Salt in broad daylight together.

"Oh hey!" he said, starting up again. "Bro, you asked about the organization I was in, right? Not about their sinister, cruel rituals but about their military power."

After a maddeningly long-winded introduction, Tsav was finally going to tell us something useful.

"The wicked band of assassins I was part of—oh, they're called Gwen Mohsa. Do you know the origin of the name? In the language of the old kingdom, it means the 'light which purges sin.'"

It was a name I recognized. The group called Gwen Mohsa had gradually gained power as the Demon Blight spread. They were originally part of the Orthodox faction in the Temple, but after their beliefs were officially declared heresy, they went underground. There they became even more militant and reemerged as an independent, radicalized religious organization.

Their doctrine was simple at first—they believed that the purity of the goddesses, the protectors of world order, needed to be maintained. However, that eventually gave rise to an insistence that goddesses shouldn't be used for war. And according to Kivia, they'd recently begun pushing the nonsensical idea that the number of goddesses could not increase or decrease, and vocally opposing Teoritta's existence.

The group had already assassinated key figures in the military and in the Temple for trying to use the goddesses for war—or in the their words, for "sinning and leading people astray." That was how Gwen Mohsa operated.

"And I was one of their elite members!" continued Tsav. "A real top dog! I excelled in every skill, and they called me a child prodigy! I was the future of their organization—the youngest, yet strongest, assassin there ever was!" Tsav repeatedly elbowed me lightly on the arm as he went on and on. "Pretty amazing, huh?"

"That *is* pretty amazing..."

I thought back to Tsav's past. This was a story I'd heard countless times.

"But don't you have a zero percent success rate?" I asked. "You never killed your marks. Just some random, unrelated people."

"Yeah, being nice is my only fault. Man, this reminds me of back when I was in training! Those days were hell. Like, when I was abandoned in the wilderness with only a knife. That was insane. I was attacked by wild animals and colleagues I'd never met before! You know how it is. They didn't let us talk or hang out so we wouldn't get attached to each other."

Tsav proudly patted his chest for some reason.

"And that's why I talk so much now! Isn't my past beyond tragic? I'm thinking about adapting it into a picture play or something. Are you interested in getting in on the act with me, bro?"

I didn't have the energy to answer and instead looked back at Kivia.

"...I didn't want to bring him," I told her, "but we didn't have any other choice, so we'll just have to deal with it."

"He's a real piece of work, for sure..." It appeared that even Kivia had never met anyone like Tsav before. "How can one person talk so much? What kind of training did he undergo to become like this?"

"I don't know the details, but his lung capacity is supposedly super-human. That might be why."

"What an aggravating talent to have."

Kivia placed a hand on her forehead as if she had a headache.

"The enemy isn't going to attack us if we keep standing out this much," she continued. "...And then all the work we did to blend in and look like tourists will go to waste. Don't you agree?"

"Yeah."

I glanced at Kivia's outfit once more: a rustic shirt under a gray cloak, slacks, and a belt with a short sword. *I see what she means.*

"You look good, by the way," I said.

"...?!"

Kivia's eyes went wide, and she quickly cleared her throat.

"Wh-what a cliché way to compliment someone. Did you honestly think a cheap remark like that would make me happy? Next time, you should choose your words more—"

"I wasn't expecting you to disguise yourself as a man. You look like a tough bodyguard, exactly the type I'd expect to be protecting Teoritta. Very natural."

Kivia's chest should have been a little too prominent for such a disguise, but her cloak was doing a good job of hiding it, so you wouldn't really notice unless you were staring at her body from the front. We didn't want the assassins to be too wary of us, but we didn't want it to be obvious that we were waiting for them to strike, either. The goddess was out shopping with three elite bodyguards selected for the occasion. That was what we needed them to think.

"Not bad," I said. "Not bad at all. If this doesn't lure them out, I don't know what will."

"...Just so we're clear. I am *not* disguised as a man!"

Kivia seemed very upset.

"And Xylo," she continued, "make Tsav shut up this instant. We need to do everything, no matter how small, to increase our chances of success."

The way she followed up with a ruthless order only made her mood more obvious.

"All right."

I complied, but I couldn't help feeling this mission would go well, regardless of Kivia's outfit or how obnoxious Tsav was being.

That was because I could feel a presence. For the past few minutes, I'd felt someone's eyes on me. We were being watched and followed. Tsav seemed to feel it, too. He looked back at me with a shameless grin and winked.

Many rare and unusual goods were brought across the Korio Bay from the West. The land route to that region was completely blocked off by mountains, and as a result, it had developed its own unique culture.

When the Federated Kingdom formed and the five royal families unified, the West was the fifth and last to join. It was not originally a monarchy, and chose its chief ruler by election. The country had no name, either, and was called by the name of its region: "Won Daolan," of which "Won" referred to the representative who unified and governed its various tribes. The area was known for producing special kinds of fragrant wood, handicrafts, fabric, and pottery, all of which were striking and especially popular among women and children.

It appeared goddesses were no exception.

"Look, Xylo." Goddess Teoritta eagerly tugged on my sleeve. "I have never seen fabric like that in my life. It does not appear to shine, and yet look at how red it is! I have never seen anything like it! Have you, Xylo?"

She looked up at me, hardly able to contain her excitement. It seemed she wanted to show me all of the rare goods.

"Wouldn't it look wonderful on me?" she continued. "Oh, and that bracelet there, too. What vibrant colors… Hey, what's that? It's shaped like a bird!"

"That's jade," I said. "And jadeite, at that. Some pretty high-quality stuff. That fabric is a well-known product from the West, too."

Nobles wore stuff like this to evening parties. I could still vividly remember the time I went to a royal banquet with Senerva and learned how much jewelry like this cost. My jaw had dropped through the floor.

"You could buy a house for the price of that piece of fabric alone, and if it was tailored into a dress, it'd be worth the same as an entire fortress. We'd be asking for trouble if we brought Dotta here."

"I am not asking you the price, nor am I worried about Dotta right now." Teoritta seemed upset by my commentary. "I simply enjoy looking and using my imagination, and I expect you to understand that as my knight."

"With all due respect, Goddess Teoritta," Kivia cut in, "I believe understanding would be difficult for a man like this."

It seemed Kivia was still pissed off, and she was doing everything she could to avoid eye contact with me. In fact, now that I thought about it, I couldn't remember her ever being in a good mood.

"He lacks imagination," she continued. "So it's only natural that he isn't able to comprehend the beauty of goods such as these."

"Yes, I suppose you are right." Teoritta glared at me as if I were some sort of ill-bred child. "Now, Kivia, if you could show me to a shop where I could find fabrics and jewelry like the ones here…"

"As you wish. I am quite familiar with the trendiest shops in this area… Hold up, Xylo. What are you looking at me like that for?"

"Huh?" I shook my head as Kivia glared at me. "I'm just standing here."

"This city is near my order's post, so I stop by from time to time."

"I didn't say anything."

"Therefore, I know enough about the city to show Goddess Teoritta around, which is more than *you* can offer. In addition, I chose this outfit after considering the nature of our mission. That is why I purposely dressed plainly."

"I'm telling you, I didn't say anything…"

"But that still does not mean that I disguised myself as a man."

She shot a hostile glare my way before picking up her pace and catching up with Teoritta.

As she moved away, she whispered, "Xylo, watch your back. You've noticed, right?"

Apparently, she'd realized we were being followed as well. All I could do was trail behind the two of them.

"Hey, bro. Rough day?" Tsav asked. He sounded utterly carefree. He'd been talking to the merchant at the next stall over this entire time.

From what I'd overheard, Tsav had caught a mouse the other day, and it had a birthmark on its back that looked like a person's face. I believed I even heard him say something like, "You've never seen anything like it, but I can show you if you pay up. Oh, and you're gonna need to treat me to a meal, too." *What an idiot.*

"But at least everything's going according to plan," he said. "They're getting really close now."

"Yeah."

Kivia and I had only one job: to fight on the battlefield. Guarding goddesses from assassins was outside our realm of expertise. Even though we could sense the enemy's presence, we couldn't be sure when or how they would attack. So I decided to ask a professional.

"Tsav, if you were going to kill a goddess here, how would you do it? Would you ambush her in an empty alleyway? Or could you snipe her?"

"Those are my two options? Not a fan of either, to be honest," mumbled Tsav, while munching on a chicken skewer he'd bought from who knows where. "It's not like the order has hundreds of assassins at their disposal. They can send maybe five or six at a time, tops...I think."

"So an empty alleyway wouldn't work, huh?"

"Yeah. The target's a goddess, and she probably has ten or more guards around, so an empty alleyway would be suicide. You'd be outnumbered. No advantage whatsoever."

Just as he'd said, Knights from the Thirteenth Order were positioned all down this road and in the surrounding area. And knowing Kivia, there were probably at least twenty.

"So if you can't get near her, doesn't that just leave sniping?"

"Bro, you can't keep using me, the amazing prodigy Tsav, as your point of reference. Of course, *I* could pull it off, but I still wouldn't risk it."

He looked up. It was a sunny day, but hardly any sunlight reached the ground. The light was blocked by the street stalls' colorful banners and roofs.

"If I couldn't afford to fail, I'd go with a more reliable method," he said.

"Use the crowd to your advantage, huh?"

"Exactly. Blend in and then casually stab her like some random slasher."

There were a lot of people here. Although Kivia was making sure that nobody got near Teoritta, there was a limit to how much a single person could do.

But just when I was thinking of moving closer to the goddess for her protection, she suddenly turned around.

"Xylo!"

She was waving me over to what appeared to be a shop selling metalware like pots, knives, and iron plates.

"I found something that even *you* could appreciate." Teoritta was pointing at a row of knives displayed on a table. "I want you to select a souvenir for me in remembrance of today."

"In remembrance of what exactly?" I chuckled, but Teoritta appeared to be serious.

"The day that Goddess Teoritta blessed this town."

"That's fine and all, but…" I glanced at the shop's knives. They were all finely crafted blades, but they were intended only for cutting small fruit and the like. "Knives are dangerous."

"That is why you are going to teach me. Knives are your specialty, correct? Now choose one."

There was no use arguing with her now, so I began looking them over. Blades from the West were of high quality. Their unique manufacturing process, known as "western tempering," created ripples on the steel and was popular among wealthy collectors. After selecting a knife and exchanging what little military notes I had left for it, I began looking for some straps Teoritta could use in place of a sword belt. Buckskin with a glossy dye would probably be a good match for her.

But right as I was about to pick up a strap, I stopped myself.

"Kivia." I unsheathed the brand-new knife and lifted it up to eye level. "You see that?"

"Yes."

Reflected in the blade's mirror finish were two people slowly approaching us from behind, pushing their way through the crowd. They looked like average citizens doing some shopping, but their hands were hidden under their long sleeves.

"So? Who's gonna guard Teoritta?" I asked.

"You, Xylo," said Kivia. "Don't leave her side."

"Hmm?"

Kivia nodded and Teoritta tilted her head, baffled. A little ways away, Tsav was happily snatching up the last bits of chicken off his skewer with his teeth.

"Teoritta," I said, placing the rope-wrapped handle of the knife in her palm. "Use this to protect yourself if you need to."

Then I started to move as naturally as possible, placing my hands on the puzzled goddess's shoulders to hold her still. Kivia had already unsheathed her weapon. It was a short sword used for thrusting, with a fine blade about as long as her forearm.

"Drop your weapons."

After delivering this single warning, her sword vanished in a flash of light, piercing one of the two men's shoulders. A knife fell from his hand and hit the floor followed by trickling blood. Despite this, he managed to lunge for Teoritta. Immediately, Kivia's blade pierced his thigh, skewering both his legs almost simultaneously. He fell to the ground, shrieking like a bird.

"I warned you," she said.

There was no doubt Kivia was a distinguished swordsman. At the very least, she was far better than someone who half-assed their training like me. She already had the tip of her sword at the man's throat by the time he hit the ground.

"Oops. Sorry, bro," Tsav said awkwardly.

He'd already disposed of the other one. The skewer from Tsav's chicken was now barely sticking out of the man's throat. His left eye was missing as well.

"So, uh...I know I said they'd probably send five or six guys, tops, but..." Tsav was studying my reaction. He had the face of a man who'd just realized he'd made a huge mistake.

"You lied, didn't you?" I said.

"Yeah, you know...I didn't expect the order to get this big. Please don't punish me."

"I'm not gonna do anything to you. And besides, this really isn't the time."

I watched as more suspicious characters emerged from the crowd. There had to be at least ten of them forcing their way through. How many were the Holy Knights managing to hold back? Their numbers were just too big. There must be around fifty assassins. To make matters worse, our little scuffle had caused a stir that was now rippling through the crowd. Someone even began to scream when they saw the dead men on the ground. A few fainted, some ran. Goods were knocked off their displays as chaos ensued. *This isn't good.*

"Xylo!" shouted Kivia as she stabbed another assassin and pulled her sword back out of the corpse. "This way! Change of plans! We're using the alternative route!"

"Roger," I replied, activating my flight seal and kicking another assassin. I hit him so hard in the stomach that he was briefly airborne before hitting the pavement again. I must have obliterated his organs.

"Nice, bro," said Tsav. It was meant to be a compliment, but he sounded a little horrified. "You're relentless. I see you like turning your opponents into mincemeat before killing them... Pretty scary stuff..."

"I didn't kill him, and I didn't turn him into mincemeat, either. I'm not like you," I replied, grabbing a perplexed Teoritta's hand. Her skin felt a little cold, but she glanced up at me with a bold expression, like she was trying to overcome her fear.

"Has it already begun, my knight? Is my vacation…?"

"Sorry, but there's been a change of plans. Wanna go for a little walk down another street?"

I silently wished that this would be the last change of plans we'd have to deal with. But I knew, too, that such wishes were never granted.

The location wasn't ideal, to say the least. There were too many civilians, and to make matters worse, everyone was panicking, so it was hard to move. I had to keep hold of Teoritta's hand.

"Kivia!"

I kicked a barrel forward, bowling over an approaching assassin—or at least someone who looked like one.

"Do something! I can hardly move like this!"

But I wasn't sure she could even hear me.

"We are the Holy Knights!" she called out. "I order all civilians to leave immediately! We are temporarily closing this road!"

Kivia raised a short staff into the air. It roared and emitted a flash of light from its tip. This, too, was a lightning staff, but it was the kind that used most of its power to create a loud sound. You'd have to be right next to your opponent if you wanted to do any damage with it. For the most part, it was employed by city guards as a warning, but it was also used to give commands to soldiers, so all commanders carried one with them.

"Anyone approaching us shall be deemed our enemy!" she declared, demonstrating her intent by thrusting her sword into a man's right arm when he staggered out from the crowd.

"Ugh!"

Pain twisted the man's face, and his knife dropped to the ground, bouncing off the pavement with a *clink*. And yet he still didn't stop.

"I'm telling you to stay back. Did you not hear me?"

Kivia didn't stop, either. Her blade swept at his feet, knocking down the knifeless man before he could lunge at Teoritta.

Her technique was beautiful. It resembled a skill normally used with short spears. Was that a northern sword style? It seemed to focus on thrusting and countering, with a very low stance—the polar opposite of the style I had learned in the south, where you just swung as hard as you could and chopped at your enemy.

"Uh…Ms. Kivia?" Tsav ventured. "Maybe we should, you know, have the townspeople help us?"

*I wish he'd just keep quiet*, I thought. He was slicing the throat of one of the assassins with a blade no bigger than the palm of his hand. He'd probably swiped it from one of the stalls.

"We can use them as shields," he continued. "Oh! Especially small children!"

"Wh-what…? What are you—?" Kivia was outraged.

"We can have Teoritta carry a child on her back to use as a shield until we can get her to safety. I really doubt there's gonna be a sniper, but you never know!"

Tsav was likely serious, but his tone was far too cheerful and flippant. The suggestion alone was enough to anger Kivia, and his attitude only made things worse. There was fire in her piercing eyes.

"Do you have any idea what you're saying, you villain?!" she shouted. "There is no way we would ever do such a thing!"

"What?! Why?! Don't you want to protect the goddess?! You two seemed to be getting along so well!" Tsav shot me a quizzical stare. "Bro, say something to her! How cold can a person be?!"

"Just focus on getting us out of this mess with as little damage to the town as possible, okay?" I led Teoritta by her trembling hand away from the crowded main street. "And no civilian shields. Got it, idiot?"

"Seriously?" groaned Tsav, the color draining from his face. "I mean, for real? There's something really wrong with this. It's not normal…"

He took care of yet another incoming enemy before crushing their head, complaining all the while. His style of hand-to-hand combat was unlike anything I'd ever seen. He would grab some part of his opponent's body, throw them to the ground, and dispose of them in essentially one movement.

*What Tsav is saying does make sense. If you're only thinking about you and yours, that is.*

I thought about this for a moment as I shielded Teoritta's eyes from the fighting. Come to think of it, Norgalle, Rhyno, and I were the only ones in our unit who refused to fight dirty like Tsav was suggesting.

"Xylo, look!" warned Teoritta as another man emerged from an alleyway ahead of us. Although I might have given it a little more thought in another situation, the sword in his hand made it clear he wasn't some stranger who just happened to be in our way.

*Wait a minute…*

What the hell were Kivia's knights doing? There was chaos all up and down the main street that needed to be dealt with. Were they busy dealing with enemies elsewhere? *Dammit.*

"Xylo, if our enemies are human, I…"

There was ill-concealed anxiety escaping Teoritta's voice, but it wasn't fear for herself. I understood that all too well as I held her hand.

"It seems I will not be able to help you, since I cannot attack them."

"Don't worry about it. Let me handle our human enemies."

I lifted Teoritta up in my arms. I could feel sparks lightly prickling the tips of my fingers where they brushed against her hair, and there was no doubt in my mind she could tell how pissed off I was. These damn assassins really knew how to ruin a guy's day.

"Hold on tight, Teoritta. Don't let go of my hand."

"I won't." She nodded gravely. "I will leave everything to you."

That was all I needed to hear.

"Tsav!" I shouted. "Take out the underlings approaching us!"

"Oh, so *I* have to take care of the weaklings?"

"Damn right!"

I kicked off the ground and activated my flight seal. After leaping over the head of the man in our way, I used the seal again and kicked off a wall. Even after landing, I didn't look back. The assassin probably had no idea what to do. Would he chase me? That would mean turning his back to Kivia and Tsav. One of them had probably taken care of him before he could even make a choice. I didn't look back to check who it was, though.

We'd discussed how we would split up beforehand. I had the best mobility and could communicate with Teoritta the quickest, so I was to take her and run. Meanwhile, Tsav and Kivia had agreed to handle most of the violence. I was pleased to have the easy job for once.

At any rate, I managed to safely slip into a back alley. This was one of the escape routes Kivia had designated in case something unexpected happened on the main street. I'd even memorized a map of the city, just in case.

We were heading toward a corner of the city known as Sodrick's Shell—a nest of complicated, winding streets. To put it bluntly, this was the sketchy part of town, and most people made sure to avoid it even during the day. If the map I'd used was correct, this alley should lead to an open area already under the control of Kivia's Holy Knights. We should far outnumber the enemy there, and for the most part, assassins were no match for an army lined up and ready to fight. There were exceptions, of course, but it wasn't the norm.

However, after the second turn in the road, I paused.

*This isn't good.*

I hadn't seen any sign of the Holy Knights. I began to sense restlessness in the air, like an itch on my back. Though it wasn't a hard rule, I usually tried to listen to my gut.

"Xylo, do you sense it, too? Something doesn't feel right."

Kivia had finally caught up to me, along with Tsav. Both of them were still light on their feet and showed no signs of exhaustion.

"It appears this route has been compromised, too." Kivia had an impressive grasp on the situation. She frowned, wiping the blood off her blade with her cloak. "My Holy Knights are nowhere in sight, and

I specifically deployed infantry to this district. Something must have happened."

"Probably all dead, then, huh?" Tsav began patting the dust off his clothing as if it had just now started to bother him. "Now that I've killed a few, I can tell not all of these guys are assassins from the order. They don't seem to have undergone any training."

"You mean they're too weak?" I asked.

Tsav cheerfully nodded back at me. "I mean, nobody's as strong as me, but these guys are pretty pathetic. Their weapons are definitely from the order, though."

Tsav held up a knife he'd picked up along the way. Engraved on the blade was a triangular wedge-shaped seal.

"This is Gwen Mohsa's seal. They call it the 'True Great Sacred Seal,' but it's different than the one the Temple uses. You know, that circle with a line through it."

"Then that would mean…" I didn't even need to think about it and immediately put my hypothesis into words. "They're trying to frame the order? There are way too many of them for an underground organization. It doesn't make any sense. But who would do something like that?"

"It could be the ones siding with the Demon Blight."

Kivia chose her words carefully. Her stiff profile hadn't changed, but I noticed a somber note in her voice.

"The coexisters?" I asked. "They've been a real pain in my ass lately."

"Yes, them. They would certainly benefit from killing the Goddess. I didn't think they'd infiltrated the military or the Holy Knights, but…" Once she finished wiping clean her blade's sacred seal, Kivia glared into the depths of the alleyway. "For now, we need to focus on getting out of here alive."

I'd been expecting our enemies to come from that direction, too. I could hear a few sets of footsteps in the distance, when…

"Whoa?! What are those?!" shouted Tsav, his voice cracking. The assassins, or men who appeared to be assassins, emerged in helmets and full suits of armor. There were three of them, each with a two-handed lightning staff. "You see what I'm seeing?! Are they allowed to have those?!"

"They most certainly are not," declared Kivia, astonished, as she began to move forward. "How did you get those, you scum?! What is going on with the military?!"

Kivia hurled insults and complaints at the enemy. Tsav was right—those staffs were exclusively distributed within the military and not available to the public. Not many were made, and ownership was highly regulated.

"The hell is going on?" I yelled, taking a step in front of Teoritta to shield her.

The assassins fired their staffs almost immediately, but their aim was amateurish. Two of them weren't even close to hitting us, and Kivia was already dealing with the third.

She muttered the word "Niskeph," as she lightly thrust the tip of her sword into the ground. This activated her sacred seal, and the air vibrated as a cloudy blue curtain took shape, blocking the lightning staff's shot and scattering it into faint sparks. Niskeph was a common protection seal, and while it could only be used continuously for a short period of time, it created an extremely strong defensive wall resistant to heat and physical attacks.

Meanwhile, I was just finishing a strike of my own. I'd brought only two knives with me this time, so I had to use something else. Shoving my hand in my pocket, I promptly grabbed the first thing I touched: a coin. It was new kingdom currency issued by the Allied Administration Division, but it had far less value than the money of the old kingdom, which incorporated real gold and silver.

I infused the coin with Zatte Finde's power before flicking it at the enemy. It was lightweight, allowing me to send it right into the group of assassins up ahead before it exploded with a flash of light. Of course, unlike with a knife, I couldn't lodge it in their flesh, so it wasn't able to blow them up from the inside. But it was more than enough to send a person flying and knock them out cold—three at once, in fact.

"This is a lot easier when there's no one else around to worry about," I said.

"Sure, but…" Kivia looked back at me, perhaps to crack a joke, but her relaxed gaze suddenly sharpened. "Tsav! Above you!"

"Ack." Tsav grunted, mildly surprised.

I was shocked, too. The enemy really was right above him.

It was a lanky figure in all black, swinging their right arm with… was that a blade in their palm? No. They weren't holding anything. They were simply swinging their fist, and Tsav reacted with beast-like instincts.

He moved out of habit, the result of constant practice. After evading the punch effortlessly, he swung his knife into the air at the enemy's throat. It was precise and immediate, but his opponent dodged as well.

Tsav was unfazed. He spun his blade around in his hand to aim it once again at his target—all while reaching out to grab his enemy's lapel and sweeping their legs out from under them. The move was very smooth and precise.

But just when I thought it was over, Tsav suddenly hopped back like a grasshopper. I could hear a series of hard, metallic sounds, and before I knew it, the slender, shadowy figure was standing on the ground, blocking Tsav's knife with their left hand and burying part of their right palm into his side. Tsav appeared to have blocked most of the attack in time, but…

"What the…?"

Tsav's lips tightened into a forced smile.

He still looked somehow flippant, but I could tell he was in pain, and I could see cold sweat on his skin. He'd protected his side with his left arm, and blood was gushing out from it, painting the pavement red.

"Something's not right with this guy," he said.

Tsav's left arm was badly injured. The area from his forearm to his bicep had been gouged out.

"This guy's doing something bad, bro… It hurts…real bad…"

There were countless holes in his arm, as if he had been bitten by a wild, fanged beast. *What the hell did that guy do to him?* The knife in

Tsav's right hand was broken as well. And just like that, the sniper fell to his knees.

The slender, shadowy figure in black shifted their gaze in my direction, but a piece of fabric completely concealed their face. I could just barely make out their eyes, and I saw they were locked on Teoritta and me.

They were the eyes of a wild animal.

We were too close—right in the enemy's striking range.

The slender assassin in black didn't waste their breath pointlessly chattering. They simply extended their right arm forward, as if they wanted to shake hands.

*That must be their battle stance.* It was an unusual style. They didn't lower their center of gravity or form fists. Their left hand was pulled back around waist height, and they were standing about four steps away. Teoritta was right behind me.

*This isn't good.*

They'd cut off most of my means of escape, and if I wanted to grab Teoritta and use my flight seal to put some distance between us, it would mean briefly turning my back to the enemy.

"Xylo, I—," Teoritta began.

"Stay behind me," I warned, cutting her off. "I'll make this quick."

"...As expected of my knight."

Teoritta briefly but tightly squeezed the hem of my shirt from behind. It wasn't going to be easy, but we weren't in any danger. This was nothing compared to the shit we penal heroes had been put through time and time again.

That gave me confidence, and I called out to Tsav, who was still crouched on the ground.

"Don't try anything stupid, Tsav."

"I can't even move, bro. This is bad."

Tsav was trying to tighten something around his left arm at the shoulder, to stop it from bleeding. It looked like some beast had bitten deep into his flesh. But while he seemed to have lost a lot of blood, he shot me a carefree smile as sweat dripped down his forehead.

"This arm's useless now," he said.

"That's rough."

"More importantly, bro, did you see their arms? They—"

But the slender assassin made a move before Tsav could finish speaking. Technically, all they did was shift their weight a little, but that was enough to let me know they were about to strike. They kept up their guard all the while.

*I really don't want to end up on the defensive. Especially against an assassin.*

That was why I chose to attack, unsheathing a knife from my belt and throwing it all in one motion. I'd practiced this technique over and over, until I was sick of it. What's more, I always hit my target even in midair, so there was no way I was going to miss while standing on the ground.

I aimed right for the middle of their forehead. I thought they were going to sway in an attempt to evade, but they chose to intercept the knife instead, blocking it with one of their gauntlets—the one covering their right hand. And that was when I activated Zatte Finde.

I had to limit the blast, since we were relatively close, but it was powerful enough to blow someone's arm clean off. And yet the slender assassin somehow charged through the blast, their right arm unscathed. They were totally unharmed... How? Their fingers cleaved through the air until they were right before my eyes, forcing me to lean back as far as I could.

Just then, a tall figure with long black hair blocked my view.

"Hff!"

Someone exhaled. Kivia's sword thrust into the assassin's right arm from the side. I heard the sound of sharp metal colliding as Kivia briefly held her breath, and the assassin narrowed their eyes. Were they laughing? They swung their left arm, aiming for Kivia's stomach.

Just then, I sensed it. Kivia was stepping in to strike, and even I could tell.

"Stop!"

I grabbed Kivia's shoulder and jerked her back as hard as I could, causing both of us to fall to the ground on our asses like idiots. She shot me a reproachful glare, but I didn't care. We'd avoided a fatal blow.

Then I heard something crack. It was the assassin's arm, or rather, the lead-colored gauntlet protecting it. When they'd thrust out their right hand, I'd seen it—the bizarre gauntlet had appeared to be coming apart. It seemed it was actually a bundle of cord, or perhaps steel rope.

Once it came apart, it changed shape, weaving and winding around and around, eventually taking the form of a beast's jaw, complete with a row of sharp fangs.

That jaw snapped shut in front of Kivia's eyes—right where she'd been standing seconds earlier.

A grunt escaped her pale throat. If she'd been any farther forward, her windpipe would have been torn wide open. This must have been what shredded Tsav's left arm, and I bet it was a small shield formed from these steel ropes that blocked my explosion. Not only was the gauntlet quick, it seemed like it could reshape itself into just about anything.

*It has to be some sort of seal compound.*

It was probably specially manufactured and not yet in use within the military. From what I could tell, it was a kind of strike seal that raised one's physical abilities. It wasn't that complicated, but it was hard to deal with in close-range combat. I'd need a pretty powerful explosion to defeat it.

Was that even possible, though? Exactly how big and powerful of an explosion would I need? One wrong move in this back alley could bring down the surrounding buildings on us. As long as Teoritta was here, I needed to keep the blast as weak as possible.

The slender assassin rushed forward to strike while we were still down, but I wasn't going to let that happen. While I was falling, I'd thrown a coin with my left hand.

*Eat shit.*

I'd aimed it over their head. The blast and impact were even more powerful than my previous shot. The assassin swiftly blocked it with their gauntlets, but they were forced to leap back, landing on all fours.

They didn't make it out unscathed, however. The enemy's black mask had been partially burned in the explosion, revealing the face of a thin woman. I'd expected as much, based on their size and movements.

Her savage eyes—the eyes of a creature assessing its prey—darted from me to Kivia and then to Teoritta.

"...You saved me," groaned Kivia, her eyes still locked on the enemy. She wore a sour expression, but I realized this was her way of thanking me. That meant she could keep fighting.

"You still good, Kivia? Feel free to lie down if you need to."

"Who do you think you're talking to?" She frowned and slowly got back on her feet. "Enough chitchat."

Bending her knees, she assumed her battle stance and took a step forward while I took a step back. We positioned ourselves on either side of Teoritta. We had to—the situation was only getting worse. I could hear more footsteps approaching from behind us, and soon six assassins emerged from the other end of the alleyway. Five were holding lightning staffs.

*Seriously, what the hell is going on?*

I was sick of these guys. The organization behind this must be a hundred times bigger than I'd imagined.

"...That's enough, Shiji Bau," instructed one of the newcomers with a deep, hoarse voice. I lowered my center of gravity and swiftly shifted my gaze in their direction.

"Your chance of defeating the penal heroes and their goddess is only one in a thousand," they continued listlessly. "It's time for you to withdraw. There is no benefit in continuing a meaningless battle."

This person, dressed in a filthy black robe, was clearly a man—the only one among the new arrivals without a lightning staff. His back was rounded almost into a hump, but he would probably be around the same height as me if he stood up straight. His face was pale and sickly. Even his words sounded gloomy, as if he was muttering to himself.

"Did you hear me, Shiji Bau? You claimed to be a professional assassin, yes? If so, you should know when it's time to withdraw."

"You're clearly still an amateur," said the woman called Shiji Bau, her face twisted into a blatant frown. "Stop blabbing people's names like that. Never give out information. That's just common sense for a professional, Boojum."

Shiji Bau called out the slouched man's name like she was trying to get back at him. *Boojum*. Was that his name? Or was it just an alias? Whatever the case, Boojum bowed to her politely.

"I see. I had no idea. I'm not familiar with what's considered common sense in this business, so I am counting on you to—"

"H-hey, is now really the time for this?" interrupted one of the assassins with a staff, cutting off what was beginning to sound like a very long-winded dialogue. "We need to get out of here! If we don't hurry, the Holy Knights—"

"I'm sorry, but I need you to be quiet." Boojum turned around and lightly waved his left hand. "I am having a conversation with Shiji Bau, and it is rude to interrupt."

From where I was standing, it almost looked like he was slapping the man. And just like that, the assassin's jaw disappeared—no, it was knocked clean off. I had no idea what had just happened, but the man shrieked and dropped to his knees. Blood poured out as he curled into a ball in agony.

Teoritta's eyes opened wide, and she gasped. I held out my hand to block her view.

"Hmph," Shiji Bau glanced at the jawless man and snorted. "Now you've gone and done it. Did you forget we were told not to kill any more than necessary?"

"'Kill'? I didn't kill anyone. I have a heart."

"You broke his jaw. There's something really wrong with you. In fact…"

Shiji Bau continued to chitchat as she casually walked toward us. Both Kivia and I could feel it in our guts—she was about to attack. We knew what she was capable of, and we wanted to avoid engaging her in close combat, if at all possible.

"Kivia, let's split up," I suggested. "The other assassins seem dangerous, too."

"Very well. I'll take care of the woman with the gauntlets."

Light began to illuminate the ground as Kivia pierced it with the tip of her sword.

"Niskeph!"

"*Tsk.*"

Shiji Bau clicked her tongue as a pale, misty wall appeared in her path. She swung her fist, turning her gauntlet into the jaws of a beast, but the barrier deflected her attack. The sound of the impact echoed down the alleyway. It wasn't going to be easy for the enemy to break past something like Kivia's barrier, especially when she was using her sacred seal solely for defense.

Meanwhile, I planned to use this time to dispose of the other assassins. I unsheathed a knife—one I'd picked up from a defeated Gwen Mohsa assassin.

"Since Shiji Bau is so serious about this, I'm going to help her. Don't fire your lightning staffs. I don't want you accidentally hitting me. It stings." Boojum moved forward, dragging his feet across the ground. "Now if you'll excuse me."

Narrowing his eyes, he suddenly accelerated. He was far faster than I'd imagined. He jumped to his left, kicked off the wall, and flew into the air. It seemed he, too, intended to use the narrow alley to move and attack in three dimensions.

*He's coming from above!*

I threw my knife, figuring he wouldn't be able to dodge easily in midair—but that was a mistake. Boojum twisted his body, accelerating even as he came down. I had no idea what he was doing, but for a brief moment, it looked almost as if his right arm bent like a whip. At the same time, I heard a *pop* like a bubble bursting.

*Just who is this guy?*

The knife I threw missed, exploding in midair with a flash of light and a roar. Maybe it surprised him. Otherwise, I don't think I could've leaped back in time to dodge. I landed somewhat clumsily, but managed to survive. Another *pop*, and a crater formed where I'd just been standing. I got lucky and managed to evade it by a hair. Slashes, as if from a sword, appeared all over the ground and walls. What was he doing? What kind of weapon was he using? It didn't look like he was holding anything, but maybe it was a hidden weapon like Shiji Bau's? A few things were still unclear, but there was no time to think about it now.

"…An explosion. The work of a sacred seal, I presume. You must be the penal hero, Xylo Forbartz, I've been hearing so much about."

Boojum closed the distance between us in the blink of an eye. His speed was unbelievable, his movement beast-like. His back was so arched, he had to look up at me, and his eyes were filled with a surprisingly genuine admiration.

"I never expected to run into you here. When I thought through all the things that could go wrong today, this was one of the worst-case scenarios."

"What are you trying to say?" I asked, carefully getting back on my feet. This guy was too unpredictable. How was he able to move like that in the air? What were these clawlike scars digging into the walls and ground? He wasn't wearing gauntlets engraved with sacred seals like Shiji Bau's—he just looked like some hunchback in poor health. And yet his presence made me strangely uneasy.

"'Boojum,' was it? What was that crazy dodge just now? Were you an acrobat in the circus or something?"

"No." He refused to play along with my joke, and there was an uncanny, chilling luster in his serious eyes. "You, too, are skilled in your craft. The precision with which you threw that knife was remarkable. Perhaps *you* are the one fit to join the circus."

"Actually, I *was* in the circus for around three years as a professional knife-thrower. I was really good on the trapeze, too."

Boojum nodded at my stupid joke.

"Interesting. No wonder you are so talented."

Was he being serious? Did he just take what I said at face value?

"You're the best in the world as far as I know," he continued. "I respect that."

"Boojum, shut up," Shiji Bau scolded in a low voice. "You're talking way too much, idiot. Stop giving him so much information. You're really starting to look like an amateur."

"I see. Professionals don't offer explanations, yes? Very well."

"Ha-ha... There's something really wrong with these guys, huh?" At some point, Tsav had crawled all the way to where I was standing. "The one with the slouch is dangerous, too, but Shiji Bau... I've heard of her before. She's a famous adventurer, not an assassin from the order."

"I bet she has a high success rate when it comes to killing her target, unlike you."

"Probably. She seems like a really terrible person. Nowhere near as lovable and kind as me... Heh..."

You wouldn't guess from his joking, but Tsav was still bleeding profusely and his voice was weak.

"You probably shouldn't be moving around, Teoritta," he said. "Here, come sit with me. My bro Xylo and that tomboy lady are strong... I'm sure it'll be...fine..."

"Who are you calling a tomboy?" said Kivia with a frown. Clearly, she could still afford to joke around. That came as a relief. When you tensed up, your brain and body slowed down as well. I could see why Kivia had become a captain at such a young age. Teoritta, on the other hand, wasn't feeling so confident right now.

"Xylo." She grabbed on to the hem of my shirt from behind once again. "...Are you in need of salvation, my knight? Surely, I could..."

Her face was wan but serious, and it was clear to me that she was trying to make a decision.

"I could...save you... I could make it...r-rain swords..."

"Don't."

I placed a firm hand on her shoulder. She was pushing herself too hard. She was terrified, fighting against her fear and going against her instincts—if you wanted to call them that—through willpower alone. I knew just how unbearably painful it was for goddesses when they tried to harm humans.

*There's no way I could forget.*

I knew that pain. I could still remember it. I forced my thoughts back to what happened that day.

"Stop, Teoritta. You don't need to do that. This isn't your job."

"But I...can save you. I can...do it...!"

She was trying to justify her actions by framing it as a way to save us.

"Stop." I grabbed her shoulder again and squeezed tightly. "It's fine."

"But..." She grabbed my hand. "It's strange... There's something odd...about that man..."

"Wait! Bro, Teoritta...! They're here!"

Teoritta was about to say something, and I wanted to hear her out, but Tsav cut in, interrupting us. *About damn time*, I thought, nodding back at him.

"They made it, Teoritta. You don't have to force yourself to do anything."

"Huh?"

"We're not alone out here anymore." I looked up as a large shadow soared across the sky. "Get down!"

I grabbed Teoritta's head and pulled her to the ground. Kivia joined us and Shiji Bau leaped back as if blown by the wind. The others, however, didn't make it in time.

A surging stream of fire rained from the sky—so powerful it could cook you to the bone. The back alley glowed a bright red, and then, in the blink of an eye, it was overflowing with flame. The assassins shrieked in agony, almost dancing as they were cooked alive, before dropping to the ground. Boojum was right there with them. Engulfed in flames, he staggered before crashing into a wall. In an instant, the alleyway had become a scene from hell. Kivia was in a daze, and I covered Teoritta's eyes with my hand—the horror wasn't over yet. Covered in flames, an assassin tried to escape, only to have his skull shattered by a spear thrown from the sky.

"Hey there," came an indifferent voice from above. The azure dragon, Neely, then spread her wings, rapidly descending to the ground with Jayce. Tsav had called for them.

With our dragon knight back on the roster, we would no longer run the risk of being isolated on the battlefield.

"The hell is wrong with you, asking us to come to a narrow alley like this?" complained Jayce with his usual scowl. "I didn't want to, so you better thank Neely. You owe her."

"I know." I didn't bother arguing. I would have to treat them to dinner or something later. "Sorry, Neely."

"You're a lifesaver, Neely," Tsav said, smirking awkwardly.

Neely snorted. I didn't know if that was her reply, or if she was laughing at us, but whatever the case, she raised her head as Jayce rubbed her throat.

"You sure? You're so sweet, Neely... Of course. We'll take another day off to make up for this. We can take a trip to the sea tomorrow, and fly as far as you want."

This might sound crazy, but there was something very picturesque about seeing Jayce talk to Neely like this amid a sea of flames.

"Call the fire brigade!" shouted Kivia in a panic as she got to her feet. "Xylo, get in contact with the local government! We need to put out this fire immediately!"

...This was the problem with using Jayce.

He didn't think twice about civilian casualties. In fact, he didn't think he should have to. You had to keep him on a short leash with his sacred seal, or you were asking for disaster. And since there was a dragon involved, you could expect far more damage than with Tsav.

*We're going to get more than a slap on the wrist for this. That's for sure.*

I looked back over my shoulder as gloom filled my heart. Of course, Shiji Bau was nowhere to be seen. She'd probably run away already. The problem was the other guy: Boojum. The rest of the assassins cried out in agony as they perished in the flames, but I hadn't heard so much as a groan from him. He simply stared at me, almost indifferently, as he was engulfed in the fire.

"You called a dragon for backup, I see. Very impressive, penal hero," he said as his skin bubbled. It almost looked as if his flesh were regenerating as it burned.

"Interesting. The flames of a dragon are overwhelmingly hot. I'm a bit short on blood right now, but this has been a learning experience… Now, if you'll excuse me…"

I hesitated briefly, wondering if I should ask him something.

"Until we meet again," he said.

Then he leaped into the air, leaving a shower of sparks behind as he kicked off the walls and made his way to the top of a building. He had the physical ability of an animal—of a goddamn monster. Jayce watched the man escape, looking fed up.

"He just…ran away? Who *was* that man? Neely lit him on fire, for crying out loud."

"I don't know. But…"

I paused, unsure of what to say.

The man called Boojum didn't make any sense. He had survived being lit on fire. It was like he wasn't human.

"Teoritta." I turned to the goddess. She was still tightly holding on to my hand. "What were you about to say a minute ago? About that man with the slouch. What was odd about him?"

"I am not sure, exactly. It's just…when I thought of attacking those people… He was the only one…I felt like I could…strike…"

Her momentum gradually weakened the more she talked. It was as if she was beginning to doubt herself.

"Don't worry about being wrong. Just say what's on your mind. What's your gut telling you?"

"…It's possible that man isn't human."

I felt more certain than ever.

*Was that Spriggan, then?*

Spriggan was a demon lord that could disguise itself as a human, and the very creature that Frenci and her men were after... He'd called himself Boojum, but that was obviously a fake name. Nobody would be stupid enough to give their real one.

Maybe the marks he'd left behind contained a clue. But when I lifted my head, I saw a group of Holy Knights rushing toward us. *A little late*, I thought. Some of them looked exhausted, and a few were injured.

*Looks like they had a rough time, too. But why?*

Shiji Bau, Boojum, and the assassins... Did they really want to kill Teoritta that badly? Why had they come with such a large group? Not to mention how easily the Holy Knights' security had been breached. Their positions must have been leaked before the fact. That was the only way to explain this.

*Just great...*

I watched the flames as they continued to spread.

*I'll think about that later.*

Venetim would have a better idea of the extent of the fire damage.

Fortunately, thanks to the rapid evacuation, no civilians had died.

To make a long story short, there was a traitor among us. That was the only thing that made sense.

The guards Kivia deployed around town had been separated from one another and isolated. Looking at a map instantly made the situation clear. The enemy had sent concentrated groups of assassins to specific points, cutting off communication. Over a hundred Holy Knights had been deployed, and over half of them were dead or severely injured.

The attack had come as a surprise, and it had been brutal. This wasn't something just anyone could pull off. We'd taken a decent number of survivors prisoner, but most of them were either low-level grunts or adventurers, who weren't much better, and the rest took their own lives with poison they'd hidden somewhere on their body. *If only Jayce had held back a little*, I thought.

…Back at the barracks, we were busy discussing the situation.

"We" being Kivia, those in charge of the deployed units, and me. I was the only one from Penal Hero Unit 9004, since I didn't want Teoritta to hear. Normally, our so-called commander would serve as our representative in meetings like this, but you couldn't expect anything from Venetim when it came to military affairs, and he was busy writing a letter of apology detailing our mistakes. So, through process of elimination, the duty fell to me.

"...Then, Captain Kivia...," grumbled a young man as he looked up from a map. "What you're trying to say is...that we have a traitor among us?"

This was the officer in charge of the infantry—I believe his name was Rajit. He wore a humorless, overly serious expression—exactly the kind of guy you'd expect to find in a military uniform.

"We don't know for sure yet," replied Kivia calmly. It sounded like she was actively keeping the emotion from her voice. "They might very well be in another unit. I contacted Galtuile about our security measures and touched base with Ioff's defense force, who we have been working with, as well."

These were both natural reactions for someone in the military. She could have set up a trap herself, but she wasn't a risk-taker. I understood and respected that decision.

"...It doesn't make much of a difference anyway." The officer in charge of the cavalry shook his head, his arms crossed.

This man was named Zofflec, if memory served. He sat up straight, but spoke roughly from time to time and seemed to always have a cynical smirk on his face.

"It could be one of us, one of those in power, or even one of our allied forces," he continued. "And we can't put up a decent fight if we can't trust one another. We're in an extremely bad position right now." He heaved an overly dramatic sigh and shifted his gaze toward the corner of the table. "Wouldn't you agree, Officer Siena?"

"...Yes, I agree," said a petite woman. Her voice sounded somewhat restrained.

Siena, who had been quiet up until now, was in charge of their sniper unit. I wished she could give our sniper a little bit of her reserved attitude.

"Our unit suffered the most casualties," she continued. "Almost every sniper deployed was killed."

"That means we need to figure this out, and fast," said Rajit, nodding cautiously. "Captain Kivia, I believe we should rethink how we're guarding Goddess Teoritta. First, we should gather only those we can trust, starting with those of us here, and consider—"

"I don't know about that. Sounds pretty pointless, if you ask me."

*I should probably keep my mouth shut*, I thought as I spoke up, unable to resist. This was about protecting Teoritta, after all... The moment that thought crossed my mind, I sighed inwardly.

*Could it be that I...?*

Was I trying to make sure the same thing didn't happen to Teoritta? Did I think this would help me take back something I'd lost? *Dammit.* Teoritta wasn't going to replace Senerva, no matter what. And yet I continued:

"'Only those we can trust'? First off, we should be skeptical of everyone in this room."

"...The audacity." Rajit glared at me just like I knew he would. "That includes you, penal hero... In fact, the 'goddess killer' should be at the top of our list of suspects."

He had a point.

*Can't argue with that.*

I smiled wryly, and Zofflec started to laugh.

"Good point, Rajit! I completely agree. Captain Kivia, are you sure we should allow this hero to join our meetings?" Although he was laughing, there was a sharpness to his words. "I'm suspicious of him, too. After all, he's the one who stole the goddess from us in the first place. Nothing he does makes any sense."

With Rajit and Zofflec criticizing me, I was growing more uncomfortable by the minute. The remaining officer, Siena, observed me in silence, her expression giving away nothing. *How like a sniper.* I couldn't afford to back down, though.

"At the very least, we need to do some undercover work," I said. "We should get in touch with the Twelfth Order of the Holy Knights via Galtuile."

I knew that unit, and they specialized in intelligence. They occupied a special role, and were the only order that didn't show themselves in public. Only a limited number of people knew what they looked like. Even when I was a captain, I never once met them. There were rumors they didn't exist at all. But I knew there was a group specializing in such matters: the National Intelligence Corps.

"We can't fight if we don't trust each other. You're right about that," I said. "And yeah, of course, I must look the most suspicious of all, but in this situation, you can't trust *anybody*."

"...I understand what you all wish to say."

Kivia slowly got to her feet, then turned to someone else—a man not at our table, but seated at the desk at the back of the room.

"What do you think, Uncle Marlen? I believe we should reconsider our strategy, report our findings to Galtuile, and conduct an internal investigation."

"Yes...," said a man with a heavy, somewhat husky voice.

This was High Priest Marlen Kivia, Kivia's uncle. He occupied a seat at the Temple's sacred council meetings, and was basically at the top of the Temple's hierarchy. He was a skinny man at the end of middle age, and his hair was peppered with white—each strand evidence of worry and stress. His overly serious expression was much like Kivia's, but in his case I got the impression he was more high-strung. Maybe it was because his eyes were sterner than his niece's.

"I was just assigned to this investigation, but..."

Marlen Kivia wasn't exaggerating about that. He had arrived from the First Capital not long ago, commissioned by Ioff's city government to serve as a consultant for the defense force. For the past ten days, he had been working to get a grasp on the situation and secure the authority to preside over the case.

The division of roles between the military and the Temple was complicated in cases like this. Especially when goddesses were involved, there tended to be exceptions and special cases. The current balance of power and political state of the kingdom usually decided who was in charge.

"The fact that we don't know who we can trust, including me, is a matter of concern," he admitted, busily drumming his fingers on the table. "That said, we don't know if the Twelfth Order can or even will help us... Therefore, our priority should be to revise our current security plan. I believe our only choice right now is to increase the number of guards protecting the goddess as much as possible."

He heaved a long, soft sigh—conveying what sounded like days' worth of exhaustion.

"It is extremely unfortunate that we weren't able to capture anyone with useful information. How did the questioning go, Patausche?"

I'd almost forgotten that Patausche was Kivia's first name, since I never had any opportunity to use it.

"Less than ideal," she replied, straightening her posture. I could tell she was nervous. "Most of those caught were adventurers, and it seems they don't know who hired them."

"I see." The high priest nodded coldly. There was something very unnatural about his relationship with his niece. They were way too formal with each other. Maybe it only seemed that way because of Kivia's personality. Yeah, that had to be it.

"You have my deepest apologies. If only we'd been able to capture the ones who seemed to know what was going on, then..."

As Kivia bowed politely, the high priest's lips curled into a faint smirk.

"Don't let it bother you," he said. "You're far too harsh on yourself. Too much regret and anxiety will only hamper your work."

"I will keep that in mind."

"You're so serious. Eh, I suppose it can't be helped. If you were any different, you wouldn't be Patausche Kivia."

High Priest Marlen let out a whispery sigh. I wondered if that was his way of laughing. He must be unable to laugh cheerfully, just like his niece.

"At any rate," he continued. "All we can do now is prepare for the next attack—"

"One moment, High Priest Marlen," I interrupted, raising my hand, despite once again thinking that I should probably keep my mouth shut. "There's still something we can do."

The moment I spoke, he turned to look at me. But he wasn't glaring—he seemed more intrigued than anything.

"Oh my. How troubling. I don't remember asking you for your opinion, penal hero Xylo. Although you may have forged a pact with the goddess, we can't have you ignoring rules and regulations in a place like this. Otherwise, our organization will cease to function."

"Yes, I understand that, but I think my opinion will come in handy."

"Xylo! Stop! You—"

Kivia grabbed my elbow in a fluster, but there was no way I could back down now.

"We can probably get some information out of the middlemen who hired the adventurers," I continued.

High Priest Marlen didn't tell me to shut up, but his sharp gaze narrowed further.

"...Are you claiming to know who these people might be?"

"Yes," I replied. "At the very least, I know of someone we should investigate right away."

I met Kivia's anxious gaze with a tiny smile and a nod. I let her know not to worry by lightly patting the hand she'd placed on my elbow, though she didn't seem to understand what I meant.

"Mmn...!"

Her eyes opened wide, and she immediately looked away from me, causing the high priest to breathe another whispery sigh.

"Hmph. Very well. I will allow you to speak. I am sure you must have a wonderful idea you are just dying to grace us with."

"You could say that. If I didn't, I wouldn't raise my hand in front of someone as important as you."

"The way you speak is provocative and yet eases the tension in the room. Take note, Patausche. You needn't be as laid-back as him, but you could learn a thing or two."

Kivia swallowed her reply, but she was clearly annoyed.

"Now, penal hero Xylo... Who is it we should look into?"

"The mediator who arranges jobs for adventurers in the city."

"It seems you're quite familiar with such underground enterprises. And who is this mediator?"

"It isn't one person." I paused before giving a name. "It's the Adventurers Guild itself."

There's one more thing I need to add to this report.

Venetim was waiting for me when I got back from the meeting.

"…Is everything okay?" he asked. Incidentally, Dotta was lying on the ground, drunk off his ass and snoring, with a bottle of booze still in his hand.

"What do you mean?" I asked.

"Oh, uh…" Venetim smirked uncomfortably at my confusion. "I was just worried that maybe we were being punished or something…"

"No, we're good. That high priest is a real serious guy, just like his niece. He didn't do anything to hurt us out of spite."

"…I see." Venetim covered his mouth as if to suppress a yawn. I had no idea what he was trying to say. "So…how were the others in the meeting acting?"

"What? Is there someone you're concerned about? Don't tell me you're trying to get with that female sniper? Don't even bother. She seems like a lot of work, and I'm sure not gonna help."

"No, it's not that…" He hesitated for a few seconds, then shook his head. "Never mind."

"The hell's gotten into you?"

Now I was even more confused. I grabbed Dotta's bottle of booze without remorse. I was probably going to need this to prepare for the next day's task.

"Time to get to work, Venetim," I said. "But first, I need your help selecting the right people."

In the end, Venetim was the only one I could count on when it came to discussions like this. His useless remarks and clueless responses helped me process my thoughts.

"Are we going to discuss strategy over drinks?" he asked. "I suppose I could help with that."

"Not like you've got anything else to do. In return, I'll listen to whatever it is you want to talk about, since it sounds like something's bothering you."

"Nothing's bothering me." His smile didn't inspire confidence. "That's not it. That's not it at all."

Venetim was a total mystery to me. But maybe all con artists were like this.

Lideo Sodrick was in his room when he received a shocking report. He was speechless—of course he was. And he was restless, too.

The attack against the Holy Knights had been a success. The lightning staffs obtained were put to good use. The knights were carefully surrounded and separated from one another. And most importantly, Lideo had sent in his two most skilled adventurers. Though they were expensive, they were well worth their price.

*I can't believe both of them failed.*

He directed his gaze to the two people in question, now back— the slender female dressed in all black and the man with the slouch: Shiji Bau and Boojum. Neither, he suspected, used their real names. Shiji Bau meant "spike" in the language of the ancient kingdom, and it was a reference to the spikes people used on the soles of their shoes in the north.

Boojum's name was a mystery. Unlike Shiji Bau, who was moodily crossing her arms and gazing down at Lideo, he had taken a seat in the corner of the room and appeared to be reading a book.

"It was a dragon knight," Shiji Bau said in a whisper. She seldom made a sound and preferred to move, speak, and work in near silence. "And he didn't seem to care how much of the city he destroyed in the process. It was completely unexpected. I can't work under such conditions, Guild Master."

*Guild master*—that was Lideo Sodrick's title. He was in charge of the Adventurers Guild, a kind of mutual aid society. The port city of Ioff was a commercial center with an endless number of guilds, and his was one of the most influential. Only the merchant guild and the Adventurers Guild had a private army at their disposal and thus the ability to resort to more forceful means.

And it was the Adventurers Guild, naturally, that specialized in violence.

*Great…* Lideo fell into a black mood. *This kind of failure is not gonna look good to our clients.*

Violence was one of the Adventurers Guild's tools of the trade. More specifically, it was the resulting fear and intimidation that created and ensured profit. In fact, promoting their reputation of violence was more important than the violence itself. That was how these adventurers made a living.

"Considering the risk, I'll be expecting a greater reward." Shiji Bau stared at Lideo, her eyes devoid of emotion. Perhaps it was more of a glare than a stare.

"I understand where you're coming from, but…"

Lideo stared right back at her. He was the guild master. Although he was technically her boss, she was far more powerful than he was. Nevertheless, he couldn't allow himself to show any fear.

"You two failed, and from what I heard, you had plenty of time to get the job done before that dragon knight appeared."

"Hmph. The penal hero guarding her was far stronger than your intel made him sound. And that man back there…" Shiji Bau pointed at Boojum with her thumb. "He's a complete amateur. He might be good at killing, but he gave the enemy far too much information. You should remove him from this mission or kill him right away."

"…Are you talking about me?" Boojum didn't look up from his book. "Why? What is the problem? I followed orders, and withdrawing when I did was the right call."

"That's not the problem. You said I wouldn't be able to defeat that hero. Why?"

"Because it's true. You wouldn't. You had only a one thousand-to-one chance of winning, at most."

"Excuse me?"

Shiji Bau looked back at him and glared, but he simply turned the page of his book without a care in the world.

"Oh, my apologies. I was simply trying to be kind. In reality, you had only a ten thousand-to-one chance, at most."

"...See what I'm dealing with?" she said, exasperated. "What's wrong with this man? Did you hire him to lower morale or something?"

"'Lower morale'...? I see... So that's how you perceived my remark," Boojum said seriously, his eyes still focused on his book. "Lideo Sodrick, you have my apologies. It appears I have upset her, when that wasn't my aim. I was simply telling her the truth."

Lideo didn't say a word.

Unlike Shiji Bau, Boojum was an unknown adventurer who had appeared on the scene only recently. Lideo first learned of him when Boojum got into a fight at a gambling house run by the Adventurers Guild. Lideo didn't know the details—what he did know was that ten adventurers had ganged up on Boojum and lost. Not a single one survived. Each of them had fatal gashes from what appeared to be the claws or fangs of a beast. None of the witnesses could say how Boojum had done it, but that was of little interest to Lideo. All he wanted was a bodyguard who could be controlled. And so he secretly took in Boojum at the Adventurers Guild, allowing him to stay for free.

*At first, I thought he was some ex-adventurer who had fallen on hard times, but...*

There was something strange about him. He was an excellent bodyguard with beast-like reflexes and the preternatural ability to sense danger. But although he would loyally follow orders, he didn't understand how the world worked at all. At first, he didn't even understand how money worked. So while he was merciless and excelled at violence, Shiji Bau wasn't wrong—he was an amateur when it came to anything else.

"...Boojum stays for now," said the guild master. "I've made my decision."

He was strong. While you couldn't predict what he was thinking, he was loyal, and that made him a valuable pawn.

"Shiji Bau, I want you to look after him," Lideo continued. "If you feel that he's an amateur, give him guidance."

"What am I? His trainer?" She gave a haughty snort before shooting a glance at Boojum, who was still reading his book, and shrugging. "He's going to hold me back. Plus, those guards are strong. I'm going to need a little more money."

"Hmph! Excuses, excuses. You're adding fees just because the enemy is a bit strong?"

"...Oh, you're taunting me now?"

Her gaze sharpened at his provocative grin, but in the blink of an eye, another individual had stepped in between them.

"Brother," came the low voice of a small, shadowy figure. "Please stand back."

It was a girl with dull blond hair. She was young enough to be considered a child, but her eyes were eerily dark. Though perhaps that was only Lideo's guilt talking.

"This woman is a stray dog. She doesn't have an owner...which makes her dangerous."

This girl was called Iri and was one of the children Lideo personally kept. Iri was the most violent of the bunch, but while she was decently skilled, it was her loyalty that made her so much more valuable than a hired mercenary or adventurer.

Lideo was raising twenty children altogether. This was something he'd been taught by his predecessor. He invested in the city's orphanage via donations from the Adventurers Guild. And in return, he would take in the most promising children and have them undergo special education and training. This would provide him with a private army not reliant on any third party.

Other guilds were doing the same thing. Organizations for merchants and craftsmen would find children with potential and train them from a young age. The only difference was the type of "products" they handled.

Lideo referred to these children as his younger brothers and sisters and had them call him "Brother" in return. This, combined with special treatment, promoted a strong sense of loyalty.

"Brother, you're always letting your guard down," Iri insisted, almost reprimanding him. "I can't believe you allowed these people into your room… I can mediate if you need me to."

"I'm just doing things as my predecessor taught me," Lideo replied. It was the excuse he always gave if he wanted to end a conversation quickly and save himself a headache. "Whenever you have important business to discuss, you should meet face-to-face. That way, you know if you can trust the other party. You have to listen to your gut."

Of course, not all of that was true. The reason he'd summoned Shiji Bau and Boojum to meet him in person was because this room was the safest place for him to be. One of his "little brothers" was waiting in the room next door with a special weapon already aimed at the adventurers, and he had Iri by his side as well. The desk between Lideo and his two guests was even engraved with some sacred seal traps.

Lideo was something of a coward, you see—even he acknowledged it.

*This is how I've survived so long in such a precarious post.*

Shiji Bau was aware of the traps in the desk, of course, but Lideo wasn't sure whether Boojum had noticed. He carefully chose his next words.

"At any rate, Shiji Bau, I trust in your skills, and in your loyalty to the contract you signed."

About this, he was being serious. Honoring agreements was important for an adventurer, and you especially didn't want Lideo, the guild master, to speak ill of you. If that happened, you'd have problems finding work even in other towns.

"Let's discuss how to proceed. Something unexpected happened, and security around the target will most likely increase. In light of the heightened risk, I'm fine with raising your pay. However…" Lideo tapped the small cloth bag of coins on the desk—silver coins from the old kingdom. "You'll have to accept another job as well."

He took out another cloth bag of the same size and placed it on the desk.

"You haven't finished the assigned job. In fact, if you ask me, expecting the unexpected is just part of our line of work. If you back out now, I will not be paying you your completion bonus." His lip curled slightly. All he needed was for her to think he had the upper hand. "We aren't the army, after all."

He was trying to hint that he knew about her past. Shiji Bau's peculiar sacred seal weapons and combat style were uncommon. This had caught Lideo's eye, and he'd looked into her background, eventually digging up her real name. To make a long story short, she was an army deserter, and her name was on a list of soldiers assigned to an experimental unit. After escaping the military, she fell on hard times, fighting and doing whatever she could to make money. Although the details weren't clear, if he were to let her former employer know she still had her sacred seal–engraved weapon, it would most certainly make her life difficult in the future.

"I believe we can establish a profitable relationship," he finished.

"All right."

Shiji Bau's movements were quick. Iri reacted as the adventurer shifted her right hand, but her gauntlet had already changed shape in the blink of an eye. The steel wires formed a sickle, swiping the two coin bags off the desk.

"How dare you…!" shouted Iri, unsheathing her knife. She was enraged.

"That won't be necessary, Iri. Stand back," ordered Lideo calmly.

He understood what Shiji Bau was doing. She could easily kill Lideo, even in a situation like this. The traps in his desk didn't matter. It would be nothing to take him out with her. That was what she wanted to say.

*I know how she feels.*

You couldn't let people disrespect you in this line of work. Lideo understood that better than anyone.

"I'll come back for the rest once the job is over," she said. "Have three bags ready."

"You're being unreasonable. Can't we negotiate a little?"

"No. I have necessary expenses," Shiji Bau spat, before turning on her heel. "Those guards were tougher than I imagined. I'll have to hire more people."

"I can introduce you to some adventurers if you'd like," offered Lideo. Shiji Bau snorted.

"Useless thugs are a waste of money, no matter how many you get. As long as our enemy has a dragon, we'll need people who can use sacred seals. Professionals, unlike this idiot."

"Wise words," Boojum replied. "I will not be very useful to you in battles within the city. By the way, Lideo Sodrick…"

Only then did Boojum finally look up from his book. Every time Lideo saw his eyes, he felt as if he were staring into two bottomless black holes.

"I would like to request additional pay for my services as well," the man continued. "I wish to purchase another book."

"Another one?" Lideo asked.

Boojum was an avid reader and asked for a new book every time he completed a job. Although a cheap and easy request, it did make Lideo a little curious.

"Are you sure that's all you want?" he asked.

"Positive. I've taken a special liking to this author, Altoyard Comette. What a brilliant poet."

"If you say so."

Lideo couldn't comprehend the value of poetry, but it seemed an interesting hobby for a man who knew only violence.

"Very well, then. In return, I expect you to follow Shiji Bau's commands at all times."

"All right. Shiji Bau, I'm ready for orders."

"…Then let's get a few things straight." She shot Boojum a brief but piercing glare. "First, no small talk. And when you speak with someone, look them in the eye. Got it? Now follow me."

"As you wish."

Iri waited a full thirty seconds after Boojum followed Shiji Bau out of the room, before turning to Lideo with a worried gaze.

"…Do you really think they can do it, Brother?"

"There's nothing for you to worry about."

Feeling stifled, Lideo shifted his gaze toward the world outside his window.

For a second, he was struck by the feeling that someone was watching them from the building across the street. The presence was soon gone, but he couldn't simply dismiss it as his imagination. *They* were everywhere. The first one he'd met was a man with a sacred seal hanging over his chest—proof of his position as a priest.

He'd approached Lideo with a deal—a deal that Lideo couldn't refuse. Obey, coexist, or die. Those were his choices, and if he didn't want to die, he was going to have to prove that he could be useful.

*…Coexisters.*

He recalled the name of their group. Humans coexisting with the Demon Blight. By reaching an understanding with intelligent demon lords, they would ensure the survival of the human race. Lideo was familiar with such deals, and he understood them.

*In other words, they want a system of slaves, people who control the slaves, and rulers.*

…Or at least, that was how it looked to him.

The coexisters would allow the demon lords to rule and in return would be made into overseers with control over the slaves. Whatever the case, they had far more influence than Lideo had ever imagined.

*At this rate, humanity is going to lose.*

He was almost certain of it. And if that was inevitable, he needed to at least secure his place as an overseer. Only then could he guarantee a good life for himself and his family: his brothers and sisters. Iri and the others were no longer just tools of the trade to Lideo. He had become emotionally attached.

Perhaps he wasn't cut out to be guild master. That's what his predecessor would have said anyway. But there was nothing he could do about it now.

*I'm probably already a traitor to humanity…*

He felt Iri's stare as the guilt slowly swallowed him up. To Lideo's way of thinking, guilt was a privilege reserved for those in positions of power like himself.

*…I don't have a choice. I have to do this for my family.*

We penal heroes hardly had any freedom when it came to our meals. We couldn't complain about the food, nor could we choose where to eat it, though there were exceptions when on the move during missions. Some people brought back booze and snacks to enjoy in their rooms, but you couldn't get your hands on stuff like that without special skills.

There were only two designated eating areas for heroes in the barracks in Ioff: a corner of the soldiers' cafeteria and a spot beside the dragon stables. The latter was a special dispensation only afforded us because Jayce had to tend to the dragons.

For that reason, Jayce hardly ever ate in the cafeteria. But that day was one of the rare occasions when he did. Arriving at our designated corner, I found Jayce and Dotta sitting side by side, eating breakfast.

"You don't see this every day," I commented, speaking my mind as I took a seat by Dotta. "What's wrong, Jayce? Neely kick you out of the stables?"

"Yep," admitted Jayce grumpily, though I'd only meant it as a joke. "Neely got jealous."

Our dragon knight stuffed his mouth with rye bread, as if to say he didn't want to talk about it. This happened from time to time. Dragons had a peculiar love for Jayce, and he liked to take care of them, so naturally, they were always around him. When a female dragon approached him, however, Neely tended to get upset.

Things could get especially messy during mealtime. Occasionally a dragon would try to eat by Jayce's side, or Jayce would share his food with one of them. This was the kind of thing that put Neely in a bad mood. I couldn't tell you what it was that set her off, but I knew it happened.

I'd even witnessed it once. Random dragons were laying their heads in Jayce's lap and on his shoulders. Some were even offering him the meat or vegetables clamped between their fangs. It reminded me of how young noblewomen might approach the sons of royalty or high-ranking nobles at an evening banquet.

"Hey, Xylo...? Just let him be," whispered Dotta, poking me with his elbow. "I'd rather you guys not start another one of your stupid fights."

"We don't fight."

"You do, too. You guys are basically the embodiments of anger and violence. It's so bad, I wish they'd have you eat at different times..." Dotta glanced behind me, then scanned our surroundings. "Hey, where's Teoritta? Is she not with you?"

"She's still asleep, so I didn't bring her. Besides, I have a favor to ask of you, Dotta, and I didn't want her to hear."

"Seriously?" He couldn't have looked less thrilled. "Actually, I'm good. You're just gonna make me do something I don't wanna do."

"Yep."

"And it's gonna be dangerous."

"Yep."

"Something so dangerous you can't even bring Teoritta."

"Wow, you're good. Saving me a lot of explanation here."

I shifted closer to Dotta and began biting into my rye bread. That day we had bread, cheese, and pickled cabbage. *I could kill for some meat right now.*

"Rejoice," I said. "You'll get to see the town shackle-free."

"Yeah, yeah. I heard what happened to Tsav."

Fortunately—or perhaps unfortunately—Tsav didn't have to go in for repairs after losing a good chunk of his left arm and only wound up in the hospital.

"So what's the mission?" asked Dotta.

"Well, we have several objectives this time around, but our first priority is to infiltrate the Adventurers Guild."

"Just great..." Dotta looked like he was struggling not to vomit.

We needed to look into the relationship between the Adventurers Guild and the people who attacked us the other day. That was our best way of finding out their identities. We couldn't bring Teoritta along, however, since it was clear that would only cause more trouble.

"If you're going to the Adventurers Guild," said Dotta, "wouldn't it be better if you brought Rhyno?"

"He's still in the hole. Besides, you never know what that guy's gonna do, and I don't want to take any risks."

Rhyno was our unit's artilleryman, but he was currently in solitary confinement for violating orders. He was originally an adventurer, so he probably had a lot of contacts in the guild, but he wasn't someone you could count on during missions like this.

"You still don't need me, though. What about Venetim?"

"He has to pick up King Norgalle today."

Those in charge had finally repaired Norgalle's leg. That is to say, they'd finally found a body part they could attach to him.

"Plus, I need your skills," I said.

"Mmm...," Dotta groaned, but he couldn't refuse. Even if he did, Kivia would eventually hand down the same orders.

"Sounds like you need help, Xylo," said Jayce suddenly, breaking his silence. "I can go in Dotta's place if you want. Not like I've got anything else to do today."

"Wait! Really?! Then—" Dotta leaped to his feet, grinning from ear to ear in pure bliss. But before he could stand up completely, he froze. I was grabbing his shoulder.

"Sit down, idiot. You really want Jayce working in the city?"

There was a fundamental problem with getting Jayce's help,

especially when it came to working undercover. You were basically betting on a dragon who couldn't understand the rules to not mess things up.

"We can't take that kind of risk. Plus, he doesn't even know what we're doing."

"I know. I was listening. The Adventurers Guild… You need to sneak into some building, right? Piece of cake. How many guards are there? A few puny humans can't stop me."

"See what I mean, Dotta? That's why you're coming."

"Fine…" Dotta closed his eyes and flopped down on the table. "I'm sick of being locked up inside all day, and if it means I can walk around town for a bit, then…sure. I'll do it."

"Well, okay then," said Jayce easily, before throwing a piece of cheese into his mouth. "Xylo, you better not cause any trouble for Dotta. Got it?"

Jayce respected Dotta and tended to be lenient toward him. He once told me: *"Not only did Dotta try to help that dragon escape, but he even let her eat his arm. He's just that kind of guy."* Almost choked with emotion, he added: *"…He fed himself to a hungry dragon. I don't know if even I could do that."* I decided not to comment on the matter.

"So? Give me the details." Dotta looked up at me, an anxious cast to his eyes. "How do you plan on sneaking inside? Will it just be you and me? No Teoritta, right?"

"That's right. Allow me to explain…"

We needed to wait until sundown before starting the mission, since that was when the Adventurers Guild conducted most of its business.

"It's time," declared Kivia. She looked so serious, it was almost painful to watch. "Dotta, Xylo. The three of us are about to infiltrate enemy territory. Our goal is to make contact with Lideo Sodrick, an extremely dangerous individual. Be careful."

I glanced at Kivia's outfit.

"Is that what you're wearing?" I asked.

"Is there a problem?"

She touched her collar. Under a dark wine-red cloak, she was wearing a rather frilly shirt with lacy cuffs and a heavy skirt. She could easily be mistaken for a wealthy noblewoman if it weren't for the sword strapped to her waist and the overly grim look in her eyes... In fact, that was exactly what she was.

"Or are you once again claiming that I look like a man? Is that what you want to say?"

She was being really aggressive, and I could tell it was scaring Dotta. He kept elbowing me in the side as if begging me to do something. *Okay, Dotta.*

"...I didn't say that." After a moment's thought, I decided to give my honest impression. "You look really good. I would have assumed you were some sought-after noblewoman if I didn't know any better."

"Oh." Her mouth opened wide for a second, then she quickly pressed her lips together. "Flattery is not necessary. It's no use trying to curry favor with me, it will have no effect whatsoever."

"Well, that's great and all," I said, "but...we're about to sneak into the Adventurers Guild, so..."

There was a time and a place for everything, and the clothes Dotta and I were wearing were anything but luxurious. We looked more like struggling merchants or craftsmen, or at best, servants working at some richer person's mansion.

"What's our story?" I asked. "We need to come up with a fake job offer."

"The most obvious choice would be a request to eliminate some faeries," said Kivia. "Let's ask them to kill some faeries that built a nest in our territory."

"I don't think that'll work," muttered Dotta quietly. "That's usually a job for the military. I know the Guild has their own personal army, but they'd never take a job like that unless it meant making some serious money."

"Then let's offer them just that," she countered.

"N-no, that still won't work. It'll just make us look really suspicious."

"I see."

Kivia glanced at me as if asking for help, and though I wasn't too familiar with the business, I did know a thing or two about the kinds of jobs Adventurers did.

"There are some bandits we need dealt with," I suggested. "How does that sound?"

It felt cliché, but we did hire an adventurer to help rid us of some bandits back when I lived with the Mastibolt family.

"Bandits have been sighted in our territory, and we need help getting rid of them."

"Aren't both of those jobs a little...violent?" said Dotta. "I'm sure you could find bandits in some more remote regions, but..."

He seemed to be choosing each of his words carefully so as not to anger us, but it kind of pissed me off to be treated like a useless child.

"We're in Ioff, you know," he continued. "...There aren't any wandering bandits, and the ones they do have are already paying the guild their share, if you know what I mean."

"Then..." Kivia knitted her brow and crossed her arms. "What do you think we should do? What kind of job would this city's Adventurers Guild accept?"

"Well, uh..." Dotta looked back and forth between Kivia and me, until at last he seemed to come up with something. "Judging from your appearances, I think we can assume you're the wife of a nobleman, and you're her secret lover."

"Excuse me?"

"Huh?"

"You're plotting together to kill the husband," Dotta concluded. "So, any nobles you're itching to kill?"

The history of the district known as Sodrick's Shell was that of the Adventurers Guild itself. You could even call it the city's own history of violence, and I knew a little about it.

Back when maritime piracy was rampant off the coast of Ioff in the Korio Bay, the leader of a certain group of fishermen built a personal army to eliminate the threat. That was Sodrick's ancestor.

After that, Dayir Sodrick, the dauntless champion and Sword of the Sea, announced he was founding his own group to promote the city's independence…or something like that. The story had most likely been altered and romanticized over the years. In reality, it was probably nothing more than a fight between two opposing pirate crews over territory.

Regardless, the Sodrick family cared enough about appearances to push their version of the story, and they had the power and influence to do so. That much was true. The current head of the family was a man named Lideo Sodrick. He represented the Adventurers Guild, and on the surface, he was one of the most notable individuals in the city.

The district known as Sodrick's Shell was the part of town over which Lideo Sodrick held the most sway. The streets wound around in circles like the whorls of a shell, all converging in the center, where the

Adventurers Guild was located. There was no sign, but once you got up close, you couldn't miss it.

After walking through the burnt and partially destroyed back alley, we finally made it to the heart of the district. The place was pretty lawless, and each step we took toward the Guild only made that clearer. The way was littered with street stalls with a plethora of illegal offerings: tools engraved with sacred seals, faerie carcasses, stolen goods, moonshine, humans, and even the forbidden plants that Jayce had cultivated and released into the world. Kivia narrowed her eyes sharply at everything she saw.

"Disgusting. What is the Temple doing?" she said. "This entire district should be eradicated."

"It'd probably be a waste of time," I said. "Get rid of this one, and another'll just pop up in its place."

"How is this in any way acceptable, Xylo?" Kivia bit back. "This is all a consequence of poverty, right? Better management and economic assistance would put an end to places like this."

"I wonder."

It wasn't so simple when the desires of man were involved. While they could probably do something about human trafficking, solving poverty might not fix people's cravings for things like Jayce's illegal plants.

"Xylo, you're being evasive," said Kivia. "Don't tell me that you've purchased goods at places like this before!"

"Of course not."

To be honest, that was more an issue of not wanting to cause any trouble for Frenci's father than anything else. Plus, Frenci herself absolutely abhorred these kinds of places. She would have killed me for even getting near one. But explaining all that to Kivia would be a hassle, so I kept it to myself.

"*Haah...* The Temple should be pouring their resources into projects like this... How frustrating," she said.

"Yeah, yeah. Now do you think you could stop glaring at people?

And stand closer to me, too. We're probably already being watched by the guild."

"M-mn…!" Kivia grunted, almost as if she'd choked. "Y-yes, you're right. We're supposed to be lovers after all. I admit, it does make sense to walk more closely by your side in order to increase our chances of success… But do not get the wrong idea! I am only doing this for the mission! *For the mission!* Got it?!"

After this rapid-fire monologue, Kivia took my arm, albeit somewhat reluctantly. It was more of a firm grasp than a loving hold, however. I hadn't asked her to go so far, but it really did make us look like a wealthy noblewoman and her servant-turned-lover. I felt like she was squeezing my arm a bit too hard, but maybe she didn't know how to control her grip. Either way, I'd just have to bear with it.

"Mnnn… I would die if my uncle saw me like this," said Kivia.

"Oh hey. That reminds me…" I decided to ask Kivia something that had been on my mind. "Why did you end up joining the military?"

"What do you mean?"

"Your uncle's a priest, right? High Priest Kivia. Er… This is getting confusing. High Priest *Marlen* Kivia is your—"

"Call me Patausche. That should make things easier. I'm only allowing you to call me by my first name for the sake of convenience, though. Got it? Convenience." She was rambling again. "Even people not close to me, who know both me and my uncle, call me by my first name. It's only logical, and sometimes it's necessary for clarity, and that's the only reason."

"Uh-huh… All right," I agreed, overwhelmed. "So… Patausche."

"…! …What? This had better be important."

"I just wanted to know why you joined the military." I'd been wondering about this for some time now. "I assume your family are priests with a large domain. So why would you go out of your way to join the military?"

"I…" Patausche paused for a moment, then nodded. "When you get right down to it, I suppose I wanted to rebel against my parents."

"…Can you be a little more specific?"

"My mother and father are priests with their share of duties at the Temple, and with that…comes various benefits. One of those benefits is land."

Priests were only granted land after the establishment of the Federated Kingdom. Such individuals were also known as noble priests, and they received court ranks from the royal family. Priests were different from soldiers in the military, however. They had authority and faith but no skills that would benefit them in the real world.

As a result, unlike soldiers or civil servants, they didn't have a salary. That meant many of them exchanged their authority and faith for money, and not always through modest means such as donations. Often, they got creative, such as buying and selling positions within the Temple via bribes, or securing territory under the guise of planned religious construction sites.

All of it was to enrich themselves and secure their family's future.

"I hated that about my parents," said Kivia. "That was why I chose a different path and joined the military. Whatever I get in life, I want to earn it through my own hard work."

*A tale as old as time.* That was the first thought that popped into my head. It really was a common story among nobles, but it was more than a trite phrase for the one living it.

"My uncle was there for me and supported me after I more or less ran away from home."

"That's—"

"I know what you want to say. Having relatives in the military can be beneficial for a high priest. But he still helped me, and I owe him for that." Kivia nodded, her expression steely. "My uncle is a man with a vision, and he is taking strong action to reform the mistakes of the past. He even plans on confiscating territory from corrupt priests and resettling the land with those who were forced to leave the developing regions."

A lot of people had been displaced by the Demon Blight, and that was especially true of settlements in developing regions. Such people were given no choice but to abandon their homes, and helping them would definitely be beneficial to society as a whole.

"I wish to be the shield that protects his vision," she finished.

This must have been yet another reason Kivia was willing to fight to the bitter end back at Couveunge Forest. It wasn't only for Teoritta's sake—Kivia had an image of what she believed a true warrior should look like, and she was risking her life to realize it. *Dammit...* I didn't want to criticize Patausche, but I was so tired of all these idiots racing to throw away their lives.

At this point, though, I was in no position to criticize.

"By the way, Xylo..." Patausche shot me a piercing stare, as if she was about to challenge me to a dual. "...I want to ask you something as well. You, uh... You said you had a fiancée?"

"Yeah."

"Then...that woman Frenci. Is she—?"

"Xylo."

A voice suddenly called out to me from the side, and I felt a light tug at my shoulder. It was Dotta. We'd split up earlier, and Dotta had gone ahead to scout. I knew he'd wind up stealing something—that much I was prepared for. But he excelled at sneaking into places, and we needed those skills. In fact, it looked like he'd already come through.

"I checked out the guild," he said.

"That was quick."

"...A little too quick, I think," Patausche chimed in.

I was impressed with Dotta's work, but she didn't seem quite so happy about it. She must have really wanted to ask me about Frenci. I bet she was just looking for something new to tease me with, but I wasn't going to let her get the upper hand so easily.

"Security's tight, but I guess that's the Adventurers Guild for you," said Dotta.

He'd sneaked inside the building and gotten the lay of the land. We wanted some idea of what we were up against, at least.

"It's a three-story building with sacred seal traps all over the place.

I already memorized the layout, so we're good there. But I saw around... twenty guards inside. Ex-military, I'd guess."

"That's surprisingly few."

"There were a bunch of weird kids, too," added Dotta, biting into something that looked like a snake on a skewer. In his other hand was a small bottle of booze. It seemed like for Dotta, there wasn't much difference between the infamous black market of Sodrick's Shell and the touristy main street. It was all just a buffet to him.

"They were doing a better job guarding the place than the soldiers. I think they're assassins of some kind, and I bet there are even more of them hiding on the third floor. I don't have an exact number, though."

"They're using kids?" Patausche's voice filled with disgust. "That's unforgivable...!"

I had heard about people raising orphans into loyal, powerful soldiers. With enough training, they'd throw their lives away without hesitation. This wasn't going to be easy.

"...Dotta, what about an escape route, if things go south?" I asked.

"I could probably make it out...alone, that is."

"Good. We'll be working separately from here on out." I started to walk toward the Guild.

"Gee, thanks... What about you two?" asked Dotta. "Are you really gonna be okay? You're not gonna mess up and put me in danger, too, right?"

"Actually, you still haven't told me any of the details of our plan," said Patausche, as if she'd just now realized this. "What will we do after sneaking into the guild?"

"Plan A," I began. "We bring them a lucrative job so we can meet Lideo Sodrick without anyone getting suspicious. If that works, then Dotta doesn't have to do a thing, and we simply capture our target."

"Interesting. Is there a Plan B?"

"Yep. Things might get messy if Lideo has a body double. In that case, Dotta will have to find and kidnap him. I'll spare you the finer details. I just need you to trust me. At any rate..." I elbowed Dotta's side. "I need you to find Lideo Sodrick and steal him. That's all you need to focus on."

"Stealing people has never worked out for me," said Dotta.

And yet I knew he'd do it anyway. He'd never learn his lesson. And that was exactly what we needed right now.

"All right, let's get started," I said. "Patausche, you're a wealthy noblewoman, and I'm your lover. Got it?"

"…I—I know. You can count on me!"

As we exchanged glances, she tightened her grip on my arm…it really hurt. *Just how strong is this woman?*

Lideo Sodrick was in his room again when he received yet another shocking report. The tension had started to give him a light headache.

"I made sure, Brother," Iri assured him. "He was a penal hero. He was covering his neck, but he fit the description perfectly. And the woman with him was most certainly a Holy Knight."

"…I see." Lideo wanted to sigh, but he stopped himself. He couldn't worry his sister. "I wasn't expecting them to really come. Bold move. Reckless, but bold."

This kind of ploy wasn't typical of the Holy Knights, which made Lideo curious as to what these intruders were thinking. Would they try to cause a scene to collect some sort of evidence or information?

"What do you want to do, Brother? Shall we capture them?"

"It depends on what happens next, but…it's probably worth a shot. We might be able to use them as bait to lure out the goddess. If that doesn't work, we could simply keep them locked up…"

Though he'd rather not do something so drastic, he was more than capable of it. He was in contact with the coexisters, and that connection gave him an advantage over even the military. The only issue right now was that both Shiji Bau and Boojum were out, so he'd have to try to make up for them with numbers.

*Yeah… As long as we're here…*

Lideo's turf extended beyond the Adventurers Guild. The whole area of Sodrick's Shell was his kingdom. Here, he could set large-scale traps and make it impossible for them to escape.

"Very well," said Iri. "Sim and I will keep an eye out for the enemy and wait for our chance."

"All right. Then—... Wait."

Lideo shook his head. His greatest strength was his cowardice.

"Let's use our secret weapon. Wake up Duhrsami. You can never be too careful."

This was one of the guild's—no, Lideo's—treasures and secret weapons. It was something he'd inherited from his predecessor, perhaps passed down for generations. Duhrsami was a former human who had been turned into a faerie. Not even Lideo knew any more than that.

"And get in touch with Shiji Bau. Have her and Boojum return immediately."

This would put him on the coexisters' good side and prove his worth. He had to protect himself and his family, no matter what the cost.

"There's someone I want you to kill," Patausche declared boldly. "And while I do not mean to be rude, I would like to request an expert in the craft."

The woman at reception was taken aback. Her mouth hung partially open, and it was clear that she had no idea how to respond. I knew exactly how she felt.

"Ahem… Listen. No, I mean… I'm sorry, but…" The receptionist shook her head, pulling herself together. "First of all, who are you?"

A reasonable question. The woman looked up at Patausche with a sickly gaze.

"Madleen is the name," Patausche replied, without a second of hesitation. "Forgive me for not giving my family name as well."

This was a fake identity she had come up with before we arrived. While it was laudable that she'd managed to say it without stuttering, she had already made a fatal mistake: What kind of noble would walk into the Adventurers Guild and directly ask for an assassin? I felt her showmanship had some real room for improvement.

I reflexively looked away from the awkward scene. Might as well get a good handle on the Guild's interior.

The building felt even more cramped than I'd expected, maybe due to the dim lighting. The first floor seemed to double as a pub for the adventurers while they waited for work. Some were drinking or smoking. A few here and there had illegal substances—the stuff called "Dragon's Breath."

The second floor was probably where they conducted business. I could see a few rooms and some men who looked like security, all with their eyes on us. It seemed we stood out, and our cover was probably already blown. Dotta was right—there were a decent number of children here as well, and the sinister look in their eyes made it clear that they weren't around to sell candy.

*Looks like they're keeping an eye on us.*

That didn't matter, though. Everything was going smoothly so far. I glanced out the window. Dotta must have crawled up the building's wall like a lizard and made it to the roof by now. He was probably waiting to see how things panned out. Walls were no different from hallways to Dotta. He could climb up them without making a sound, almost as if he were simply walking. Apparently, he had some sort of claws in his gloves and shoes. I heard he could even crawl across the ceiling if he had to.

"Ms. Madleen, pardon me, but…" The receptionist spoke to Patausche as if she were talking to a child. "We don't take just any job someone brings us, especially when it comes to assassinations. As you're a first-time customer, I doubt it will be possible. But let's talk money. How much can you pay?"

"I can pay however much it costs."

"I'm afraid that's not the issue…"

The receptionist was clearly fed up. I felt I had no choice but to join in on the negotiation.

"Sorry, miss. Milady has lived a very sheltered life and isn't used to places like this."

Patausche knit her brows in protest as I placed an elbow on the counter. She'd insisted on taking the lead with the negotiation and had stepped out in front as if to say, "Let me handle this." It was probably my fault, though. I really shouldn't have told her she couldn't do it. That said, while I was no old hand at such things, I felt confident I could do a better job than Patausche.

"It's true there's someone we need to get rid of. I know we don't have a letter of introduction, but we're desperate. If nothing else, we need you to help us disappear."

I casually pulled a leather pouch out of my pocket to give her a little peek. I was really hoping that this gesture would make us look like naive, easy prey.

"We have money," I said.

"I wouldn't even be talking to you if you didn't." The receptionist seemed to be evaluating us. "Ahem. Okay, I'll hear you out. Who do you want to kill? And why do you want to disappear? I'd rather not get involved in some mess you made and wind up taking care of your dirty laundry."

"I want you to kill a nobleman," I said, lowering my voice. "Have you heard of the Hystead family, the bridge-keepers of Ginai?"

"No," she promptly replied, though she could have been lying.

Regardless, I continued. "Well, we're having a little trouble with the third son of one of the branch families, and milady here—"

"Yes," chimed Patausche, though I wished she hadn't. "I married into the Hystead family."

It was a bold performance, but more or less what I expected from her.

"Yet ever since I was a child…I vowed to spend the rest of my life… with this man here… We made a promise to each other under a sacred hargra tree."

*I can't believe she went out of her way to make up such a bizarre background story.* All the weird details she was adding would only make it harder for me to keep up.

"Therefore, I want to kill my husband…and use the inheritance to marry this man."

Could she have been any more straightforward? You had to ease into this stuff. You know, start out trying to hide the details, then finally give up and spill the beans. Otherwise, you sounded crazy. She must've gotten distracted telling the story she'd made up.

"And if that isn't possible," she continued, "then I'm fine with simply running off with this man and getting m-married, but I need the Adventurers Guild to introduce me to someone who can help."

She couldn't have sounded more suspicious if she tried.

"U-uh... Hold on...," the receptionist said, groaning.

That wasn't a good sign. The woman turned around and started talking to someone out of sight in the back—security, I assumed. They were probably going to kick us out.

"Xylo," whispered Patausche. She sounded extremely uncomfortable. "Maybe it's my imagination, but I don't think they believe us."

"It's not your imagination."

"This isn't good. What should we do? Do you have a backup plan?"

"Yeah, let's kick some ass."

"Wait. Excuse me?"

"Kick some ass. You know, create a disturbance. What we need right now is mass confusion. Imagine we're looters, but the loot is Lideo Sodrick."

Patausche opened and closed her mouth a few times, her face pale. "Wh-wh-what kind of reckless plan is that?!"

"Not like we've got any other choice. They're already suspicious."

"You don't look panicked at all. Don't tell me this was always part of the plan."

"You're sharp. I figured this would happen, and I'm really glad I brought along someone strong like you."

"Mmm...! You're... It's really hard to be angry with you when you're complimenting me!"

I knew I could count on her swordsmanship, and she was way better at close-range combat than I was. I would've liked to have been led to the second floor before causing a scene, of course, but it was a little late for that now. With Zatte Finde and Sakara, I was confident I could escape any building. Our opponents probably knew that, too. It was going to come down to a show-and-tell with our secret weapons. It would be a bit of a gamble, but there was a good chance we'd win. If things went sideways, it didn't matter what happened to us; as long as Dotta managed to kidnap the guild master, the win was ours.

*All right, let's do this.*

I glanced at my surroundings and noticed two armed men walking our way.

*Looks like these two will be our first victims.*

But just then, I saw someone behind them, and I couldn't believe my eyes.

She had smooth, brown skin and dull, gray hair the color of iron. To top it all off, her eyes were practically glowing with a cold light that would send a chill down anyone's spine. I knew this woman. Even the cheap leather suit of armor she was wearing couldn't fool me.

"Sorry, Ms. Madleen. But—"

"Sounds like a fun job."

The iron-haired maiden—Frenci—called out to us before the receptionist could finish her sentence. I heard Patausche gasp.

"It sounds like you need someone killed," said Frenci, her voice devoid of emotion and weirdly intimidating. "I would love to hear more about this job. I do not care how sloppy or foolish your plan is. As long as I get paid, I will consider it."

She shifted her chilly gaze toward the receptionist.

"Could we borrow a room upstairs?"

"Huh? Oh, yes…Madam Renzari."

So that was the name she was going by? It looked like it was working, but who was she pretending to be around here? The receptionist had sounded very respectful.

"Room seven and onward are free to use. Please take your pick," said the receptionist.

"Thanks… Let's hear more about this little job of yours up there." Frenci looked at us as if compelling us to follow along. "You are the lady of a noble family, yes? And you, her lover?"

Though I usually found Frenci hard to read, I was painfully aware of how she felt now. She was clearly in a bad mood. In fact, I'd never seen her so furious.

◆

"You're a mess, Xylo."

I knew she was going to say that. Once again, it was so predictable that I laughed.

"You lack awareness of your situation. This is no time for laughter. Maybe I should sew that careless mouth of yours shut."

After giving me a good tongue-lashing, Frenci settled into a chair in one corner of the room and crossed her legs. Two men I assumed were her bodyguards stood silently on either side of her. Although they were using their clothes and hats to hide it, they were members of the Night-Gaunt clan as well. That would explain their silence— Night-Gaunts usually didn't speak much before the People of the Plains, in order to avoid unnecessary conflict.

"Are you listening, Xylo? Do you realize how reckless you're being right now? I clearly remember telling you not to do anything foolish." Frenci's complaints were endless. "How stupid can you be? ...They were going to tie you up and throw you into a cell if I didn't step in to save you. A man who is to marry into the Mastibolt family, captured by a couple of lowlife adventurers? Such a scandal would be unbearable."

"Hey, I had a plan, and it was going fine," I said. "We were about to kick some ass and cause a scene."

"Exactly," Patausche chimed in. "An ally of ours was going to sneak into the building to get a hold of some evidence. This plan was chosen by Ioff's defense force itself. We didn't need your help at all."

"...I see." Frenci's cold gaze swept over Patausche from head to toe. "You're a Holy Knight, yes?"

"I am the captain of the Thirteenth Order of the Holy Knights, Patausche Kivia."

"Whatever you say."

When Frenci made it clear that she didn't care about this title, Patausche reached for the sword at her waist almost instinctively.

"Do you think you could stop spoiling my soon-to-be husband like this?" Frenci continued, speeding through her words. "He is still an awful mess. He is undereducated, inexperienced, and a fool, so I would appreciate it if an outsider like you would leave him alone."

"An 'outsider'?" Patausche's fingers turned white from squeezing her sword's handle so hard. "You are the outsider. You have nothing to do with our mission."

"And that is where you are wrong. I am that foolish man's fiancée, so I should be by his side, even during the hardest of times. That's how things have always been between us. Isn't that right, Xylo? Whenever you caused trouble, I was there to save you."

"That happened like once or twice at most…," I replied.

"E-even so…!"

Patausche stepped forward, her taller frame looming intimidatingly over Frenci.

"That was the past," she said. "Yes, that's all in the past. I'm here now. We don't need any help from an ex-fiancée."

"Oh my. Are you claiming you can take care of him?"

"Of course I can. Creating a commotion and escaping a small building like this would be child's play for Xylo and me."

"Escaping the building is only the beginning. Are you planning on making an enemy of every person in this city? Of course, my fiancé could no doubt manage such a feat, but what if he were severely injured? What if it affected his memories of me? How would you take responsibility and make it right? At minimum, I would need to kill you."

"Hmph! I'd like to see you try. Besides, don't you think you're underestimating this man's skills? He has defeated three demon lords in a row. And with me by his side, no adventurer would stand a chance, even if they all came at us at once! Isn't that right, Xylo?!"

"Well, I didn't come here to lose, but more importantly…"

I took a step in between Frenci and Patausche, since even Frenci now had a hand on the hilt of her blade. I didn't want a fight to break out.

"I need you two to get along. I knew you wouldn't be compatible personality-wise, but this is way worse than I expected."

"Excuse me?"

"'Personality-wise'?"

Frenci and Patausche turned on me at the same time, and I felt like I was being stared down by two ferocious beasts, baring their fangs and growling. They were both ready to kill.

"That is your only conclusion?" said Frenci. "I sometimes wonder if your head is actually full of rocks."

"It's even worse than that," Patausche said. "His ability to judge people is the lowest I've ever seen."

"I could not agree more. He has the eyes of a susubana mole."

"That tree over there is more intelligent than he is."

"Hey! I know I said I needed you two to get along," I said, interrupting them before they could hurl more abuse at me. "But could you please bond over something else?! Listen. We can't fool around. We don't have much time, so let's use what little we have and get down to business."

Dotta was probably outside in the cold waiting for our signal, and while I doubted the temperature would affect his ability to steal, I knew what kind of person he was. His kleptomania always led to trouble, and there was a high chance he would start getting sticky fingers beyond the scope of the plan if left alone for too long.

"For starters," I continued, "you could tell me what you're doing here, Frenci. Playing adventurer?"

"I am in the middle of an investigation, of course. The same as you two, I assume, though I am operating far more gracefully." Her sharp tongue clearly enunciated each word. "I am disguised as an adventurer for an undercover mission, and I was getting very close to finally meeting Lideo Sodrick."

"Until we interrupted? Sorry about that. But I think our way is going to be faster. We're about to create a disturbance. Can you help us?"

"Yet another aggressive strategy, I see. Do you understand how dangerous that will be? I will not allow it. Stop this nonsense and go home. Now," she demanded, her tone unusually forceful. But just then—

"Ahem. Excuse me."

It was the voice of a child, most likely a young boy, coming from the other side of the door, followed by the sound of a knock.

"Do you have a moment?" the boy continued. "The guild master would like to see you to discuss your request."

Frenci silently stood up as her guards unsheathed their swords. Patausche briefly glanced at me, then signaled with her chin, pointing to the wall that separated our room from the one next door. For the past few moments, there had been some strange rattling coming from the other side.

"What are you gonna do, Frenci?" I asked. "You can leave now if you don't wanna help."

I unsheathed a knife from my belt. I had four left—they might be enough, but I was doubtful.

"I am so appalled that I am at a loss for words."

Frenci took out her weapon as well. It was a curved short sword with a sacred seal clearly engraved onto the blade. I gave a small smirk.

"See? This was way easier," I said.

Immediately, the door flew open as two short, shadowy figures—obviously children—rushed into the room. At the same time, the wall to our side burst open with a flash of light. We were barely able to dodge the bolt of lightning, and we only managed because we were expecting it.

Standing in the room next to ours was a man wielding an absurdly large ring-shaped bundle of lightning staffs. It appeared to be the new rapid-fire weapon I had been hearing about. At any rate, the man was shocked that we'd managed to dodge his attack, and his surprise had left him wide open.

"Hmph!"

Patausche dodged with a grunt, showcasing incredible speed. With a fierce rush, she leaped into the neighboring room and sliced the man's arm right off, causing the weapon to drop to the floor. I didn't spare a glance at Frenci and her two guards. I knew they would be fine. After effortlessly deflecting the knives thrown at them, they kicked the two kids to the floor.

Meanwhile, I threw a knife at the window and detonated it on impact, creating a hole in the wall. The cold, dry air from outside brushed against my cheeks.

I looked down through the gap at the ruffians below. I even saw one idiot pointing up at us and shouting.

"We're surrounded. Perfect. This should serve as a good distraction," I muttered.

"...How awful." Frenci looked back, one hand pushing up her lead-colored hair. "You're really going to do this? You must be quite brave as well, Holy Knight."

"This, uh... This actually wasn't the plan I had in mind..." Patausche frowned uncomfortably, her eyes on me.

"Hey, you said it yourself," I shot back. "This town is full of scumbags, right?"

"What are you trying to say?"

"We'll clean up the city by disposing of all its trash while we smoke out Lideo Sodrick. We'll be contributing to society."

Neither Patausche nor Frenci said anything. Frenci's guards were similarly silent. But when I peeked out the hole I'd made, I could see bad guys all around below and in the neighboring building. There was no going back now. My ungraceful, poorly thought-out, and foolish plan was already in motion.

It was difficult for Lideo Sodrick to believe the report. He had never imagined his opponents would take such aggressive measures.

"Brother...," said Iri anxiously, "we should probably start heading toward the underground escape route. I looked into those people. The man is the goddess killer, penal hero Xylo Forbartz, and the woman is the captain of the Thirteenth Order of the Holy Knights, Patausche Kivia. The other three could not be identified, but I believe they are from the Night-Gaunts."

The instant Lideo heard this, a heavy feeling of uneasiness began to weigh down on his heart. He knew those names, and he was especially familiar with that of the penal hero.

*The goddess killer, Xylo Forbartz...*

Lideo's men had done some research on the penal heroes, and this one was the worst of the worst—the enemy of mankind. Normally, someone like him ought to be locked in the lowest floor of Taga Jaffa Prison, where they kept captured demon lords. Killing a goddess was out of the question, regardless of motive. Lideo knew people who committed murder for fun or just to feel something, but Xylo Forbartz's sin was beyond his understanding.

*He's the last person I want to run into. But...*

Xylo himself chose to come here, and he'd even started a brawl in

Sodrick's Shell. His actions surpassed the words "daring" and "fearless." This was reckless violence—and for Lideo, it was both the most dangerous scenario and the opportunity of a lifetime.

*If I can kill the man who forged a pact with that goddess...*

That might just earn him some major perks from the coexisters. And in that case, he was going to use every secret weapon he could to dispose of the intruders.

"Iri, you mobilized our whole force, right?"

"Yes, Brother. I have already arranged for everyone to be here. I was told that Shiji Bau recruited the Iron Whale as well."

That was a name Lideo had heard before.

*The Iron Whale? Seems doubtful he'll make it here in time, though.*

The Iron Whale was an artilleryman—something like a mix between a mercenary and an adventurer. The concept of an artilleryman was only a few years old, and they constituted a new branch in the military, just like the thunderstroke soldiers. Artillerymen went through special training, and it was said they could even take on dragon knights one-on-one.

"All right. Then—"

Lideo paused, hesitating. There was one thing still bothering him. Why would Xylo Forbartz do something this reckless? The entire city was like a weapon in Lideo's arsenal. The adventurers and his adopted family could wipe out any intruder in their way... Did Xylo believe he had a chance at winning? Surely, his goal wasn't simply to kick up a fuss. He would probably try to escape the city very soon. Did he think that Lideo would chase after him, blinded by a desire to capture the man who'd forged a pact with the goddess?

*Is that what he's after? What kind of trap have you set for me, Xylo Forbartz?*

Perhaps he planned to use the disturbance as a distraction to capture Lideo as he pursued them. The guild master stopped and took a few deep breaths until he was calm enough to stand.

*The most important thing right now is to keep my location a secret.*

Being a coward was his best chance for survival. That was what he'd learned from years working as head of the Adventurers Guild. He could feel it in his gut, and his gut was telling him that he was in danger. Xylo Forbartz wasn't someone he should wait for and attack head-on. He was correct to summon every warrior he could, but he was going to use them to flee the scene.

"…Have the adventurers handle them while we escape."

That was the best move they could make, in Lideo's opinion.

*Yes… The only thing they can do is cause a scene and leave town. And if I chase after them, I'll be falling right into their trap. I'm not going to play their games.*

Lideo began collecting the most important documents from his drawers and shelves. These were things he couldn't leave behind, including any evidence that he was involved with the coexisters.

"Iri, don't leave my side."

"Yes, Brother." It was clear she was nervous. Her already white cheeks were becoming even paler. "I will protect you, even if it costs me my life."

"Good." Family members risked their lives for one another. That was how Lideo believed families should be. "Keep the orders simple. Kill the penal hero and Holy Knight… In fact, kill anyone who gets in our way. We have no need for prisoners."

That much was non-negotiable. The Adventurers Guild couldn't afford to look soft, especially since violence was a big part of their business. Plus, they could neutralize the penal hero for a while if they killed him, which was itself a great achievement.

*Even if we're up against the military…*

He had to make it a point, especially in this city, that if someone came at them with such lawless violence, the Adventurers Guild would crush them with twice the force.

It wasn't long before Sodrick's Shell was lit up like a festival, and just as loud. People started rushing out of buildings around the Guild, while merchants at their outdoor stalls grabbed whatever they could and ran, no time to close up shop.

I landed on a canopy of wooden planks and filthy cloth that hung over the street.

"Eek!"

A merchant shrieked and rushed off in fright. I felt guilty, but this was an emergency. I immediately activated my flight seal to increase my speed, blowing away the canopy and running up the neighboring building's wall. It seemed to house a brothel, and for a second, I spotted a scene inside—a woman in the middle of work and a panicked man trying to put his clothes back on. Of course, I didn't have time to watch. My concern right now was the ground below. As my body twisted in the air, the first thing I noticed was Patausche jumping directly out of the Guild building and onto the ground below. Her swordsmanship and athleticism were outstanding.

"Hey, get back! Stay away from that woman! That's the one the guild master's after!"

"Surround her, but do not engage!"

The instant Patausche landed, adventurers and common delinquents pushed and kicked merchants and their customers out of the way and began to encircle her. They lunged at her with hatchets and short swords, but none of them could get near.

"*Tsk.* Xylo... Was this really all part of his plan?" Patausche's shoe scraped against the ground. "What a reckless fool!"

She deflected a pursuer's blade, then pierced the ground to activate her shield before blocking another strike and thrusting her blade into the attacker's shoulder. Any arrow shot at her from a crossbow would only be deflected by her sacred seal barrier. Patausche's defense was the true heart of her swordsmanship. Or maybe it was her footwork.

At any rate, she took on the group alone. As she fought the enemy in close combat, she had to attack and defend while limiting the other side's opportunities to snipe at her. I, on the other hand, had a relatively easy job. I had plenty of time to aim at my target while infusing my weapon with the power of my sacred seal. After unsheathing my knife in midair, I threw it straight down toward the ground. The blast sent flying numerous reinforcements and snipers targeting Patausche from the shadows, and took the surrounding street stalls, pavement, and buildings along with them. Stalls exploded into pieces, stone blocks shot into the sky, and walls came crumbling down.

It may have looked like I was merely destroying the city, but I was actually closing off the area to reinforcements. It was the easiest way to create panic while reducing our enemy's numbers.

The job was easy with a skilled swordsman like Patausche on my side. When I landed, I had my back to a wall and around ten enemies lying on the ground around me.

*The only issue now is—*

"Xylo!" shouted Patausche. "There's a child assassin. Wh-what should I do?"

A child with a small blade was charging right for her. Fighting adult adventurers was far less troublesome. With children's youthful decisiveness came great speed, and the small assassin's footwork made it clear that she was willing to sacrifice herself to take out her opponent. To make matters worse, Patausche seemed uncomfortable fighting children. I knew where she was coming from. The military didn't train you for this sort of enemy. But things were different for Frenci and me.

"There is no need to fear the energy and agility of a child. They do not have the muscle mass of an adult." Frenci swung her curved sword, hitting the child's arm. "All you need to do is focus on blocking their attacks from a lower angle."

She had delivered a blunt strike, not a cut. In fact, the blade of her sword was no blade but a meaty slab of steel—fine when using a weapon with a sacred seal. A flash of light sent the knife-wielding child's body into convulsions, causing her to hop a few times before dropping to the ground.

Franci's seal was called Gwemel, a seal of violet lightning. Her weapon was structurally similar to a lightning staff, allowing her to immobilize her opponent with an electric shock from the so-called blade. The design was meant for fighting warriors with heavy armor and faeries with armor-like skin, and it was one of many sacred seal technologies developed by the Southern Night-Gaunts.

"Do you see what I mean, Holy Knight?"

Frenci kicked the child on the ground without a second thought, then looked back at Patausche.

"Mmgh..."

As expected, Patausche was frowning. Frenci, however, expressed no concern. She was busy reprimanding me, now that the threat was neutralized.

"Xylo, what's next? Surely, you have a plan. I hope there's something in that tiny head of yours besides rocks. How are we going to get out of here?"

"Who said we were running away?" I countered. "We're gonna fight. We need to create even more chaos."

"Then what? Do you plan on eliminating every single person living in the slums?"

"Yep. We're going to continue fighting until Lideo Sodrick can't afford to keep ignoring us."

"I was giving you far too much credit when I said your head was full of rocks. I have never heard a more poorly thought-out plan."

Frenci may not have agreed, but we had a good chance of winning this battle. For now I needed to focus on creating as much chaos as possible while sealing off any street I could to prevent reinforcements from arriving. Merchants and customers were already pushing one another in a mad dash to run away, kicking up dense clouds of dust.

Just then, an angry shout came from somewhere in the crowd.

"That's as far as you go, penal hero!"

The speaker was a bearded man pointing the tip of his short sword at me. He was probably an adventurer. He coughed as he stumbled over a small pile of wreckage.

"We, the Giant-Hunter Brigade, will make you pay for disturbing the peace of the city! Come on, men! Get 'em!" he shouted, signaling behind him.

A group of men came crawling out of one of the buildings I'd partially destroyed. They were covered in wounds, but they still hadn't lost the will to fight. Each of them held a lightning staff in hand.

"Who are they?" Patausche sounded disgusted. "*These* are the people they're trusting to protect the peace of the district?"

"Looks like it, and that one seems to be their boss. Hey, boss-man, don't do this. I don't want to fight you." I tried to warn them. I didn't want to kill them unless I had to. "Do you really wanna get hurt that badly?"

"Heh! I should be asking you the same question." The bearded man shot me a smug grin. "Looks like you criminals don't know who you're dealing with. We're the seasoned adventurers who cleared out the Western Shenvoo Crystal Cemetery—the Giant-Hunter Brigade! And guess what? My reputation even earned me an invite to join the famous Molchet's Northern Expedition Corps!"

"No clue who that is."

My comment was enough to make the bearded man's expression twist with rage.

"Don't you dare underestimate us... Fire! Did you see my skills, men? I stopped him in his tracks with the art of conversation, and now he's wide open! A fat bonus to whoever hits him!"

The men behind him fired their lightning staffs, but their aim was poor and their timing, sporadic. Both Patausche and Frenci simply moved to the side and easily dodged their shots. This was going to be a piece of cake.

"Don't stop! Fire, fire, fire!" shouted the bearded leader. "Hit 'em with whatever you've got! Use fireworks for all I care!"

One of his men did just that, in fact. Red, green, blue—a bouquet of beautiful colors dispersed as it exploded. Lightning staffs used to make flashy lights like that had minimal attack power. They were brought out during summer festivals or for New Year's celebrations, so most of the technology went into making the colors and sounds pretty. In other words, they were just trying to distract us. The real attack was going to come from elsewhere.

"You guys handle this joker's lackies," I said. "I'll take the one up top."

"H-hey, wait!" Patausche shouted. "Don't leave these nutjobs to us!"

"I agree," said Frenci. "You explained nothing, and now you are going off to do something reckless again."

But in spite of Patausche's and Frenci's complaints, I kicked off the ground and began running up the nearest building's wall. I'd seen someone on the roof with something quite unsettling—a ring-shaped weapon composed of multiple elongated lightning staffs. It was the same weapon I'd seen earlier inside the Adventurers Guild, capable of firing multiple shots simultaneously. From what I could remember, the military called this weapon the Halgut Blaster Seal Compound, and it was still in testing. I didn't want to think about what would happen if that thing started taking potshots at the ground below, so I activated my flight seal continuously until I made it all the way to the rooftop, then leaped into the sky and launched a knife.

"What the hell?!"

The rooftop adventurer reflexively fired the lightning staff seal compound the moment he saw me, but his aim was poor. Trying to be accurate with a rapid-fire weapon like this was an impossible task to begin with, and it was definitely not meant to shoot down an airborne target.

The multiple bolts of lightning didn't even come close to me. Conversely, there was no way my knife would miss. It struck the Halgut Blaster head-on, blowing it to pieces and silencing the man holding it. The top of the building was partially destroyed in the process, causing rubble to come crashing down—perfect for creating even more chaos. I landed not on the ground but on the wall of another building. Thunderstroke soldiers with flight seals like mine achieved our highest mobility in labyrinthian districts like this, and we had the advantage over dragon knights, thanks to our ability to turn in confined spaces. They were welcome to come at me with arrows or bolts of lightning…

…*But they aren't gonna hit me.*

That much I was sure of. Leaping over an alleyway, I threw another knife, blowing a hole right into the wall of a house and creating yet another avalanche of rubble.

"Aaah!"

I heard the bearded man scream below as his men were cut down by Patausche and Frenci before they could even fire their lightning staffs.

"Threatening me or Xylo is tantamount to a declaration of war upon the Mastibolt family," declared Frenci as she swung her curved sword like a vortex. "You will regret this."

Both Patausche and Frenci were covering each other's blind spots as they moved. It was pretty good teamwork. In fact, they seemed surprisingly compatible.

...All that was left was for me to finish the job as I descended from the sky.

"I need precision, men! Now, fire!" shouted the bearded man, pointing his sword up at me, but he was asking the impossible.

Leaping off the walls to either side, I dodged their attacks while closing in on them, all in a single breath. Now I just had to continue toward the bearded man and kick the stuffing out of him.

"Gwah!"

He released a short scream as I kicked his body into a wall. With their leader gone, the team's will to fight evaporated. Some of the men threw down their weapons and ran away, while others rushed forward, only to have my fists introduce their faces to the ground.

"How stupid are you guys?" I muttered.

The skirmish was over in five seconds. I searched the unconscious leader's overcoat and found a short sword and a massive knife, both of which I kept. I ran my finger down their blades and found them sharp enough. *Passable*, I thought.

"Pardon me," said a deep voice. When I turned around, one of Frenci's bodyguards was holding up a round shield in front of us. The two of them seemed to have been handling some of the adventurers on their own. But before I could thank him, I heard a dry pop. An arrow, fired by the last standing member of the Giant-Hunter Brigade, skewered his shield. Frenci promptly coldcocked that adventurer as well.

"...Please take better care of yourself...," said the bodyguard. "I'm the one who gets scolded when you act recklessly."

SENTENCED TO BE A HERO, VOLUME II

"Well, we wouldn't want that. My bad. I really appreciate the help, though."

"I'm just glad you're safe."

I'd carelessly let my guard down. While that arrow wouldn't have fatally wounded me, it could well have done some damage. I would have expected a Night-Gaunt to tell me I was a mess or something.

"You're not gonna insult me, huh?" I asked.

"Of course not. Why would I?"

"I mean... You know how Night-Gaunts are. Insults are as common as breathing."

"Oh...? You still believe that? I feel your pain, but Lady Frenci simply—"

"Kalos!" Frenci called out, her tone stern. "Enough chitchat. Do not bother Xylo with such useless information. We are in the midst of battle."

"My apologies." Kalos smiled wryly. His expression gave me the impression of a boulder grinning.

Then, out of nowhere, Kalos's brawny body was blown straight to the side, followed by a painfully loud thud as he hit the alleyway wall. At least, that was what I assumed happened. I didn't have time to check—I had to move.

I caught sight of a large black shadow lunging toward me from the back of the alley. The figure must have thrown some rubble and hit Kalos. It...was humanoid, but colored a bluish-black with a sort of slimy luster to it. Its body was 50 percent bigger than mine, its head was covered with eyes, and fangs were protruding from its mouth. But what stood out most of all were its thick, long arms, hanging down to its feet. Occasionally, its knuckles would hit the ground, and the pavement would split open, shooting gravel into the air and reducing the pathway to dust.

I had to get out of there. The creature, now roaring at us, was obviously a faerie.

"What the hell?" Patausche put everyone's curiosity into words.

"Isn't that a faerie?! It looks like a troll! Was Sodrick keeping this monster as a pet?!"

"It seems he failed to properly discipline it," said Frenci. "Tahg! Go make sure Kalos is okay!"

The two of them might have been joking around, but they were getting the job done. Patausche shifted her gaze toward this new target, then stepped forward and thrust her blade, aiming for the groin. She stabbed twice—no, three times in the blink of an eye, all the while dodging the troll's counterattacks with unbelievable speed and grace. However, the enemy's legs were so massive that she only managed to take off a little bit of flesh from its knee and calf.

"Foul creature," she cursed as she activated her sacred seal barrier to block one of the troll's attacks. Its arm bounced off her shield of light with a heavy thud, causing the beast to stagger before leaping back. "I need a more powerful weapon! I knew I should have brought my lance and armor!"

"If you did that," I said, "they would have captured you before you even walked into the building... Frenci!"

"Yes, I know. Good work drawing its attention."

Patausche's attacks were only a distraction. Frenci promptly threw her curved blade as I, too, infused one of my precious knives with the power of my sacred seal and threw it.

...However, neither of our attacks struck home. The troll was far more agile than it appeared and quickly guarded its head with its arms. Although some damage was done—the lightning from Frenci's curved sword burned its arms, and my knife managed to take out a chunk of its shoulder in the explosion—neither attack was close to fatal.

*It's too damn big.*

This troll appeared to be particularly large and tough, and defeating it was going to take a while. We needed to make a definitive strike to its head. That meant our only option was...

"Xylo!"

Someone called out to warn me, though I couldn't tell if it was

Patausche or Frenci. The troll screamed in agony, then reached out and grabbed a street stall's pillar before throwing it with all its might, destroying countless shops in the way.

*Dammit.*

I wouldn't be able to dodge in time, not with the collapsing stalls to worry about. I ended up using my flight seal to kick chunks of wood out of the way.

Had Patausche and Frenci made it?

It appeared Patausche had dodged in time, but her leg was bleeding as she tried to get back up. She'd been hit with a piece of wreckage. Frenci managed to jump on top of a still-standing street stall as she put some distance between herself and the troll. I could tell she was yelling something, probably hurling insults at me, but I didn't have time to check.

Chunks of wood and gray dust soared into the air, and on the other side was the howling faerie. I'd thought we were finished with the adventurers, but now more began to emerge. It seemed their supply was endless. Here and there, I could see them crawling out of buildings, armed with bows and crossbows. It looked like they intended to let the troll fight us head-on while they showered us with arrows from the periphery.

"Dammit," I said. This was absolute chaos. But if that was how they wanted it…

*Heh. Bring it on. Don't get too cocky, you assholes.*

If they wanted chaos, then I was going to give it to them. I looked up.

*This should be far enough.*

I'd arrived at a street intersecting an alleyway connected to the main road. I had already led them right where I wanted them, all the while blocking off smaller side routes. I could feel her.

"Teoritta! I'm over here!"

Holy Knights and goddesses could detect one another's presence to an extent, and Teoritta had probably already sensed me, just like she had in the tunnels of Zewan Gan.

"Save me with your divine blessing," I called out. "I'm sorry for leaving you behind."

Teoritta was here. Of course she was—the reason wasn't all that complicated. When I'd met with Dotta that morning, Jayce had been there as well. He hadn't shown much interest in our plan, so when Teoritta asked him where we went, he would surely have told her.

That was why she'd come.

And of course, she'd brought along some guards to watch over her.

"It appears you needed my protection, after all." Her proud voice was even closer than I'd expected. "This situation is obviously your punishment for leaving me behind, my knight. However, I am a generous goddess, so I shall help you. Follow my lead, men!"

Beyond the cloud of dust and the troll stood Teoritta, her arms crossed. And standing behind her were King Norgalle, Tatsuya, and Jayce. Norgalle looked confident, while Tatsuya's eyes were vacant and expressionless. Jayce, of course, looked bored out of his mind. I had no idea what any of them were thinking, but I knew exactly what was going to happen.

"People of Sodrick's Shell! Run away now, or surrender! If you choose to fight, you'll die!"

I shouted loud enough that everyone in the district could hear. Offering a warning was the least I could do, since this wasn't going to be pretty for those who still wished to fight.

"Bow before me!"

King Norgalle's voice carried through the streets, in spite of the chaos.

"I am Norgalle Senridge the First, king of the United Kingdom of Zef-Zeyal Meht Kioh."

He sounded impressively dignified and absolutely confident, and that was why every single person there turned to look at him.

"I was told that this district has become a nest of criminals and sinners threatening my rule, and the moment I arrived tonight, it became clear that was true!"

The king raised his hand. In it was a small metal tube, and I could see plenty more sticking out of the rucksack on his back. I couldn't be sure, but my gut was telling me those metal tubes were some sort of powerful, highly destructive weapon.

"I am giving you a choice! Submit to lawful punishment as my loyal subjects! Or—"

"Can it! What are you babblin' about, you old kook? Move!"

"Die!"

"Outta the way, geezer!"

The bearded leader of the Giant-Hunter Brigade, along with a few adventurers, began sharing their extremely reasonable opinions as they rushed to leave the slums, pushing Norgalle and the others out of their way. King Norgalle's face was overcome with pain and grief.

"It pains me to make this decision. Nothing is more regrettable for a country ruled by law than to be forced to carry out extralegal punishment. But as it must be done, I shall take on the unenviable role." King Norgalle threw one of the metal cylinders. "For the crime of treason, I sentence you all to death by explosion."

The instant the cylinder hit the ground, it exploded with a flash of light. A deafening shock wave sliced through the air, swallowing one— no, two—street stalls that had managed to survive the earlier fighting. They were blown to bits, leaving nothing behind. Screams followed, as the adventurers trying to make their escape were sent flying. Weak building walls in the area crumbled. Cracks spread, and destruction gave birth to yet more destruction. The chaos and panic grew, catching even the troll's attention.

This was our chance. I traded glances with Patausche and held out a hand to help her up.

"Hey, can you move?" I asked.

"Y-yes... I-I'm fine. It's merely a scratch..." A troubled expression flashed across her face, but she managed to stand, undeterred by the fresh wound on her leg. "Ahem... Um, that troll... It's extremely tough. We should probably aim for its head."

"I agree."

A half-assed attack would only tickle a troll of that size. I started racking my brain for ideas, but time was running out, and we had to stop this monster before things got any worse.

"Tatsuya, Jayce, move out!" shouted Norgalle, as he threw another explosive tube. "Fight and protect our Goddess!"

"Guh."

"Fine..."

Tatsuya grunted as he moved forward, while Jayce spoke through a yawn, assuming a battle stance with his spear. Both of them moved swiftly and mercilessly, after their own style.

Hearing that, I promptly shouted to the goddess:

"Teoritta, I need your help! Our enemy is a faerie!"

"Heh. Do you regret leaving me behind, my knight? I am sure you are now painfully aware of just how important and dependable I am."

"...Yes, extremely aware."

"Of course you are!"

Teoritta joyfully ran straight over to me without so much as a glance at her surroundings. And that was a good thing—she didn't have to see any of the chaos, destruction, or tragedy. Tatsuya and Jayce stood to either side of Teoritta, disposing of whatever obstacle came their way.

"Gubba... Buh... Buh..."

Tatsuya continued grunting intermittently, using only his right hand to swing his battle-ax into a pack of adventurers. They instinctively countered, but his weapon didn't care if you were a strong warrior or a delicate child. Tatsuya was like an autonomous killing machine. Challenging him was tantamount to sticking your hand into moving saw blades—it was essentially your own fault.

"Guuuh." Tatsuya released a nonsensical battle cry from the back of his throat. "Bujiiiruaaah!"

He then swung his ax, cutting down a series of incoming arrows. One adventurer appeared to have lost it and came running at him screaming something awful, only for Tatsuya to split his head wide open. Meanwhile, a young assassin tried to pierce Tatsuya's stomach with a knife but was met with the ax before he even got in range. Tatsuya didn't spare the corpse a second glance. Instead, he reached out with his left hand, grabbed the nearest adventurer by the leg, and began spinning him around to use as a shield.

"Who the hell *is* this guy?!"

Someone tried to hit him with their lightning staff, but Tatsuya deflected the shot with his weapon. His reflexes were superhuman.

"Eek! Stay back!"

"This is bad! That guy's a monster, too!"

Tatsuya rushed across the ground, seeming almost to hover. This charge was a weapon of its own, and each step he took tore into the pavement. Getting hit by him now would feel like being run over by a chariot.

"Fff," grunted Tatsuya ominously. Nobody could stop him now, not even Tatsuya himself.

Those who tried to run away were caught up in his attack and slammed into the alley walls, reducing them to rubble. Impressive as always.

I'd heard that Tatsuya had been a hero ever since the days of Penal Hero Unit 9001, so long ago no records of it remained. Unit 9001 was created during the First War of Subjugation, when mankind's war against the Demon Blight first started... But that rumor came from Venetim, so it was most likely false.

"Forget about the guy with the helmet! Just aim for the guy with the moustache and that bratty goddess!"

"You got it! Outta the way, shorty!"

That insult was hurled at Jayce, causing him to raise one eyebrow.

"Dammit," he said. "...I should have never told the goddess where Xylo was."

Although in battle stance, Jayce seemed to lack motivation. This was how he was when Neely wasn't around. That said, his skills with a spear were useful, even when he wasn't in the sky. Jayce used to frequently participate in and win martial arts tournaments all across the continent, though he did it only for prize money, which he used to take care of dragons.

I had heard of him long before we ever met. They called him Jayce the Rumbling Wind, since he went from tournament to tournament, sweeping every one. He was so strong that a certain princess from an extremely wealthy noble family had once asked for his hand in marriage, but I never heard what happened after that. Then again, I didn't really need to.

"*Tsk*. All right, assholes. Shut up and get in line, or get out of my face," he hissed, making his annoyance clear as day. "Stop wasting my time."

To Jayce, people were no different from wild animals. He claimed that humans were important symbionts to dragons, but that didn't stop him from killing them without much hesitation. I didn't know much about his past, but Jayce's code of morals did not seem to afford a special, superior place for his own kind. Personally, it made no sense to me.

"Stop while you can," he said. "I'm serious. I'm warning you."

But the adventurers didn't listen to Jayce's advice. After all, they were lowlife goons in the middle of an adrenaline rush.

"Shut your mouth! Cavalry, attack!"

A neigh rang out, and a bunch of men suited in armor immediately charged toward Jayce on horseback. I had no idea what they were thinking, but it looked like there were some ex-cavalrymen among the adventurers. While this surprised me, Jayce simply sighed as if he found it all very tedious.

"Cavalry? You know what?" His short spear bounced off the ground in an arch-like motion as he scooped up one of King Norgalle's sacred seal–infused cylinders. "…I'm in a really bad mood today."

The cylinder flew into the air and exploded in a blinding burst of light over the ex-cavalrymen's heads. The horses reared, stopping the men in their tracks, while Jayce lunged forward, swinging his spear.

"You asked for it."

The tip of his spear cut a single stroke through the first row of enemies, and that was all it took. Jayce's small frame flew through the air, piercing a man's head. I witnessed the weapon pass right through the enemy's steel helmet before shattering his skull. This wasn't a show of Jayce's own strength. His short spear had a sacred seal engraved in it for when he was fighting from the back of a dragon. Normally, his weapon was for throwing, and the sacred seal was meant for sniping flying faeries while he sailed through the sky. Even if Jayce was still holding the spear, a strike from it was like being hit by a lump of iron with enough force to drill a hole through your body.

"Hyaaah!"

Another cavalryman charged forward in a frenzy while spinning his long spear, but there was no way an attack like that would hit Jayce.

He effortlessly dodged it before swinging his own spear once more, gouging a hole into the man's breastplate.

"I warned you all. Stop this. Are you really going to force your horses to join you on this suicide mission? …Go, you're free now. Get out of here," urged Jayce, patting the man's horse on the rear to get it to leave, which it obediently did.

He seemed to sympathize with the horses and skillfully made sure to kill only the riders. The cavalry weren't going to last much longer at this rate.

"Surely, you have realized you are no match for us! Surrender!" shouted Norgalle. "If you yield to the laws of my kingdom and pay for your crimes, then you shall be forgiven!"

The dreadful scene was rapidly growing grimmer. The slums would soon be reduced to ruins. One man surrendered to King Norgalle, throwing his weapon to the ground and clasping both hands above his head. It was a depressing sight.

"Just who are you people?!" Even the bearded man from the Giant-Hunter Brigade had dropped to his knees, with tears in his eyes. "This is insanity. Pure insanity…!"

Norgalle's presence alone seemed to be bringing the conflict to a close on that end of the battlefield, and things over here were almost taken care of as well. After all, Teoritta's arrival had basically solved our troll problem.

"Xylo, it's coming," warned Patausche. "And it's angry, too. Do not let it get near Goddess Teoritta."

"I won't."

Blood was dripping from the troll's half-open mouth and from the wounds we'd inflicted. It screamed, pulverizing the ground and the walls as if it were in a great deal of pain. Stones flew through the air, hitting a few adventurers.

*The hell is wrong with Lideo Sodrick, keeping a faerie like this as a pet?!*

I sprinted to the right while Patausche went left so we didn't get caught up in the troll's frenzy. It was simple, but it worked. I reached out to Teoritta as she raced toward me, grabbed her, and held her in my arms.

"Sorry for leaving you behind," I said. "I only did it in case of an emergency like this."

"I do not need your excuses, my knight," she replied.

"Yeah, I figured."

I kicked off the ground, leaping over the faerie's head while Patausche remained on foot and kept the enemy distracted. As the tip of her blade touched the ground littered with broken pieces of pavement, she muttered: "Niskeph Rada," activating her sacred seal. A blue barrier appeared, sending a few stones from the rubble flying as it flickered. The barrier then bashed into the troll's head beautifully. While this was hardly an attack and inflicted no pain on the troll, it did a good job of distracting the beast. The troll's gaze instantly turned on Patausche. It didn't last long, but it was more than enough time. With Teoritta by my side, a single faerie—not even a demon lord—was hardly a challenge. Against a nonhuman enemy, she could strike with her full power.

"Finish this quickly, my knight."

She stroked the air before her, and over a dozen swords instantly emerged from the void, raining down upon the troll below. I grabbed one, twisting my body before launching the weapon with plenty of energy from my sacred seal. The shower of swords skewered the troll's massive body to the ground, and it screamed for only a moment before the sword I'd thrown exploded.

The entire district shook with the blast. The light was so blinding it could burn your eyes just looking at it. I wasn't expecting it to be that powerful or that loud...and that was apparently King Norgalle's fault. Some of his tubes must have been caught up in the explosion. Whatever the case, the blast quickly engulfed the district, and by the time the air had finally cleared, the troll's upper body and most of its lower body were gone. Its remaining flesh dropped to the ground, oozing a black, sticky, bubbling fluid into the city's drainage channels.

"I owe you one, Teoritta. You saved us," I said.

"Is that all you wish to say?" she replied. "Are you sure you are not forgetting something much more important? Such as praising me?"

"...Do I really have to?"

"Yes." Teoritta snorted proudly. "I require praise from my knight and my knight alone, Xylo, and that is you. I want *you* to tell me how incredible I am—tell me that I am 'one hell of a goddess,' especially since I am still angry that you left me behind! Now speak! Shower me with praise!"

"Yes, milady! Uh... You're one hell of a goddess."

I couldn't deny her a compliment after she'd said all that. This felt different from the innate desires that these living weapons were saddled with by the disgusting humans that created them. What Teoritta wanted was honor as a soldier. She wanted to be complimented by someone she thought was strong. That was the kind of praise she was after, and even I could understand that. *At least, I really hope that's all this is*, I thought, and with that simple wish in my heart, I placed a hand on her head. Sparks shot into the air with each rub.

"You're amazing, Teoritta. I can't lose with you on my side. You really are one hell of a goddess."

"Of course I am!" Her lips curled into an ear-to-ear grin. "I am the goddess of swords, and I promise to eliminate every last demon lord and bring peace and freedom to you all."

"...What's happening?"

Lideo Sodrick looked on in utter amazement. He had hidden himself among the other adventurers and was in the middle of trying to flee, when he suddenly realized that all of his escape routes had been sealed off, and he was now stuck in the middle of a storm of violence and destruction. Explosion after explosion—it was barbaric. The entirety of Sodrick's Shell had been reduced to a vortex of screams. Any building might come crumbling down at any moment. This district was like a castle for the Sodrick family and had been passed down to Lideo from his predecessor.

*How did things end up like this?*

He had placed sacred seal–engraved traps and mechanisms all throughout the district, just in case there were ever any intruders or double-crossers. He once thought he would always be safe here, but now he felt the best plan was to mix into the crowd and flee.

And he still didn't understand what the intruders were thinking. Once they'd made an enemy of everyone in Sodrick's Shell and were surrounded, they should have immediately prioritized escape. Never in his wildest imagination did Lideo expect them to start aggressively destroying the city, fighting off all challengers. Perhaps he'd underestimated the penal heroes. He couldn't believe all his safety nets had been destroyed by a bunch of irredeemable, foolish savages' random acts of violence.

"…Brother!"

It was Iri's voice that brought Lideo back to the present and made him realize that he'd become separated from her in the midst of the fleeing crowd. He glanced around in search of her, but someone else found him first.

"Hey, uh. Sorry…," came a voice from behind. It sounded truly remorseful. Someone was standing behind him—and soon an arm wrapped around Lideo's neck, and a small piece of metal like a blade pressed against his throat. "I'm sorry about this, but a really bad man asked me to steal you away, and he even threated me. I honestly don't want to do this anymore, but I had no choice." He sounded more embarrassed than frightened.

It's true they were in a crowd of panicking adventurers, but Lideo was still stunned that he hadn't realized someone was sneaking up on him. He scowled.

"I need you to come with me," begged the man. "Please? I don't wanna have to kill you…" He had a small, childlike frame—it was Dotta Luzulas. "You'll be fine. Trust me."

*Ridiculous…*

Lideo had said the same things Dotta was saying countless times, and he knew they were meaningless. Lideo saw Iri's despairing face out of the corner of his vision.

*I'm sorry.*

He gently closed his eyes. It was all he could do.

*...Just bear with it a little longer.*

He would simply have to wait and see if the last ace up his sleeve was going to make it in time.

Under the blanket of night, the city was eerily chaotic, and in the center of all that activity was Sodrick's Shell. Fires spread and rose toward the sky, and explosions could be heard in the background as adventurers ran down alleys, trying to escape.

Shiji Bau stood in a back street beneath the pale crimson moon and watched. It appeared the situation had gotten a little out of hand. She wanted to get a handle on what was going on, but she also knew that the first thing you had to do in times like this was move before it was too late.

"Quite the commotion," muttered Boojum apathetically. He was seated on a stack of wooden boxes, reading again. Shiji Bau found his behavior especially aggravating.

"You know," he continued, "in my personal opinion, this is far too dangerous. You should keep your distance."

"I never asked for your opinion...but you're right. Lideo's probably already dead, and if that's the case, we won't get paid."

"Damn... This is bad. The hell is going on here?" complained another strangely muffled voice from behind them. "I came all the way here, and the client's already dead?"

This man was called the Iron Whale, and he sounded fed up. He worked as a mercenary and was known as an artilleryman—a rarity in their line of work. Getting in touch with him hadn't been easy, and now it looked like it had all been for nothing.

"I'm not going to work for free," he said. "I'm out. That okay with you?"

"I suppose it's inevitable... We should probably withdraw."

Shiji Bau began racking her brain. Lideo was a very cautious person, but you couldn't predict what the penal heroes would do. They were out of their minds. Nobody had expected them to start destroying the city so quickly.

"The Guild seems to be in a state of confusion as well, so I think we should go in, collect our reward, and get out of town. What about you, Boojum?"

"Hmm... I'm going to save Lideo Sodrick. That would be the polite thing to do, I think."

"Seriously? What are you so loyal to him for? He's probably already dead, and I'm not going to help you."

"I can't save a corpse? I owe him, and I would feel bad for him if nobody went to his aid, regardless of whether he's alive or not."

"You would feel bad for him? You..." Shiji Bau didn't know how to respond. There was something wrong with this man. It was as if he wasn't human.

"I wasn't planning on asking you to come with me. It's just— Wait." Boojum suddenly waved his hand and stopped Shiji Bau. He lifted his head from his book to reveal an even gloomier expression than usual. He even sighed. "...I see. How unfortunate. It appears this is as far as I go."

"What?" This was the first time Shiji Bau had ever seen him express something akin to emotion. "What's wrong? Did you notice something?"

"No... I was contacted. That's all. I feel sorry for Lideo Sodrick, but I was given an order."

He waved his hand around his ear again. There seemed to be a small bug—a fly-like creature buzzing in between and around his fingers. Boojum stood, then looked to Shiji Bau.

"I can offer you two a new job, Shiji Bau and Iron Whale. What do you say?"

"What?"

"You two are after money, yes?" continued Boojum. "That can be provided, or so I was told."

Shiji Bau studied his expression. At first she thought this must be some kind of joke, but Boojum never told jokes, so that couldn't be it.

"Unfortunately, we are cutting ties with Lideo Sodrick," he said. "What a shame. I feel truly sorry for him."

"Wait. Where's the client? Who's hiring us?"

"We are."

A number of shadows emerged from the darkness of the back street as Boojum audibly shut his book. Shiji Bau immediately realized they weren't human, or any other normal creatures. They were faeries, and relatively small ones, at that: a cir sith, a fuath, and a kelpie.

"Are they—?" she began.

The cir sith bared its fangs and growled, perhaps perceiving repulsion in her gaze, and Boojum began to softly caress its neck.

"Stop. You're being rude," he said to it.

To Shiji Bau, it looked like something was growing out of the tips of Boojum's finger. Crimson blades...or some sort of claws.

*Riiip.* She could hear the muffled sound of the cir sith's throat being torn open before the creature collapsed to the ground and began to convulse. It was silent, but it was obvious this was no quick and painless death. The other faeries took a step back in fear. Boojum looked at them and nodded.

"Good. We are asking them for help, so be polite. Now then...what was I supposed to say again? Oh, right... We can pay you more than Lideo Sodrick would have."

Boojum stared at Shiji Bau with his bottomless black eyes. It was at this moment that her suspicions grew into certainty. This man was a demon lord, the center of an outbreak of the Demon Blight. Unlike Lideo, he wasn't simply a traitor to the human race.

"You will be rewarded," he said. "Humans will do anything for money. I learned that."

Shiji Bau briefly closed her eyes, though not because the black abyss of Boojum's stare had overwhelmed her.

*I probably don't have much of a choice*, she thought.

This man was far stranger than she had imagined, and he was most likely a demon lord. *I was naive*, she thought. *Where did I mess up? It's too late now, though. I'm surrounded by faeries.* The threat was clear, and she had no choice but to accept the mission she'd been offered—to obey orders.

"Works for me," Iron Whale chimed in, with a hint of cynicism, before Shiji Bau could answer. "I don't care if you're an adventurer or a faerie, as long as I get paid. You're just a client to me."

Iron Whale moved slowly, accompanied by the sound of creaking steel. Shiji Bau looked at him in his black suit of armor. It made him look like a cavalryman with no horse, but he was shorter and stockier than a cavalryman, slower, and his body was covered in sacred seals.

The suit of armor he wore was the sign of an artilleryman, and the armor itself formed a single cannon. It covered even his face, concealing his expression.

"So, as our new client, what would you like us to do?"

"Technically, I'm not your client…but I have been given orders to destroy evidence." Boojum pointed ahead, nodding. "We need to completely erase any connection between us and Lideo Sodrick. The *Adventurers Guild*, I believe it was called? I want that building destroyed without a trace."

"All right. That's my specialty," said Iron Whale.

In truth, that was the only thing he could do—the job of an artilleryman.

"I appreciate your cooperation," Boojum replied. "What about you, Shiji Bau? I owe you for all you have taught me, so I'd rather not kill you."

"You know you're asking me to turn against the human race."

"Is that a problem?" Boojum tilted his head to the side as if this was a completely reasonable question. "I learned something important from Lideo Sodrick. Nothing is more important to humans than their own safety and that of their family. That is far more pressing than the fate of your race as a whole. Am I wrong?"

*Hmph. Can't argue there. In my case, all I care about is myself.*

On that point, maybe Lideo had been a better person than she'd thought.

The man Dotta captured didn't seem frightened at all.

He was the one and only Lideo Sodrick, and he was glaring at us like we were a nuisance. Maybe this was just the way he acted after all his years as a guild master, or maybe he simply didn't like us. I had no idea. What I did know was that he'd hardly fought back as his arms were being tied. Perhaps he knew that resisting wouldn't get him anywhere.

We decided to use the large hall of the Adventurers Guild to question him, since there was too much going on outside. The guild building was falling apart, thanks to us, but at least it was essentially empty. Every person in the district who wanted to run away had already made it out. I was sure Lideo Sodrick had some kind of right-hand man, but I hadn't seen anyone like that around since things began to settle down. That said, I wasn't sure if whoever it was had run for it or if they were simply biding their time.

"I want a man on watch on all sides of the building," ordered King Norgalle before taking a seat in one of the few chairs that had miraculously survived the chaos. Looking around at the remaining adventurers, he said, "I am offering you a chance to atone for your crimes. Obey my commands and dedicate yourself to our nation."

Though clearly bewildered, those he was speaking to had no choice but to start moving. These were the men who had surrendered after witnessing the violence Tatsuya and Jayce were capable of, along with the destruction Norgalle had visited upon the district. There were nine of them. They exchanged timid glances, then approached the crumbling walls and windows and began keeping watch.

Patausche and I would be doing the questioning. Tatsuya and Jayce couldn't handle such a task, and Dotta was busy throwing back shots of booze as if he'd just finished a hard day's work. After verbally abusing me, Frenci got her two guards who had already recovered and began to search the inside of the guild. If they managed to find physical evidence, that would probably be more useful than any confession we might manage to extract. Meanwhile, as for Teoritta...

"Repent." The goddess crossed her arms haughtily before Lideo Sodrick, who had been forced to sit on the floor. "You kept a faerie as a pet, turned to wrongdoing, and attacked us! You have committed a grave sin, and if you understand that, then you need to repent this instant."

She looked back at me. "What do you think, Xylo? Look at his solemn expression. He must be in awe of my presence."

"You think so?"

"I know so! Impressive, huh? ...Now, for you. Tell us everything."

I had offered to do the questioning, but Teoritta wasn't having any of it. Her mood seemed to have improved immensely, and she was now trying to prove her usefulness. To be completely honest, she wasn't doing a very good job.

"I don't know much," replied Lideo gloomily. "Yes, I hired those adventurers and tried to have you all killed, as the master of the Adventurers Guild. But my client communicated via a messenger in a black mask. I don't know any more than that."

"Mmm..." Teoritta looked back at me with a frown. "This is not good, Xylo. This man does not seem to know anything."

"Don't trust people so easily. He's lying."

"Ohhh! ...How dare you lie to me, a goddess! Such insolent behavior shall not be tolerated!"

"Indeed," said Xylo. "Let me see if I can get anything out of him."

Teoritta wouldn't be able to pull this off. Goddesses lacked both the experience and the know-how required to negotiate with people, and their innate nature probably didn't make it any easier. And so I crouched in front of Lideo and looked him directly in the eye.

"You realize you're in a bad position, right? Normally, I'd hand you straight over to the Holy Knights, but I don't have to."

"Excuse me, Xylo?" Patausche furrowed her brow. "You don't have the authority to make any deals with him."

"Then should I threaten him with a little violence? Of course, I'm sure someone like him is used to that kind of thing."

"If I made a deal with you…" That was when Lideo finally spoke up, a hint of nervousness in his voice. "Would you be willing to accept my conditions?"

His lips curled into something resembling a smile.

*Looks like it worked.*

"I guess we could hear you out," I said. "I'm curious what kind of shameless requests you'll make."

"All I ask for is my family's safety—that you not harm my brothers and sisters."

"Oh…" He was probably talking about those assassins, though the look in their eyes was unlike that of any child I had seen before. "We couldn't hold back during the battle, so some of them are already dead."

"…I will consider a deal with you as long as you promise not to search for them."

"In other words, don't lay a finger on them?"

"Exactly."

"All right," I agreed. Patausche grimaced distastefully.

"Xylo, I said you didn't have the authority to make deals with him. They may be children, but they are criminals. Those in power already have their eye on you. Do you really want to make things worse?"

"You're telling me to find this guy's siblings and kill them? I guess we could bring them here and kill them in front of him as a form of torture. I mean, we'll do it if you want. Just give the orders."

"…I never said I wanted you to do that."

"Then we have an agreement," I said. Patausche fell silent. I decided to take that as assent and shifted my gaze back to Lideo. "Just tell us everything you can."

He must have been weighing his options. He was probably hedging his bets to make sure he'd be okay, no matter what happened. But for now, he seemed to understand he was in far more danger with us than with whoever hired him. Plus, I guessed he was just as worried about his "siblings" as he was for himself, and that seemed to be his weakness. He would probably betray his client if it meant saving their lives.

"Hey, Lideo. This is a pretty simple deal we have here. But you gotta give us something first."

"…You already know what they were after," he said, groaning. "They want to kill the goddess. My client called his people coexisters."

Coexisters. It was a name I'd heard not so long ago. The group had been around ever since the Demon Blight began, and they were adamant about coexisting with the faeries. That might not sound so bad on the face of it, but in reality, they wanted to welcome the demon lords as our rulers. Humans would become slaves, and the coexisters would be in charge of those slaves.

*I feel like I've been hearing about them way too much lately.*

Some people claimed that they were nothing more than the delusions of conspiracy theorists, and I'd thought so as well until pretty recently. But even if people like that did exist, I'd always thought they were few and far between. Never did I imagine there were enough to put together a force this large. But they existed. I couldn't deny that any longer. They were a threat, and they were my enemy.

"I don't know much about the coexisters, either, but…" Lideo lowered his voice somewhat, then shot me a cynical smirk. "I met the man in the black mask for the first time ten days ago, and we only met three times after that. He did tell me his name, though."

"It was probably a fake name, but let's hear it."

"Mahaeyzel Zelkoff."

"…Hmph. Ridiculous." Patausche was the first to react, and she fixed Lideo with a stern glare. "Mahaeyzel is the name of a saint at the time of the First War of Subjugation. In addition…" Her expression shifted somewhat. "Zelkoff. Zelkoff is…"

But before she could finish her sentence, a blinding light poured in through the window.

"Aaaah!" We heard the scream of an adventurer keeping watch. "Y-Your Majesty…!"

I felt bad for a second that Norgalle had made them all use his royal title, but stopped caring the instant I looked out the window.

"Shit."

I grabbed Teoritta, then swept Patausche's legs out from under her, dropping her onto the ground.

"What the…?!" she shouted.

"Get down!"

There was no time to listen to her complaints as the light and noise reached a crescendo. It was a bizarre sound, like an explosion. The pillars holding up the building crumbled as the wall was blown in. Chunks of wood swirled through the air as dust rose to the ceiling. Fire crossed the floor, spreading throughout the building, and the previously sporadic creaking of its frame increased considerably, signaling the final moments of the Adventurers Guild.

"Run! Get out of the building!"

I knew what this was. Dotta and Norgalle probably did as well. Jayce scowled and clicked his tongue.

"It's a damn artilleryman," he muttered in aggravation before swiftly rolling outside through the destroyed wall. The building was about to come crashing down.

"Xylo, we have to get out of here!" Teoritta took my hand in a panic.

I completely agreed with her, but were Frenci and the others okay? …Just then, I saw Frenci and her two guards drop down from a window. They'd been quick to react, and we needed to do the same. There was one idiot who didn't seem to understand that, though.

"Patausche! What are you doing?! Let's go!" I shouted.

"Wait. That man just…"

Lideo. It appeared that he'd taken off running the instant the blast hit us, heading toward the back of the crumbling guild. Was there some sort of secret passage there? I was sure we'd tied his legs as well, so he must have been hiding some sort of blade on him— Wait. There was no time to worry about that. I could regret my careless mistakes as much as I wanted later.

"Run!"

I knew another blast was coming soon, so I decided to give up on chasing him and focus on evacuating instead. I promptly grabbed Patausche and dragged her outside with me. We soon heard another impact, followed by a roar and radiant light—the finishing blow.

"Why did I have to get caught up in this mess?" After fleeing like a skittish rat, Dotta slipped behind Tatsuya to hide. "What's going on?!" he yelled. "What kind of person does something like this in the middle of a city?! This isn't normal!"

"Yeah, and there's nothing we can do about it," I said.

The only way to deal with a long-range attack like this was to have a sniper like Tsav or another artilleryman. If we had Neely, we might stand a chance. But without any of those, we were like sitting ducks.

"Let's get out of here," I suggested. "We now know the enemy has an artilleryman, and while I can't say I'm excited about it, we're gonna have to get Rhyno released from solitary. I'll have Venetim pull some strings."

"Seriously?" Dotta was clearly disgusted. "I mean, do we really have to? I don't like that guy at all."

"Me neither. But do you know anyone who can do his job better than him? He's our only choice."

I cast a final glance at the crumbling Adventurers Guild as the sound of shots continued sporadically. Then we began our retreat.

"Come on, pull yourself together. This is no time to space out," I demanded, patting Patausche on the shoulder as she stood in a daze.

"O-oh, right…"

"It's a shame we don't have a lead anymore, but Lideo Sodrick is still alive. We can go after him again later."

"Yes…" Patausche's complexion looked unusually pale as she spoke. "Let's do that. We can find out if he was lying or not once we catch him."

The underground passage beneath the Adventurers Guild was created as an escape route for use during crises just like this.

Lideo stepped into the darkness. The smell was awful, but that was inevitable, since this passage was made by modifying an existing sewer system. It would get him out of town, but it would take some time. All he had to aid him was a small sacred seal–powered lantern, which cast a pale light on the path ahead.

"Brother!" Iri rushed straight over to him. She'd come here ahead of time to secure the route. "You're okay!"

"Somehow." Lideo wrapped her in his arms and rubbed her head. "We lost the guild, but we're alive. I made sure you guys would be safe, too… I had to make a little deal with them, though."

"A deal?" Iri's eyes narrowed with uncertainty. "Are you doing something dangerous?"

"As long as we get out of here, we should be fine. It's nothing you guys need to worry about."

"But I am worried." She looked up at him with her deep blue eyes. "Did you tell them anything?"

"I didn't have a choice. Nothing important, but—"

That was when Lideo noticed something was wrong. Iri's eyes. The words she chose. *Why did she ask if I told them anything?* he wondered.

"I see." Iri nodded, and Lideo felt something warm at his chest. Pain followed shortly. "Then I have to do this, just in case… I'm really sorry, Brother."

Her voice was mechanical. Before Lideo realized what was happening, he had dropped to his knees, looking up at Iri. Intense pain meshed with confusion.

"Who...?" Lideo struggled to speak. "...Are you...? Where is... Iri...?"

"She's dead. I'm using her body and brain right now." A bashful smile covered Iri's face. That alone was the same as always. "Farewell, dear Brother."

Those were the last words she left him with. Then she turned around and faced three others in the darkness: Shiji Bau, Boojum, and a man clad in armor, who must have been the artilleryman he'd heard about, Iron Whale.

"It's over. Come on, let's go," said Iri.

"Very well. I'm sorry, Lideo Sodrick." That was Boojum's voice. His shoulders were slumped in his usual gloomy manner as he leaned that sickly looking face of his down toward Lideo. "I personally wanted to save you."

"And disobey orders, Boojum?" Iri's voice again.

"I would never. I will obey, but I have to wonder. Did you expect for all of this to happen?"

"No. I still could have used him. I never thought the entire district would be burned to the ground. What a despicable act of barbarism... So those were the penal heroes?"

"I knew they weren't to be taken lightly after they defeated Iblis, but I never expected them to go this far. I'll have to rethink how I approach them going forward."

"I agree. We'll need to speed up the plan. We have to dispose of that Holy Knight and kill the goddess at all costs." A roughness entered Iri's mechanical voice. Whether due to anger or fear, Lideo wasn't sure.

"...Could I have a little time off before our next mission?" asked Boojum. "I wish to bury Lideo Sodrick."

"There will be no need for that."

"But I must pay my respects to him. That is the proper etiquette when it comes to the dead."

"I said there will be no need for that. You were given orders to follow my commands. Did you forget?"

"...All right," Boojum replied, after a brief moment of silence. "As you wish. I'm sorry, Lideo Sodrick. Thank you for buying me those books."

He held his head low in what looked like a bow of apology. But that didn't matter to Lideo any longer. The air felt bitterly cold. Everything began to blur.

"I need all of your help for our next mission," said the one with Iri's voice, "not only Boojum's. Of course, you will be paid as promised."

"All right, but I have a question." Shiji Bau's voice was cold. "What should I call you? Do you want me to call you by the name of the girl whose body you took?"

"Spriggan."

The little girl's smile lit up in the darkness—the smile of someone who used to be Lideo's "sister." How long had she been gone? When did this monster steal her body? Lideo hadn't even noticed.

"Call me Spriggan."

"All right. So what do we do first?"

"Get ready to destroy the city. We must eliminate all its inhabitants, including the penal heroes and their goddess, and reduce this place to dust. They are in our way, and I need your help to get rid of them."

Lideo had finally realized his mistake—his failure—but it was too late to regret any of that now.

The man's methods were not what Theodney would call impressive. Horrific was a far better descriptor.

Once he'd checked the records on hand, Royal Inspector Theodney Nantia was certain: This man—the young man sitting before him— was a ruthless killer, and the rumors about him devouring his victims were sounding more and more plausible.

*We inspectors are told to throw away our preconceived notions when conducting interviews, but...*

Theodney Nantia stared fixedly at the man in front of him.

*...sometimes, that's easier said than done.*

At a glance, the man in front of him was a little scruffy, with a cheerful smile. He seemed so carefree that it was hard not to let your guard down. But when you really thought about it, being so laid-back in an interrogation room wasn't normal.

The man's name was Tsav, but on the streets, he was known as the Man-Eating Ghoul. He didn't have a family name, or a family, for that matter. He had been raised as an assassin by the group known as Gwen Mohsa, and he was almost certainly behind the disappearances of eight people. And those people didn't simply disappear, either. This man had killed them.

"Eight people, huh?" Theodney read out the number written in the report—the number of this man's victims. "That's about one per month. You've had a pretty busy year, huh?"

"Wait, wait, wait! I'm sorry, Inspector, but that's not true." Tsav corrected Theodney with a smile. "I'm an honest guy, so I'm going to tell you the truth. I actually killed twelve people. That's a fifty percent increase. I mean…I'm a real earnest person when you get down to it, you know? And I'm kind. I have empathy."

Tsav sighed as if to say that being a "kind person" had been a real burden for him over the years.

"Whenever I mess up or I'm having trouble at work," he continued, "it hurts my boss's reputation, and I feel really bad about it. That's the kind of person I am. And because of that, I always get the short end of the stick. Being serious just hurt me in the end, too. I mean, look at me now! They abandoned me."

Theodney started to get a headache as he listened to Tsav ramble. The assassin didn't seem to think killing people was a big deal at all. He was a monster. A terrifying monster was sitting right across the table from him.

"Don't you feel any remorse?" he asked. The words escaped his lips almost unconsciously. "You killed people. Don't you feel bad at all?"

Theodney knew of a man who had been raised by dragons. When he'd looked into it, he'd learned the man felt no remorse when it came to humans. *Maybe Tsav was like that, too*, Theodney thought.

"Oh, sorry! Are we talking about good and bad right now? Like morality? I honestly don't know too much about religious stuff like that… That's why I was considered a problem child even in the order." Tsav gave a lighthearted chuckle. "The thought of killing someone I like makes me feel sick. That much I get, but the rest doesn't make a lick of sense to me."

Theodney felt as if he were conversing with a creature from another world. Without any clear reason, he began pouring himself a glass of water from the pitcher to his side. But when he drank it, the liquid left only a vague, lukewarm aftertaste. This man called Tsav made him indescribably uncomfortable.

"The reason why the order couldn't—… How should I put it?" But Tsav continued to talk. It felt like he might never stop. "I'm too stupid to understand that stuff, you know? And that's probably why the order couldn't brainwash me. Know what I mean? Oh hey. Wait… What if I'm the chosen one? Oh man. That'd be too much for me to handle. I have a strong sense of responsibility, and that would really weigh me down. What if destiny has something even greater planned for me, though? What should I do?"

In a sense, Tsav might be right. Theodney knew how the order of assassins did things. They used countless techniques to instill a sense of right and wrong in children's minds. They would use anything, from drugs to pain to pleasure. And yet Tsav still hadn't understood the order's morality. He must possess a very unique mental disposition.

"…Are you not scared?" Theodney asked. He was hoping to draw out some hint of Tsav's humanity. He wanted to believe that Tsav was human, just as he was human. "If you're lucky, they'll lock you up for the rest of your life. And if you're unlucky, you'll get the death penalty. Does that not terrify you?"

"It does," Tsav replied immediately. "It's really scary, but being scared isn't going to change anything, so…" He smiled foolishly. "Why not have fun while I still can? I'd be wasting what little time I have left, otherwise. I mean, it's not like heaven and hell are real, and once people die, it's over, right? So why waste that time trembling in fear?"

Theodney was certain now. Tsav truly was a monster.

"Most people might understand that in their head, but their emotions and instincts overpower them. Maybe your situation simply doesn't feel real to you? Do you suffer from a poor imagination?"

"Ouch! I have a great imagination! I often think about what other people's lives are like. But even then, some things just don't make sense to me." Tsav's smile faded as he looked at Theodney with a serious expression. "Why should I care about anyone other than myself and the people I like? …It's all about the positives and the negatives, and you'd do anything if it benefited you or people you like, right? And when you really think about it, being afraid of the death penalty is a huge negative. Man, do you think I'm *too* serious about this stuff?"

Theodney was at a loss for words. He felt like he was witnessing something deeply repulsive, and he almost wanted to throw up.

"Tsav, you—"

"—are one interesting guy," cut in a voice from the side.

The speaker was sitting at the same desk as the other two men, and while he seemed like a cheerful fellow, there was something sinister about the way he smiled. Theodney didn't know his name. All he'd been told was that the other man was an inspector as well, and of a much higher rank.

"Tsav, my friend, you killed twelve people, but I was wondering…" The man leaned over the desk to get a closer look at Tsav. "How did you choose them? What were your standards?"

"I don't know," Tsav replied. "I guess they seemed easy to kill?"

"So they were easy to kill. Interesting. Then what about this man here—Taldy?" The mystery man picked up a document consisting of a single sheet of paper. "He disappeared not from his home but from the government office where he worked, and in broad daylight. The window of time in which he disappeared was a mere seventy seconds. You killed him and took the body home with you, correct? Are you saying he was easy to kill?"

"Wait, wait, wait. I'm not talking about my methods," Tsav said, laughing again. "I'm talking about feelings. Like, I'm a prodigy, right? It doesn't matter what these random defenseless people in the city do or where they do it. It doesn't change anything. In terms of difficulty, they're all exactly the same. So, like…"

Tsav lowered his voice as if he were letting the man in on a secret.

"I just picked people who wouldn't make me sad if I killed them."

"And how do you decide that?" the man asked.

"I dunno. A gut feeling, I guess?" Tsav seemed to ponder the question for a moment, but soon gave up. "Once I become emotionally invested, I can't kill them anymore. Sorry, but I'm just too nice of a guy. I was born kind. Know what I mean?"

"Yes, you've said that already. Now, about these twelve people you killed…" The nameless man tossed a stack of documents onto the desk. "Are you saying you empathized with none of them?"

"Exactly," Tsav said, nodding, looking totally relaxed. "That's why they were easy to kill."

"I see." The nameless man's smirk curled into something more sadistic.

"Perfect," he muttered. Theodney had no idea what he meant by that, but the nameless man proceeded to nod a few times, flipping through stacks of documents before turning his gaze back to Tsav. It almost looked like he was enjoying himself.

"Tsav," he said. "I believe the death penalty would be too light of a sentence for you."

"What? Are you saying I'm getting a punishment worse than death?"

"Yes." The nameless man paused as if to build up suspense. "I am sentencing you to be a hero."

"Wait." This was the first time Tsav had shown any sign of panic. "No, no, no! Wait! Hold on! This is completely different! Being afraid of the death penalty or whatever else would be a waste of time, but being a hero… That's—"

"Yes, it's exactly how you're imagining it." The nameless man's grin deepened. "Not even dying is permitted."

"Permission denied," the officer in charge declared, as if he were the law itself.

Although he was young, he was imposing. It looked like he'd been through a lot, and now he managed the prisoners in solitary confinement.

The officer—Rajit Heathrow—was also in charge of the infantry within the Thirteenth Order of the Holy Knights, and he looked like he'd been born to serve in the military—exactly the kind of person who Venetim didn't get along with.

"I cannot allow penal hero Rhyno to leave his cell before he finishes serving his time," Rajit insisted.

"Yes, I understand that very well," Venetim replied. He was lying. He had no clue how long Rhyno had left to serve, but he had to play along and adapt. People like Rajit hated when you were irresponsible. "However, the situation has changed. This is a special case and you must release him immediately."

That was what Xylo had told Venetim before ordering him to get Rhyno out of solitary, and Venetim had sensed violence behind his words. He had the distinct feeling he would get pulverized if he failed. But it didn't look like this Rajit fellow was going to give him the time of day.

"I cannot make any exceptions," he said. "The only way I will release him is if High Priest Marlen Kivia or Captain Patausche Kivia order me to do so."

"I have already received permission," Venetim replied quickly, holding out a slip of paper.

"Is this—?" Rajit's eyes opened wide in astonishment, for on the paper was the official seal of the Ioff city government. "Is this real?"

"You are free to check and see for yourself."

Venetim wasn't bluffing this time. The paper was genuine—an official request for release issued by the Ioff city government. This was the same government that had entrusted the city's defense to the high priest, making a note of permission from them even more effective.

Of course, there was a trick to all this. For the most part, governments were compartmentalized, and most of those in charge were dead set on avoiding responsibility, so personnel administration was extremely complex. Venetim had used this to his advantage. If he had gone directly to High Priest Kivia or Patausche, then he would have never gotten Rhyno out of his cell. They would never have agreed to releasing a penal hero who had disobeyed orders.

But what about the local government? All Venetim had to do was bend the truth a bit when he met with the defense force's director—a man who would have little understanding of their situation. Venetim had met with him as Patausche's representative, too, not as a penal hero. This lie was the foundation of Venetim's con.

What's more, it just so happened that the director wouldn't be able to contact either Patausche or the high priest that day, even if he wanted to, since they had both left that morning on private business.

Requesting to release a penal hero from solitary confinement wasn't anything unusual, either. To begin with, locking a hero away wasn't a real punishment. Solitary confinement was a safe place away from the threat of death, where you could loaf around all day, snoozing. At least, that was what anyone who didn't know Rhyno would believe.

No matter what order he'd disobeyed, Rhyno needed to be punished.

Allowing him to stay in a safe cell all day was outrageous. It was the opposite of punishment. The defense force's director had barely even questioned Venetim's claim. In fact, Rhyno was always in and out of solitary confinement, and this was a common method of busting him out for emergencies.

"Patausche Kivia will take full responsibility for whatever happens," said Venetim.

Those were the magic words. Once someone heard that, they'd stop caring if Venetim was lying. Whether or not Patausche Kivia would actually take responsibility wasn't an issue. If something happened, they could simply place all the blame on Venetim. That quickly eliminated all foreseeable problems. The clincher was Venetim's bold confidence and the menacing, powerful aura of his partner, Tatsuya, who he'd brought along.

In the end, releasing a single penal hero wasn't going to cause any trouble, especially since the sacred seals on their necks prevented them from getting out of hand. So who cared?

"All right. Let me get in touch with Ioff's government office to confirm."

Rajit looked skeptical, but he accepted the documents Venetim handed him.

*Sure. Knock yourself out*, thought Venetim. All he cared about was that his job was finally over. *I really hope Xylo doesn't give me any more unreasonable tasks.*

The only thing still bringing Venetim down was the thought of taking Rhyno back with him.

The morning started with an unreasonable request from Teoritta.

They were sitting in the penal hero's corner of the barracks' cafeteria, and the goddess was having breakfast.

"I want to go out today!" she declared, while spreading zeff butter on some fried bread. Zeff butter was a type of cream made from stirring heated sheep's milk, and Teoritta seemed to have fallen in love with it. She ate it almost every day. "I want to go out today, my knight! Let's go into town!"

"Hmm…"

She'd gotten the attention of Norgalle, which made the situation ten times worse. King Norgalle was always in the cafeteria for breakfast, but that day Jayce was there as well. That was a surprise, since I was sure he'd already made up with Neely. He had a huge blueprint unfurled in front of him, which he'd been working on all morning. He would sometimes turn to Norgalle for advice, so I assumed he was working on improvements for his dragon's equipment.

"Why not take the goddess to town, Xylo? Show her around." Norgalle elegantly used his knife to cut into the grilled fish Dotta had supplied. "The people of my nation will surely feel blessed simply to be in her presence."

"Right?! You know what you're talking about, Norgalle!" she replied.

"But of course. I am the king after all. So… Where do you wish to go?"

"Huh? Oh, uh… Err…," Teoritta groaned. It seemed she hadn't thought that far yet. But that was only natural, as she still knew almost nothing about the city. "D-do you have any recommendations? I wish to go somewhere fit for a walk with my knight!"

"Hmm… Then I recommend you stop by the Dujin Art Museum."

Norgalle gracefully stroked his moustache. The museum in question was pretty famous—even I had heard of it. Ioff was a strategic center for maritime trade, and lots of things, like works of art, gathered here. The Dujin Art Museum, run by the local merchant association, had used that to their advantage.

"They have numerous mid-classical masterpieces," he explained. "And the building's architecture itself utilizes modern Nashida techniques. There is much to see if you have the time."

"…I don't get it. What's so fun about art museums?" said Jayce. He continued to work on his blueprints, not even glancing in our direction. However, it seemed he'd been paying attention to what we said.

That was the kind of person he was. "If you want to go for a walk, go to the beach. The view is wonderful when you fly toward the sea, and if you head slightly south, there's a forest perfect for hunting as well. Flying through the ravine isn't so bad, either."

"Listen to this asshole, acting like we can all fly...," I muttered. None of his advice was helpful. At all. The man looked at everything through the eyes of a dragon. "What do you even hunt? Bears?"

"No, that'd be boring. I'm talking about hunting faeries, of course." Jayce briefly looked up and flashed me a competitive smirk. He was usually in a foul mood, but he seemed to find special joy in taunting me. "It's hundreds of times more exciting than some museum. How about we make a bet, Xylo? Let's see who can kill the most faeries."

"Hell no. What's wrong with you? Who in their right mind would waste their day off doing something like that?"

"Yeah, guess you're right," Jayce said, shrugging.

But I knew his game. This was all an act.

"I get it," he continued. "I'm already beating you seven to six, and this would just be adding another loss to your record."

"Wait. What was that, Jayce? Seven to six? Are you still counting what happened half a year ago? That's not fair. Tsav's the one who—"

"That is enough, you imbeciles!" King Norgalle's thunderous shout instantaneously ended our argument. "I will not have my nation's two greatest generals bickering like children! Use that energy against the Demon Blight. Now go cool off!"

Jayce and I had no choice but to shut up. I couldn't believe Norgalle had told us to "cool off." In fact, it was so unfair I didn't even feel like arguing.

"U-um... I'm not really sure what is going on, my knight, but...!" Teoritta grabbed my arm. Maybe she sensed that this conversation had been one huge waste of time. "I am fine with wherever you wish to take me, be it the art museum, the beach, or even the forest. Norgalle has given us permission, so let us be off!"

"What are you talking about? How does getting Norgalle's permission change anything...?" Of course, I wasn't going to take her anywhere. That would be madness. "Did you already forget that people were trying to kill you?"

"I have not. I had a really good time seeing the market before that happened. I even wrote about it in my diary! So let's go back and—"

"Oh, so you're trying to lure the enemy out again, huh?" I said, cutting her off.

"…!"

"Don't. It's a waste of time."

I could see her swallow her words. Teoritta wanted to help us, even if it meant putting her life on the line. I had to admit it: The reason why this kind of attitude pissed me off so much was because there was a part of me that would do the same thing.

I was willing to acknowledge that. But this was different. Using Teoritta as bait wouldn't help us. We'd learned a few things from our failure. We could prepare the best defense possible, but it was meaningless if the enemy went right for our weak points. Someone was leaking information, so what we had to do now was find the mole. Everything else would have to wait.

"Just give up," I said. "We won't get permission to go out again. You know who's in charge of making those decisions, right? Patausche."

"Mmm…"

Teoritta lowered her head and stuffed her last piece of deep-fried bread into her mouth. She wasn't happy, but there was nothing I could do about it. It was too dangerous to use Teoritta as bait when someone was leaking information to the enemy.

But just then, someone very unexpected reached out a helping hand.

"Actually, I think taking Goddess Teoritta out for some fresh air might not be such a bad idea."

My shoulders jolted. I wasn't expecting to hear Patausche's voice coming from right behind us. She had a tray loaded with breakfast. Apparently, she'd been passing by and happened to overhear our discussion.

"I can grant you permission to visit the nearby temple. It's just around the corner, and it's well secured."

"Really?! Patausche!" Teoritta's eyes instantly lit up. They were practically sparkling. "You make the most wonderful suggestions sometimes! Is everything okay?"

"Yeah, this seems unusual," I said.

I examined Patausche's expression. Something felt off. I had the impression she'd been lost in thought ever since the events at Sodrick's Shell the other day.

"Everything is fine."

She stubbornly shook her head—exactly what I'd expected her to do. Patausche wasn't the kind of person to easily admit that something was bothering her.

"Yo, Xylo… I've been wondering for a while now, but who is this woman anyway?" Jayce pointed his quill pen at Patausche. It appeared she'd finally registered with him as a new human in his periphery. "I don't know what's going on, but I've noticed she's always hanging around you. Are you being kept under surveillance?"

"H-how dare you even suggest such a thing!" exclaimed Patausche. "I have never once 'hung around' Xylo! Retract that accusation immediately!"

"Oh. Well, I don't really care, but could you keep it down?" Jayce said, turning back to his blueprint.

The exchange had taken some of the gloom out of Patausche's expression, at least. Jayce could be useful like this from time to time.

After briefly clearing her throat, Patausche lowered her voice and continued:

"Xylo, you need to start thinking about Goddess Teoritta's circumstances. She has been more or less forbidden from leaving ever since what happened at Sodrick's Shell. I know going for a walk isn't much, but you need to consider her mental health."

"You heard the lady, Xylo!" said Teoritta. "Help me cheer up!"

"Yeah, yeah."

I supposed it wasn't worth arguing if Patausche herself had approved the outing. The temple was just around the corner, like she'd said. Going there would be about the same as moving from the cafeteria to our sleeping quarters or the training grounds.

"Fine."

I nodded and took a bite of my bread. It was hard, like tree bark. This was the kind of stuff we penal heroes got for breakfast.

"Ready to go?" I asked. "I haven't been to a service in ages."

"Yes, let's go!" exclaimed Teoritta. "Thank you so much, Patausche!"

"I will do what I can for you, within reason, Goddess... Ahem, Xylo." Patausche addressed me, but turned away for some reason, refusing to make eye contact. "Go tell my uncle—High Priest Marlen Kivia—that you will be going to the temple. I'm sure he'd be thrilled to get a few followers together for Goddess Teoritta's sake. I'll call for some soldiers I can trust as well. Head to the inner courtyard in half an hour."

"Oh, so this is gonna be that kind of trip?" I said. "Great... What a pain in the ass."

"It is not a pain at all!" cried Teoritta. "Hurry up and finish your breakfast so we can go!"

"Yeah, yeah. Patausche, you're coming, too, right? You are her guard, after all."

"No, I... I'm busy today."

Patausche shook her head, still refusing to make eye contact. It was obvious she was hiding something. She was awful at lying. Whatever was bothering her must have been serious.

I didn't press her for answers, though. If she was this troubled, it probably involved someone close to her. Did she have an idea who the mole was?

When it came to problems like this, some people simply weren't able to talk about their worries. To them, doubting someone close was like insulting that person, and the closer they were, the more difficult the issue. Patausche probably wouldn't say a word until she found concrete evidence. I understood that. After all, I was the same.

For that reason, I simply nodded in response.

"All right," I said. "I'll make sure Teoritta's safe, then."

"Good." She looked at me, her gaze tense and serious. "Do not leave her side, no matter what." She then turned to the other two heroes, who were acting like the matter had nothing to do with them. "Norgalle, Jayce, I want you two to guard Goddess—"

"Unfortunately, I have other matters I must attend to," said Norgalle.

"Same here," said Jayce. "I don't have time to fool around."

They both answered immediately. Jayce seemed to have finished with his blueprint, and he began loudly folding the large piece of paper, his quill held in his mouth.

"I need to make a new saddle to snap Neely out of her bad mood," Jayce continued. "Come on, Norgalle—ahem—*King* Norgalle. We need to pay a visit to the leatherworker and the metalworker after that. Only the highest-grade materials will do."

"A tour of the city's shops, eh?" said the king. "Then you shall be my guard, Jayce. You never know when a terrorist will strike."

"I know... Outta the way, giant human female. We're in a hurry."

"...Xylo, is it just me, or is...something wrong here?" asked Patausche. "I'm your superior. I should be the one giving orders, and yet..."

"Don't bother with those two," I shot back.

Norgalle and Jayce were the two worst listeners in our unit, and not even killing them would fix their insubordinate behavior.

"Come on, Teoritta. Let's go."

...And that was how we ended up here.

To make a long story short, Teoritta's visit to the temple turned into quite event. All eyes were on her the moment she took a step inside the chapel. She was so instantly popular that a crowd began to form around her. Children and elderly followers were especially excited.

"It's the goddess!"

"The goddess of swords, Teoritta! Can I have your autograph?!"

A swarm of kids were the first to approach her, starting an impromptu signing event.

Signings were a unique custom held at temples worshipping the goddesses. Followers believed the handwritten signature of a goddess had sacred seal–like powers that warded off disaster...or at least, that was how it was in the past. The Temple's current stance was that this belief was mere superstition. The custom, however, remained. A goddess's signature was still recognized as a token of good luck to the faithful.

"Goddess, please sign my clothes!"

"Please sign my book! And this book for my little sister, too, please!"

Teoritta surged with excitement as children pressed in around her.

"Heh-heh. Gather round. I, Goddess Teoritta, shall bless each and every one of you."

As people received their signatures, we guards would have to pull them away before they got too close to the goddess. Incidentally, there were thirty of us in total. Patausche had personally selected each one, and the sheer number struck me as a little overprotective.

Nevertheless, it ended up coming in handy, since Teoritta was *very* popular. We managed to get everyone lined up so they could each have a turn to speak with her, get her autograph, and shake her hand, but it was a long, difficult task. I had no idea why she was so popular with the children, but I could see why the elderly liked her. She was like a grandchild to them.

"I'm so proud of you, Goddess Teoritta."

"You're just a little girl, and yet you defeated all those demon lords for us."

"My son lives in one of the northern settlements, and well... Thank you. What you did means a lot to me."

They showered her with praise and offered her candy. Teoritta accepted all of it with a huge, satisfied grin. I suspected she was trying to smile benevolently and with grace, but she looked like a kid being praised by her grandparents.

I made a note to check all the candy for poison later.

"What do you think, Xylo?!" Teoritta puffed out her chest. "Look how popular I am! And as you know, being worshipped is a goddess's greatest desire."

She must have been in an extremely good mood. Her hair had begun to spark.

"As my knight, you must be very proud. I suppose I could share some of this praise with you! I will split my candy with you later as well! Here, hold on to it for me for now!"

"Great. Thanks." I nodded humbly, the picture of a goddess's Holy Knight, then accepted a surprisingly full bag of candy. I would have to ration it so she didn't try to eat it all in one sitting.

That was when I realized that a few of the children who had received Teoritta's autograph were now staring at me.

"Need something?" I asked them.

But the children immediately looked away, flustered. Perhaps they had never seen a penal hero before. Or maybe they were simply afraid of me. They began to whisper among themselves.

"*Psst.* That's the guy, right? Goddess Teoritta's Holy Knight..."

"The Lightning Bolt! The Demon Lord Hunter! Thunder Falcon!"

"Yeah, that has to be him. My dad said he'd seen him...!"

"I knew it. That's Xylo Forbartz. D-do you think he'll give me his autograph?"

*The hell?* I thought. They knew who I was?

All of a sudden, somebody patted me on the shoulder from behind.

"You seem to be quite popular yourself."

"Huh?" I responded absentmindedly and turned around, only to find High Priest Marlen Kivia behind me. His sharp stare was similar to his niece's, but his seemed a little gentler.

"How the hell—? Ahem. How do these kids know my name?"

I tried to speak as politely as I could, since he was the highest-ranking individual on the city's defense force at the moment. Patausche was in charge of military affairs here, and he was clearly her superior.

"You're the one and only Holy Knight who forged a pact with Goddess Teoritta, and you appear to have quite the following among this city's children after your stunning victory at Mureed Fortress and the impressive performance you put on at Sodrick's Shell."

*This is ridiculous*, I thought, shaking my head. "I'm a penal hero."

"The children do not yet understand what that means. I was surprised as well. I never imagined that *the* Xylo Forbartz would be so service-minded and caring."

"That's 'cause they'll activate the sacred seal on my neck and blow my head off if I violate orders."

"I am still amazed. I have heard a lot from Patausche about you, but...you have far exceeded my expectations."

"She told you about me? What did she say?"

"She praises you often."

Those were the last words I expected to hear. I'd been sure she was bad-mouthing me whenever she got the chance.

"She says she could learn a lot from you as a knight and as a person," he continued.

"...Did she really say that?"

"She phrased it differently, of course. She often says things like, 'He's always so reckless,' and 'I can barely stand to watch him. His actions go against everything I've learned in the military.'"

"Figured as much."

"Hmmm. I know her very well, you know." The high priest looked me right in the eye. His face was serious. I had no idea what he was getting at. "My niece has a habit of valuing honor over her own life. Perhaps you could say she wants to be a true champion of the people. A very troublesome wish. Wouldn't you agree?"

"...I guess," I replied ambiguously. I couldn't blame her. Teoritta and I were the same, after all. "Though it's common to find aspiring generals in the military with hopes like that."

Especially among those who fight the Demon Blight, rather than other humans.

"You must be worried, being her uncle and all," I said.

"More than you know. Patausche is like a daughter to me. I treasure her, and I will not forgive anyone who betrays her or makes her sad."

Where was he going with this? I met his gaze and tried to read his expression, but I couldn't figure out what he was thinking. I wasn't good at things like this. In fact, I was a little wary of making assumptions based on the way people looked and acted. This guy could be two-faced like Venetim, for all I knew.

"My darkest fear is that someone with bad intentions will try to seduce her. Listen, Xylo Forbartz. I hear you have a fiancée, so let this be a warning. If you—"

What in the world did he mean by that?

But as I cautiously waited for him to finish his sentence, a deafening clamor suddenly drowned him out. The air around us shook with the raucous ringing of a bell. *Claaang, claaang.* The sound went on, echoing harshly through the temple, causing a stir among the believers. A few flustered priests took off running.

I knew this sound well.

"Xylo?" Teoritta looked back at me uneasily. "What's going on?"

"Sorry, but it looks like your meet-and-greet's gonna have to wrap up early. This is an emergency. We're—"

"—under attack," cut in High Priest Kivia. His tone was urgent. "That bell means the city of Ioff is being raided by the enemy."

Patausche Kivia was in one of the rooms in the barracks when she heard the bell. Parts of the city were already on fire, smoke rising into the air, signaling danger.

"Captain! There you are," a familiar voice called from the door—it was Officer Zofflec, in charge of the cavalry. Standing behind him was Siena, the woman in charge of the sniper division.

"I apologize for disturbing you like this," he continued, "but this is a serious matter. I have sent for Rajit, but if possible, we need you to assume command right away."

"…All right," said Patausche, with a nod. She stood, placed the stacks of documents in her hand neatly back into the desk's drawer, and tried to remain calm. "Deploy the troops. Protect the city. You've already sent scouts, yes?"

"Of course. We were only waiting for you, Captain. But..." Zofflec faintly creased his brow. "What were you doing in the high priest's room?"

"I came here to discuss the town's defense, but it appears I was too late."

Patausche was well aware that she was a terrible liar.

She thought back to the documents she had been reading a few moments ago. They were daily reports on the town's defense, and they provided an indirect account of her uncle's recent actions, detailing when he had gone out or been absent during his ten-day stay in Ioff.

After examining his preparations taken, meetings attended, interviews conducted, and everything in between, Patausche found herself drifting toward a single, undeniable conclusion...

We were in a hastily constructed, temporary command center.

Then again, spaces allocated to us penal heroes always included words like "temporary" or "special." The proper facilities were for regular soldiers, not us. Even this temporary command center was nothing more than a small storage shack next to the dragon stables.

When Teoritta and I stepped into the room, *he* was already there, standing next to Venetim, his arms behind his back, a faint smirk on his lips. As always, he was aggravatingly calm.

"Well, if it isn't my good friend, Comrade Xylo," said Rhyno. "You seem to be doing well. I'm glad. It sounds like you've had a rough time of it while I was gone. My heart ached for you all every day I was in solitary confinement."

His behavior was not what you would expect from a man who had been locked up alone for so long, but he was always like this. He spoke like a priest or a teacher who loved to lecture everyone around him.

"Is that the goddess I've heard so much about?"

He narrowed his gaze at Teoritta. She visibly recoiled. *You're right, there, Teoritta. Rhyno is a* very *shady guy.* Unbothered by her silence, he continued his greeting:

"It is a pleasure to meet you, Goddess Teoritta. I am Rhyno, the artilleryman for Penal Hero Unit 9004. Comrade Xylo here is my

partner, after a fashion. Together we fight for the happiness of all mankind."

"Still talking out of your ass, I see." The second half of his claim was a lie. "Venetim, I'm starting to think maybe we released him a little too soon."

"What...? But you were the one that ordered me to break him out, no matter what..."

Venetim made it sound like he'd gone through a ton of trouble, but I was having a hard time believing him—he was always busting Rhyno out. Solitary confinement was like a favorite inn for Rhyno. He violated orders all the time, and he never showed any sign that he regretted his actions or was working toward improvement. He was a real habitual offender, and he was usually locked up for half the year.

...I recalled the last time he'd fought alongside Jayce.

All of a sudden, Rhyno had left his post and taken off for a nearby settlement. There he started attacking a horde of faeries on his own, forcing the military to defend the settlement. Apparently, the military's strategy at the time would have seen them abandoning all settlements west of the line of defense. But when Rhyno heard that, he'd abandoned the mission and taken matters into his own hands.

It sounded like a heartwarming story, and he'd bought the people living in those settlements time to escape, saving their lives. But for whoever was in command, it must have been an extremely aggravating experience. Regardless of whether a decision was right or wrong, a military couldn't function if everyone went off and did whatever they wanted. It made perfect sense that he'd been locked up. In fact, I could hardly believe he got off time and again with such a light sentence.

"I just can't sit back and do nothing when someone's in trouble," Rhyno said with a thin smile. "And I believe it is our mission to protect the vulnerable, abandoned by their nation, their lives destroyed by the faeries. Wouldn't you agree, Comrade Xylo?"

Only Rhyno could say something like that with a straight face. He was the only member of the penal hero unit who got here without committing a crime. Probably. I'd heard he volunteered. *Who the hell would do that? What kind of person chooses to fight an endless battle where not even death can set you free?*

I had asked him about it before, but he'd simply replied, "I'm doing it for the world, Comrade Xylo. My only wish is to serve mankind."

It didn't make any sense to me. In fact, it made me sick. *Did he really want to toil as a penal hero for all eternity for some stupid, naive ideals?*

And he might say stuff like that, but this wackjob would smile as he blew up a house or two, or even three, as long as he believed it was the best way to save lives. It made no sense. Honestly, working with him was the last thing I wanted to do, but I had to admit we needed him now.

He was good at what he did. Artillery was still a new branch of the military, and you needed specialized knowledge and an understanding of the sacred seals involved. Where he learned all that was a mystery, but he had a set of skills none of us could replicate.

"At any rate, this is no time to fight among ourselves," said Rhyno, his voice disgustingly calm. "We must work together and overcome the obstacle before us. I'm counting on you as well, Goddess Teoritta."

"O-of..." Teoritta stuttered a little, but managed a firm nod. "Of course. You can depend on me! ...What should we do first, my knight?"

"Hmm..."

Teoritta was pumped up and ready to go, so I held in my complaints. I cast a quick glance at Rhyno's vacant smile, then shifted my gaze back to Venetim.

"First, I need to confirm the situation," I said. "Is the city under attack?"

"Yes." Venetim pointed at a map on the desk. It featured a few handwritten notes and showed the city of Ioff, which took up an elongated strip of land from north to south. The tip of Venetim's finger was on a northern section of the harbor: Ioff Cheg. The name meant "north side" and referred to Ioff's port district.

"Right here. Witnesses saw faeries coming in from the ocean, or possibly the coastal waterway. The horde headed here, first..."

His finger wandered the map for a few moments until he eventually pointed to its corner, at a building by the ocean—a man-made island with a red tower poking out toward the sea, with fortress walls surrounding it in the shape of six flower petals. The tower was used for Ioff's coastal defense, in addition to functioning as a lighthouse.

"Tui Jia, the Coral Tower, suffered a surprise attack and fell. The enemy now has control of it."

I looked out the window and saw smoke rising faintly from the red tower. Tui Jia—these words were derived from the language of the former island kingdom of Kioh in the east. They had built the tower and its man-made island as a token of goodwill when the Federated Kingdom was formed.

The purpose of the island was to defend against any Demon Blight coming from the sea, and it was equipped with numerous weapons. So how was it so quickly occupied? Maybe the tower simply wasn't prepared to handle lightning-fast attacks from land.

Venetim heaved a deep sigh and continued his explanation.

"There is a demon lord within the horde that attacked the tower, and the effects of the Demon Blight are rapidly spreading. It's only a matter of time before Tui Jia itself is tainted by the Blight and transforms into a faerie."

"That's a trap."

"Definitely a trap."

Rhyno and I spoke almost simultaneously. *Ugh.* I glared at him, but he simply smiled back, then returned his attention to the map.

"It appears my partner and I share the same opinion. I'm glad," he said. "Considering the wind's current direction and speed, I believe nearly all of Ioff Cheg can be hit by artillery from Tui Jia, making it nigh impregnable."

"Sounds about right. Our best bet would be to call for a goddess who can attack from outside the enemy's range, but—"

"—That would take a long time, and we would have to abandon Ioff Cheg."

"In other words, they're holding every single person in the area hostage. Dammit. This is obviously a trap."

But it was a trap we couldn't ignore. We had to consider the pros and cons. Ioff was an extremely important center of commerce within the Federated Kingdom, and this port was a key hub. The damage would be catastrophic if the ships, warehouses, or shipbuilding yard were destroyed. There were a lot of people here as well.

*I don't want to agree with Rhyno, but...*

I glared at the artilleryman as I continued making up excuses in my head. Yes... This was nothing more than an issue of pros and cons. We had to weigh our options. How could the military continue this war if they couldn't even protect their own citizens? They were on the defensive, and nobody knew how much longer it would continue.

That said, I had a feeling I knew what the higher-ups would say...

"Venetim, what do we need to do? What are the orders from Galtuile?" I asked.

"It seems they agree with you and Rhyno. This is a trap. Therefore... Uhm..." Venetim tried hard to put on a serious face as he spoke. "The Thirteenth Order will be deployed near Ioff's government office building. The city guards are to immediately withdraw while the penal hero unit defends the port of Ioff Cheg in their place. We are to hold out until the Ninth Order arrives with reinforcements to regain control of Tui Jia."

"Is this some kind of joke?" Was I hearing things? Galtuile's orders were always reckless, but telling us to hold out for reinforcements in this situation? "A large percentage of the population is concentrated in Ioff Cheg, not to mention assets. This could start a riot."

"...The assets of the noble class will be fine. They're all stored farther inland, where we are...safe from ocean-based attacks." Venetim hesitated another moment, then pointed at the government office building. We could see a group of warehouses separated from Ioff Cheg by a few streets and internal city walls.

"Knowing how much influence the nobles have over Galtuile," he continued, "I wouldn't be surprised if they pulled some strings to get us to prioritize their assets."

"They're out of their damn minds."

"P-please don't get mad at me," said Venetim. "I'm just the messenger."

What were those nobles going to do after mankind was wiped out? Offer their accumulated wealth to the demon lords in exchange for their lives? It was like they were telling us to gradually lose the war in a way that benefited them.

"Hey, uh... I have a suggestion..." Venetim first tried to gauge my mood, then took a chance and said what was on his mind. "I believe putting ourselves at risk would be pointless. Instead, how about we lie low for a while? We can get as close as we can to the outside of the designated combat area and start yelling. It'll look like we're trying to lure the enemy out."

"Excuse me? You should be ashamed of yourself, Venetim!" Out of nowhere, Teoritta, who had been quiet the whole time, suddenly spoke up, her voice firm and furious.

"How can you call yourselves brave knights of Goddess Teoritta with a straight face! The situation may seem bleak, but the people's lives are in danger! ...Xylo!"

Her tone sounded demanding, but it was clear she was pleading and hoping I would agree with her.

"The people need to be saved, and right now, we're the only ones that can do it...right?" Her eyes lit up like flames. "This is a battle worth risking our lives for."

"Ugh. You're always so damn eager to sacrifice yourself for other people."

"Heh-heh. You should see yourself, Xylo. You are only angry because you know I am right." She straightened her back and stuck her head out toward me. "What do you say, my knight? My words are admirable, are they not?"

But right when I was about to answer her, Rhyno suddenly opened his stupid mouth and ruined everything.

SENTENCED TO BE A HERO, VOLUME II

"What incredible determination, Goddess. Beautiful, even. I humbly agree. We must protect the lives, livelihoods, and happiness of the people who live at the port." He smiled and narrowed his eyes. How obnoxious. "Comrade Xylo, now is the time for us to fight. Am I wrong? Let us join hands and work together for the happiness of all mankind."

"Shut up already. This is just work."

I waved my hand to get Rhyno to stop looking at me, but Venetim still seemed uneasy.

"We're soldiers," I said. "If we're given orders, we follow them."

"I understand that, Xylo, but do you have a plan?" Venetim asked. "To be blunt, I don't have a single good idea right now."

"That's nothing new."

"Should I try to convince them to ease up on our orders?"

"Don't even think about it. I know how you negotiate. You'll just try to save your own ass."

Relying on Venetim, our so-called commander, to solve things with the military would be a mistake.

*Looks like it's up to me... Think, think...*

I racked my brain for some way to save the people of Ioff Cheg. There was no way we could go around the district to help evacuate every single person, so what could we do? What was our best option? Did we even have an option?

...Could I really pull something off?

"Xylo." Teoritta quietly called my name, and I noticed she was smiling. "You will find a way. I believe in you."

*She's right.*

I knew she was right—or at the very least, I convinced myself she was.

*I work well under pressure. I'll figure something out just like I always do.*

There was something malicious about our orders, as usual. Sometimes it would feel like we were being set up to fail, while other times, it felt like the higher-ups were trying to mentally break us. There was someone in the shadows pulling the strings and saddling us with impossible tasks.

*I'm not going to play your game,* I thought.

Like hell I was going to let them push me around. If there really was someone who took delight in seeing us panic and fail, then I was going to smack that smirk right off their face.

I needed to focus on the problem in front of me. This was both a defensive battle and a tactical retreat. I needed to remember the fundamentals—the basics of war: Attack the enemy's weakness, avoid playing to their strengths, and only fight battles you can win. Perhaps these were nothing more than ideals. After all, if they could, every military would be doing just that.

*But they're ideals I should always pursue.*

I thought of the faeries' weaknesses, or rather, the weakness of the Demon Blight itself, and the answer came naturally.

"All right, let's do this," I said. "We'll fight to win."

"Wonderful. That's Comrade Xylo for you," said Rhyno. "Could you enlighten us with your plan?"

"First, we need to prepare for battle. Go put on your armor. I'll explain while we're moving."

I placed a hand on Teoritta's head and rubbed her golden locks. It wasn't like I wanted to, but I didn't have any other choice.

"We're finally doing work fit for a goddess's band of knights."

"Yes! Yes, my knight. This is an honorable battle with a worthy cause!"

Sparks tickled the palm of my hand as Teoritta smiled. This would be another desperate, hopeless mission, and yet she was still so fired up. She really was one hell of a goddess.

"Venetim, you've got a role to play as well," I said.

"Huh? M-me?"

"I need Jayce and Neely in the sky, and I need you to get permission, since they prohibited us from using the dragon after the two of them lit the town on fire the other day. Now go."

"Yet another one of your reckless plans, I see... Why me?"

Venetim looked like he wanted to cry... *Good*, I thought.

No matter how reckless the plan, we still needed a base, and I wasn't talking about the barracks. We needed something on the front line. If our aim was to evacuate the populace, then we had to have some place relatively safe. Norgalle, of course, was the perfect man for the job. The instant he arrived at the city wall separating Ioff Cheg's port from the inland district, he emphatically declared:

"We shall build my fortress here!"

It didn't take long after that.

The guards unfortunate enough to be stationed nearby received the king's orders. Confused and being yelled at, they had no choice but to move to protect themselves. The military had ordered the gate to the inland district to be sealed off, and the low-level guards unable to evacuate in time had been left behind. Now they had no choice but to become Norgalle's lackeys. After all, he did have the arrogance and distinguished appearance of a king. Those traits, in addition to the fear and confusion of the situation, compelled the guards to obey him.

What truly surprised me were the adventurers who came crawling out of the woodwork to follow Norgalle's commands. Even more shocking, I recognized them from the fight at Sodrick's Shell. Even the man with the beard from the Giant-Hunter Brigade or whatever showed up.

"Hurry, my people!" shouted Norgalle. "We must build this sacred seal–engraved wall exactly as I designed."

"Aye, aye!"

"And we must start a fire! Guards, do you have any cooking equipment with sacred seals at your station? I need water boiling now! Collect every pot and ration you can from the nearby shops! The minister of finance will compensate everyone when this is over!"

"Aye, aye! ...No dilly-dallying, men! Get it done!"

The high-spirited adventurers diligently got to work right before my eyes. I couldn't believe what I was seeing.

"What the hell is going on?" I asked. "They're actually following Norgalle's orders?"

"I'm just as confused as you are," said Dotta. He looked like he'd just seen a ghost. The adventurers were running all over, following every one of Norgalle's deafening commands.

"King Norgalle promised to hook them all up with new jobs. You know—sounds like they all lost their livelihoods after what happened to the guild and all. Scary stuff, right...?"

"What? Do you think this counts as a job?"

"Beats me... His Majesty offered them all official titles and salaries, but..."

"Seriously? Do those adventurers think he's some kind of eccentric nobleman?"

"No clue."

"The military might hire them if they work hard... Better than life as a bandit, I guess."

Whatever the case, the adventurers were dutifully following Norgalle's orders, using sacred seal–infused tools Dotta had stolen from the barracks and whatever scraps they could find to hastily make a line of defense.

Meanwhile, Teoritta and I were warming our hands over the swiftly prepared bonfire while we waited until it was time to attack. As the sun sank into the ocean, the temperature rapidly fell. Keeping your body warm was essential during times like this, and eating was just as important. You didn't want to collapse from hunger in the middle of the mission.

For that reason, I was using one of the pots that the king had "collected" to cook us a simple meal—a porridge of fish and vegetable scraps. Once it was ready, I poured it into small bowls before taking a big sip.

"This is delicious. Hot, though…" My simple meal seemed popular with Teoritta. "I want to cook this for us next time, my knight!"

"Hopefully, we'll have something better than leftover scraps… Hey, Tatsuya. Eat up before it gets cold."

"Mmmfff… Grrr…"

"Seriously?! Don't eat with your hands, dammit! I gave you that spoon for a reason!"

"Heh-heh! You're getting food everywhere, Tatsuya. You shouldn't rush your meal," said Teoritta.

"Look who's talking. You've got food all over your face… Stay still until I'm done wiping you off! Both of you!"

There was something about a hot meal that really motivated you, no matter how paltry the ingredients, and right now, I was feeling just that. One extraordinary thing about King Norgalle was that when building a base, he would always start with an area for cooking. He understood that hot meals both promoted morale among soldiers and helped civilians feel safe.

"Comrade Norgalle never ceases to impress me," said Rhyno, clearly in awe. "Thanks to him, we were able to prepare for the mission and warm up our bodies as well."

Just as he'd implied, Rhyno appeared fully put together and ready for battle.

He was wearing his familiar armor, made from a mysterious kind of steel with a dusky-red sparkle to it. He had an insect-like short, stocky appearance, and his arms were absurdly massive. His right hand served as the barrel of his armor's cannon. It was a hollow cylinder with a sacred seal engraved into its surface. It looked almost like he had a chimney attached to his arm from the elbow down.

This bizarre metal suit, known as the Neven Artillery Seal

Compound, was Rhyno's weapon. But it was still in testing within the military, so how he got his hands on it was a mystery to me. In fact, I doubted anyone knew for sure.

"I thought we'd finally be working together as a unit," he complained, sounding a little depressed. "But it appears Comrade Tsav and Comrade Jayce can't be with us. What a shame."

He always put too much emotion into his voice—to the point that it sounded fake. In a way, he was probably more of a liar than Venetim.

"Tsav's arm is still being treated," I said, "but I'm sure he'll be dragged out of bed and brought straight here with minimal care."

"What about Comrade Jayce? Did he not get permission to fight with us?"

"He did not. But I've got it covered."

Bringing a dragon into urban warfare was dangerous, and that went double for Jayce and Neely. So of course, the military was reluctant to allow it... But I had Venetim negotiating with them, and there weren't many people he couldn't persuade. I would have a great time kicking his ass if he didn't pull it off, though.

"Anyway, we need King Norgalle to stay at the base, and Dotta should stay here, too, to analyze the battle and keep an eye out for us."

"That leaves the two of us, along with Comrade Tatsuya and..." Rhyno shot Teoritta a grin. "Goddess Teoritta, yes? It looks like the four of us will be fighting side by side tonight. Let's do our best."

"...Yes." Teoritta was clearly wary of Rhyno, keeping her distance and hiding behind me. "We must hurry... Those people are waiting for us...to rescue them..."

"Oh, Goddess Teoritta! Yes! I humbly agree. What joy this brings me! With your approval, I feel we cannot go wrong."

"I don't know why you're so happy," I said, "but we've got more important things to worry about right now." I had to face the reality of the situation. "The city's guards have started to withdraw, so we're vastly outnumbered. I have an idea, but we're gonna need more men."

"Allow me to handle that. We need more soldiers, yes?" replied Rhyno, with his usual calm. "May I suggest a strategy as well?"

"...I mean, I already have a plan, but I guess I'll hear you out."

"The city wall." He pointed at the barrier behind us—a colossal structure separating the port area of Ioff Cheg from the rest of the city. "Let's use my artillery to destroy it and allow the faeries inland."

"What...?!" Teoritta was scowling something fierce. "Why would we ever do that?"

"Goddess, I believe suffering and pain should be shared among everyone. That is how humans create bonds. It's beautiful, really. Once the faeries make their way into the inland district, the Holy Knights and city guards will have no choice but to help us fight." Rhyno spread out his stubby, armor-covered arms as if he believed this plan was pure genius. "It isn't fair that only some have to suffer. So when disaster strikes, we must divide the misfortune among everyone. Anyway, what do you think, Comrade Xylo?"

"My knight...!" exclaimed Teoritta. "This man is—"

"I know. That's just who he is." I wanted to sigh—a big, exaggerated, theatrical sigh. "Anyway, thanks for wasting everyone's time, Rhyno. Maybe you'd have a point if we were just talking about the Knights and guards, but putting civilians' lives in danger? What's wrong with you?"

"Hmm? Are you suggesting you have an even better plan, Comrade Xylo?"

"Listen up, Rhyno. You may not know this, but it isn't friendship or rainbows that motivate the average person."

I pointed toward the port. Ever since I'd heard our orders, I had been thinking. I knew asking for one or two thousand reinforcements wasn't feasible, but I wanted five hundred, and I had a slightly better plan for getting them than what Rhyno was suggesting.

"It's profit—it's getting something in return," I said. "Rhyno, shoot that ship. You should be able to hit it if you get a little closer, right?"

"Interesting." Rhyno was a quick thinker and eerily sharp. "That makes a lot of sense, Comrade Xylo. It seems like our best bet, in fact."

I was sure he was smiling underneath all that armor. I could just tell.

"And this is why I respect you," he said. "I always learn so much.

Anyway, what's the next step in this plan of yours?" He sounded as if he were testing me, or trying to get something out of me. "Do you propose we rescue each lost civilian one by one? You seemed to have thought of something a moment ago."

"We're going to do just the opposite, and drive the faeries into a corner." I wasn't going to play by the Demon Blight's rules and allow its horde to push us back. We were the penal hero unit. Like hell we were going to fight fair. "We aren't going to protect the city. We're going to attack the enemy and retake what they've stolen."

I pointed at the red edifice by the sea: Tui Jia, the Coral Tower. *If we attack their nest, they won't have time to attack the civilians*, I thought. And there was no way we were going to wait for the Holy Knights and city guards to arrive.

"We're going to take back Tui Jia and kill the demon lord."

Even as I spelled it out, I realized how reckless my plan was. But that didn't stop me.

Tui Jia was highly fortified. Not only was it fully equipped with lightning staffs specialized for sniping, along with an array of other seal-engraved weapons, it would likely be Shiji Bau and other adventurers using them. That much I was sure of. After all, the reason the faeries were able to occupy the tower was because those manning it had been surprised by an attack *from land*.

Still, we had a decent chance of victory, and while I hated to admit it, it was because we had Jayce and Rhyno on our side.

*This is absurd.*

That was Patausche Kivia's first thought when she looked over their orders. But the document had, without a doubt, come from Galtuile.

"...It was inevitable, Captain," said Rajit. He could have been admonishing or consoling her. "We need the support of the nobles, just as we need support from every citizen. And besides, there are numerous buildings in this district that belong to the Temple..." Rajit looked at the map with a serious expression. "And faith is essential. It is the foundation of our hearts, especially in desperate times."

Patausche understood where those at Galtuile were coming from.

*...I* should *understand.*

Patausche tried to convince herself. A soldier must never question their orders. Doubts would only hinder her on the battlefield.

*I need to hurry and deploy the infantry.*

Zofflec's cavalry and Siena's snipers were already in position and ready for battle, and the situation would only worsen the longer Patausche hesitated.

*But...*

She stole a glance at the documents in her hand. That rude, unpleasant woman—Frenci Mastibolt of the Night-Gaunts—had grabbed them for some unfathomable reason right before the Adventurers Guild came crashing down.

The papers were a record of Lideo Sodrick's daily movements, and they showed that in between his tasks as guild master, he was making strange visits to someone—a man calling himself Mahaeyzel Zelkoff.

It was the same name Lideo had given them.

The coexisters' messenger, his face concealed behind a black mask. The fact that Lideo had kept this record might well be proof he was trying to play both sides. He made deals with the coexisters, but still did favors for their enemies, refusing to commit until it was clear who was going to win.

*If only I could capture him... But I doubt we'll ever find him,* Patausche thought. *He's probably already long gone.*

Something still bothered her, though. She was almost certain now, and if she was right...

"Captain Kivia," came a sudden voice from the doorway.

Patausche looked up to see an overly pale man with a suspicious smirk: Venetim Leopool—the penal hero unit's designated commander.

"You again? What are you doing here?" Rajit asked sternly. "The penal hero unit has already been given orders to attack."

"Yes, and it is my job as commander to fire them up and send them into battle. However..." Venetim spoke fluidly, turning to Patausche. "I have received a report from the front line that the faeries are already marching up Ioff Cheg's ninth water route toward the inland commercial district. Furthermore, for some unknown reason, they are now attacking the Temple's seal ships."

"...What?" Rajit's eyebrow twitched, and he promptly looked down at the map.

"We will handle rescuing the civilians and eliminating the faeries," said Venetim. "But we would like permission to use a dragon within the city. In addition, while we will do our best to succeed on our own, I would like to request the help of the Holy Knights to protect the Temple's property and prevent any casualties among the affluent merchants living in the area."

Venetim spoke quickly and fluently and topped it all off with a bow.

"I beg of you," he said. "Please provide us with backup as we risk our very lives to defeat the enemy."

"Captain... This sounds extremely suspicious." Rajit groaned, staring at the map. "Would you like me to send some soldiers to the front lines to confirm his claims? Is what he's saying even possible? Why would faeries prioritize attacking the Temple's ships over humans...?"

"Perhaps they instinctively sense a threat," Venetim suggested, without a moment's hesitation. "Or maybe they are simply trying to hurt the Temple financially. I suspect they are being led by a creature with some kind of intelligence."

"But—," Rajit began, only to be interrupted by a messenger rushing into the room.

"Captain Kivia!"

The messenger was holding a sheaf of papers neatly rolled into a cylinder closed with a sacred seal—proof it was an official order. The man continued:

"We have received witness reports that multiple ships owned by the Temple are under attack. Two are currently ablaze! The Temple has requested these ships be saved at all costs!"

This sealed the deal. Patausche stood up. Though these weren't orders from the military, it was still an official request from the Temple, and more than enough reason to act.

"Understood. I will have my soldiers on it immediately."

*What would Xylo Forbartz have done? Surely, he would have come to a decision more quickly, without waiting around for some justification... But such speculation is pointless,* she thought. *What do I need to worry about that for?*

She promptly chased away these thoughts.

"Relay the Temple's orders to Zofflec and Siena! I will allow the penal hero unit to use a dragon. Prioritize rescuing civilians."

"Understood. And, um..." Venetim hesitated for a few moments, a timid, ambiguous smile forming on his lips.

"What?" she asked.

"No, it's nothing."

It was a cynical, almost self-deprecating smile that left a strange, lasting impression on her.

"Please give my regards to High Priest Marlen," he said. "His support would allow us more flexibility, so I believe we should ask for his help."

Patausche's face stiffened.

High Priest Marlen Kivia. She would have to meet with him eventually... They needed to have a talk about a certain messenger for the coexisters who went by the name of Mahaeyzel Zelkoff.

Our artilleryman was back in action, and that had opened up a powerful new battle strategy—armored warfare.

Infantry could follow behind an artilleryman, using the latter's massive suit of armor as a shield. The artilleryman would boost the infantry's defense, while the infantry would in turn compensate for the artilleryman's lack of maneuverability. With a skilled infantryman and careful scouting, this kind of strategy could work even in an urban environment.

Under these conditions, Tatsuya would be the ideal infantryman, and a thunderstroke soldier like me would be better able to turn in tight spaces than a dragon knight. The battleground would be relatively small. Dotta would stay in the rear and use his abnormally good eyesight for scouting.

In short, our team was set up to quickly remove any threat that targeted Rhyno, our artilleryman.

*"Oh! They're coming from the right,"* Dotta said nervously through his sacred seal. *"Bogies! Seven of them!"*

Bogies were especially small barghests. Usually, barghests were around the size of a horse or an elephant, but not always. These smaller bogies made up for what they lacked in size with large horns on their heads and with speed, and they were a significant threat. When they charged, their horns could easily pierce thick armor. The fact that we were fighting in narrow streets made them even more dangerous, since the bogies could drop down from above or charge right at us in a group, allowing little space to dodge.

They were an artilleryman's natural enemy. Or at least, they *should* have been.

"Comrade Xylo, I'm counting on you," said Rhyno, his voice muffled inside his armor.

"I know."

As I replied, Tatsuya was already moving. He didn't have to be told.

"Vagrrr!"

He swung his battle-ax with lightning speed, chopping down a few bogies the moment they came rushing from a gap between some buildings. He let out an eerie battle cry, smashing the beasts with his ax, giving them no chance to counter.

"Keep your eyes forward, Teoritta!" I called out. "Let's do this!"

"Very well." Teoritta summoned a sword in midair. She instantly knew what I wanted. "You shall be blessed."

I launched a knife as I grabbed the sword she'd summoned. A bogie exploded, taking out another bogie with it. When the third made its way over, I slashed it with the sword, blowing it up as well.

*All done here.*

"Taking it easy like this is rather nice, and nothing beats fighting alongside my hero comrades. I am blessed to have you all," said Rhyno. Every word out of his mouth sounded insincere and shallow. I wanted to ask him if he meant any of it, but this wasn't the time or place.

"Let's keep pushing forward," I said. "Once we're in Tui Jia—"

"*Wh-what the…?! Wait! There's something up ahead!*"

Dotta cut me off and ruined my speech right as I was trying to fire everyone up. He was panicking.

"*There's…some kind of warehouse up ahead, and uh… It has Verkle Development Corporation's seal on it. There's a bonfire, too. It looks like some people have barricaded themselves inside, and faeries are gathering around the building… Wh-what should we do?*"

"Some people must be using the place as a shelter. Dammit. What a pain in the ass."

*"Right? So, uh… Maybe you should ignore it and go around,"* chimed in Venetim, via our sacred seals' communication function. *Just what I expected him to say,* I thought. *"It would be best if we ignored them, don't you think? We can let those civilians keep the enemy busy while we—"*

"I don't know about that," Rhyno said, tilting his head to one side. "I don't like it. I think we should save them before retaking the tower. What do you think, Comrade Xylo?"

Rhyno looked at me as if trying to confirm something, and while I hated to admit it, he was right. Regardless of my morals, our orders were to save the civilians, so we needed to protect them.

…And Teoritta looking up at me anxiously had *nothing* to do with it.

"Xylo, this is an honorable battle. I—"

"I know. We're going to make that warehouse our base. The fact that it belongs to Verkle Development Corporation makes it all the more convenient."

*"Seriously…?"* Venetim sounded worried. *"Verkle Development Corporation might file a complaint against us."*

"You'll manage to smooth things over if that happens."

*"What? No. We really shouldn't…"*

"Once we secure the warehouse, we'll split into two teams. I'm going to work you to death today, Rhyno, so I hope you're ready."

"But of course. This is starting to get fun." Whether he was joking or not was of little importance. Rhyno got the job done, and that was all that mattered. "Shall I open a path for us?"

He aimed his cannon at the fuathan clustering up ahead, blocking our way.

"Here goes nothing."

We were only thirty steps away from them, so there was no way Rhyno was going to miss. He got down on one knee, and the sacred seal engraved into the barrel on his right arm began to glow. It was all over in a single breath.

*Boom.* A loud pop. The silvery-white artillery shell made a beautiful arc in the air before landing right in the center of the fuathan. Flames swallowed the entire street in the blink of an eye. The impact created a powerful gust, but by the time it reached the fuathan, they were nothing more than dust in the wind. All that was left was a crater.

"Target hit. Path cleared. Let's go."

The seal Rhyno was using was called Tehwes Noots, which meant "impatient firefly" in the language of the ancient kingdom, or so I'd heard. It consumed an obscene amount of luminescence, but poor fuel efficiency was simply the price we had to pay for its wide range and powerful blast—enough to destroy a steel-framed castle wall. In addition to requiring physical artillery shells, the weapon was extremely difficult to aim. And yet Rhyno was somehow eerily good at it. He could adjust the amount of luminescence and fire each shell in the space of a single breath and still somehow easily hit his target.

*It doesn't make any sense. Though I guess nothing about him does.*

Rhyno was supposedly a former adventurer—he'd never worked for the military, so how had he learned to use this technology? Now that I thought about it, I didn't even know his family name. Whatever the case, almost everything about the guy was fishy.

"We make a pretty good team, don't we?" Rhyno lightly swung his right arm, allowing it to cool off. "And I'm especially impressed with you, Goddess Teoritta. What incredible power you possess. You and Comrade Xylo make a good pair."

"Yes, we do, though it does not sound so convincing when you say it…"

Teoritta retreated a few steps away from Rhyno and grabbed on to the hem of my shirt from behind.

"Ha-ha. You don't have to be scared," he said. "We have a lot in common, don't you think? After all, we're both fighting for the sake of mankind. I think we can learn a lot from each other."

"You're nothing alike. Just stop talking," I cut in. Teoritta had started tugging on my shirt even harder than before. "Let's keep moving. Rhyno, how many shells do you have left?"

"For large-scale strikes like the one just now? I have...around five more shots."

"All right. Use them wisely. The Holy Knights should be here soon... Right, Venetim?"

*"Huh? Oh! Right."* Venetim's voice crackled and hummed as I touched the sacred seal at my neck. *"I just heard that they're sending around five hundred soldiers. And I worked hard to get permission for Jayce to join us, so he should be there soon. I had the guards seal off the water channels as well."*

"The enemy was invading the city through the waterways? I'm impressed you tracked them down."

*"Uh... I kind of made that part up,"* whispered Venetim uncomfortably. *"I figured a sense of urgency might impair our superiors' judgment enough to meet our demands. I mean, imagining faeries right under your feet is pretty awful, right?"*

"Don't lie about important stuff like that!" I shot back. "You're tying up soldiers who could—"

"I don't think it was a bad idea at all," Rhyno said gently. "It's certainly not impossible. After all, where *did* the faeries come from? I think we should be wary of the water channels. They might well have used them."

"If they suddenly popped up in the city, I guess it's possible."

The source of this Demon Blight was lurking somewhere inside Ioff—the one behind it all: the demon lord Spriggan.

I had a hunch I knew who it was, too. That guy we'd run into while guarding Teoritta, Boojum, had raised my suspicions. Not even the flames of a dragon had been able to kill him. Plus, the athleticism he displayed as he fled was superhuman. It had to be him.

I guessed he would be waiting for us at Tui Jia, but I had a backup plan in case I was wrong: Frenci and her men. She was still leading the Night-Gaunts as they searched and patrolled the city. She had only around two hundred soldiers with her, but they were all people you could rely on in battle.

*"I will say it one last time. Do not do anything unsightly trying to save someone."*

That was her final warning.

*"Your mind and body exist solely for the prosperity of the Mastibolt family, and I will not allow you to damage either. Understood?"*

She'd said what she wanted to and left. I really needed to have a talk with her father. It seemed she was still treading on thin ice. I wondered how the Southern Night-Gaunts back home were treating her.

*"Hey, Xylo!"*

Maybe because I'd been distracted, the sudden sound of Dotta's voice irritated me.

*"Check out the rooftop up ahead! This is bad!"*

"What? What is it this—?"

Wondering what kind of vicious faeries we were up against, I shifted my gaze to the rooftop and got a shock. I could see humanoid faeries standing upright—and they were very small. These were bipedal faeries known as goblins, unable to fully transform into trolls. One or two dozen stood on the rooftop, each holding something in their hand. Were those sticks? No, they were staffs. And not just any staffs...

"Oh my. Are those lightning staffs?"

Rhyno took the words right out of my mouth. There was no doubt about it. The goblins were holding lightning staffs, though they were of an outdated, single shot variety.

"Wow, incredible. I wasn't expecting to see something like this. Faeries using sacred seals? What a surprise."

"Buhguh...mmn..."

Tatsuya looked up at the goblins with vacant eyes. He probably had no idea what he was seeing.

"Save the commentary for later!" I said, grabbing Teoritta and Tatsuya by the arms and ducking behind Rhyno. "Here it comes! Don't let it hit us!"

The rooftop goblins fired simultaneously, sending bolts of lightning straight for Rhyno, only for the shots to bounce right off his armor. This was one of the Neven Artillery Seal Compound's functions: It could produce a sacred seal barrier for defense. That said, it wasn't impregnable, nor was it unlimited.

"No damage taken, but I had to use some stored luminescence for fuel," said Rhyno. "That might've wiped out our fifth shot."

"Seriously? Dammit. Ideally, I'd like to run into an alleyway or something to get out of their line of sight, but..."

"But we don't have time for detours, right? Because there are people waiting for us to rescue them. So..."

"...Hey, wait!"

But I was too late. Rhyno probably wouldn't have stopped anyway. In the span of a single breath, he'd stuck out his right arm and activated the sacred seal, causing it to glow bright white.

"Breaking through the front should get us there faster."

The air vibrated as a flash of light was followed by a roaring explosion. The house right before our eyes was blown away, easily wiping out the goblins on the rooftop.

"People's lives are more important than property, right?" he said.

"That's not the issue here!"

*"That is not the issue here!"*

Venetim and I snapped back at him in unison, though I kind of hated that we were in agreement for once. Venetim seemed especially upset.

*"How am I supposed to explain this?!"* he cried. *"You realize I don't have an infinite number of excuses up my sleeve, right?!"*

"I'm not so sure about that. I believe in you, Comrade Venetim. I just *know* you will persuade everyone beautifully and smooth everything over." Rhyno was probably smiling behind his helmet as he continued his charge, climbing over the rubble that had once been someone's house. "Now, come on, Comrade Xylo. There are people waiting for us to save them. We must succeed."

Strategically, he'd done the right thing, especially if we were prioritizing people's lives. However, there was something genuinely odd about how quickly he made such decisions, without a moment of hesitation.

"It would be really nice if the rest of the mission was this smooth and easy," he said.

"Don't get your hopes up."

Unlike Rhyno, I was more pessimistic about the situation, especially after what I had just seen.

*Faeries using lightning staffs...*

The goblins were all dead, either from the blast or from falling off the rooftop, but the sight of them had made me very anxious.

*The coexisters... They must have somehow gotten those weapons into the hands of the faeries. Dammit.*

It was possible their reach had already spread to every corner of Ioff.

Voices could be heard coming from the darkness. They were followed by footsteps, the sound of metal scraping, collisions, roars, screaming—the sounds of battle. The demon lord Boojum heard it all.

*It seems they sealed off the channels.*

Ioff's underground waterways—Spriggan's plan was to send faeries through those channels into the city...but the enemy had seen right through it and sealed the channels off. The scouts had likely been disposed of already. The humans' intuition must have been excellent for them to have put up a line of defense in such a short amount of time. Perhaps the goddess with the power to see into the future had lent them a hand, or was one of their commanders simply an excellent strategist?

*Whatever the case, their skills are impressive and deserve respect.*

Respect was necessary in battle. It was proper etiquette. At least, that was what Boojum believed. If underestimating an opponent caused a warrior to let their guard down, then respecting them should have the opposite effect. And so Boojum came to a respectful conclusion about what had to be done.

*It is truly unfortunate, but I suppose I must kill them—every last one.*

When Boojum pulled himself up out of the darkness, he saw a blinding light—something was illuminating the space around him.

Humans with sacred seal–powered lanterns were staring at him, and one of them was readying a spear to attack.

"Something's there! Is that…a person?"

"My apologies, fellows…" Boojum stared straight into the light. "But please do not struggle. It will only make your deaths more painful, and that would be truly unfortunate."

"Huh?"

The humans' response was slow—fatally slow.

"I can make your deaths quick and painless if you hold still," said Boojum. "Allow me to explain. I—"

As Boojum extended his right hand, it began to bubble. It was as if something was swelling from inside his body before breaking through his skin and overflowing. The liquid was like bright crimson blood, and it wrapped around his right hand, forming claws.

"I-it's the demon lord! Tell the captain!" shouted one of the humans.

"F-fire! Fire your lightning staffs!"

One of the staffs flashed, and Boojum heard a dry pop as a ray of light pierced his body. His shoulders, chest, and side were filled with holes, causing even more blood to ooze out of him. But the substance merely continued wrapping itself around his body, as if it were alive.

"How rude. I was still in the middle of speaking." By the time Boojum had said this, his entire body was covered in blood armor. "Now, as I was saying… I have already replenished my supply of blood. You have absolutely no chance of defeating me. Now I am finished."

Three of the humans were still attacking with their spears and lightning staffs, ignoring his warning. Boojum had transformed into a beast, and his shadow danced in the light of the lanterns. It was over in the blink of an eye. He closed the distance between himself and his enemies in a single bound and swung his blood claws, digging into the exposed parts of their bodies between pieces of armor and easily severing their limbs. The humans desperately swung their weapons, but their blades and bolts of lightning merely bounced off Boojum's blood armor.

"It's called Blood Transmutation. While it isn't quite as tough as steel, with enough compression and layering, I can easily deflect attacks of this caliber."

"What is this thing?! None of our attacks are working!"

"B-blow him up with an explosion seal!"

"Get back! Fire in the hole!" someone yelled as a cylindrical object flew through the air. Whoever threw this explosive seemed fully prepared to sacrifice a few of his allies in the process. There was no time to escape. It blew up right above Boojum's head, releasing a storm of fire and light.

…And yet Boojum didn't stop.

"It's still alive! Don't let it get any closer! Raise your shields!"

No matter how much of his blood armor they chipped away, the humans' attacks couldn't reach Boojum's body, and it wasn't long before he was standing among them.

"I call this one Spiraling Blood." Boojum effortlessly swung his arm, creating a whirlwind of blood with his claws. "Not even armor can protect you from it."

His claws lost their rigid shape, whipping around the room and scarring the walls and floor of the underground path. The soldiers were relentlessly and indiscriminately torn apart. Their armor and shields proved useless, as the spirals of blood seeped in through the gaps, destroying them from the inside out.

One of them kept screaming, and it upset Boojum.

"I will only say this one last time." As Boojum's arm rested at his side, the blood coming from his fingertips slowly began to form an even larger blade. "You cannot defeat me, and I do not plan on letting any of you escape, so I recommend choosing a quick and painless death."

The humans didn't answer him. They simply whispered to each other and braced themselves. One even took off running, perhaps to relay a message.

"Even now, you still resist? I suppose I have no other choice…" Boojum lowered his posture until he was crouching like a wild beast in a crimson suit of armor. "I truly pity you all."

Countless blades of blood soared through the darkness.

The warehouse was already surrounded by faeries.

A quick glance was enough to see that the group included fuathan, bogies, kelpies, and even large barghests. The bonfire outside was drawing them right in, glowing bright in the darkness and signaling right where all the people were.

Thankfully, this warehouse belonged to the Verkle Development Corporation, so the walls were protected with sacred seals. Nevertheless, the faeries continued to ram the building with their horns and bodies, even if it meant burning to death in the process. There were already a few massive cracks in the walls. The building wasn't going to last much longer. We needed to make a move, and fast.

"Tatsuya, let's do this!"

I kicked off the ground, holding Teoritta in my arms and activating my flight seal. I unsheathed my first knife in midair.

An explosion. Then a flash of light. While the faeries were busy looking up in the air, Tatsuya charged into the horde with his battle-ax.

"Grrr."

He grunted with each swing, pulverizing every faerie in sight. He was literally smashing them. He charged like a beast and attacked with the force of a raging storm. It wasn't long before we broke through the besieging enemy forces and sent the rest of the faeries into retreat.

But there was still one thing we had to worry about at times like this: How would the civilians, who had no idea what was happening, perceive the situation?

"Eek!"

We heard a shriek from inside the building. Someone had looked out one of the steel-barred windows and seen us.

"There are even more faeries now...and they're humanoid! But why are they fighting each other? Agh! That one's the scariest yet...!"

They must have been referring to Tatsuya. He'd just buried his ax into the spasming body of a near-dead faerie, finishing it off. He'd smashed its head just in case and was double-checking to make sure it wasn't moving anymore.

"We're not faeries. We're humans. There's no need to worry!" I yelled, addressing the people on the other side of the window. "We're here to rescue you. We already killed all the faeries. I need you to open the front door for us."

The faeries that escaped would surely return with reinforcements, so we needed to finish preparing before they got back. We had to turn this warehouse into our base and make sure the civilians inside had a way to protect themselves.

"Hurry!" I shouted. "Do you wanna die?! This building won't last much longer if you keep standing there doing nothing!"

"Eep!"

"We don't have time for this. Hurry up and open the damn door!"

"Xylo, stop. They are terrified. Leave this to me, your Goddess!" Teoritta puffed out her chest and widened her stance. Her legs were surprisingly long and slender for someone so short. "...You'd better praise me if I get them to open the door!"

She took in a deep breath, then shouted in a clear, steely voice that could be heard all around:

"People of Ioff, I am Goddess Teoritta, and I have come to rescue you all! However, I need everyone's cooperation in order to guide you to your salvation!"

"Yes! People of Ioff, you are in danger here!" Rhyno shouted, finishing Teoritta's plea. His voice, too, was clear and booming. "However, there is no need to worry. We have the great goddess and her Holy Knight on our side: the Shining Goddess of Swords, Teoritta, and the Thunder Falcon, Xylo Forbartz!"

"What the...? Stop right there," I said, protesting.

A stir rippled through the warehouse, and I kicked Rhyno in the shin. Of course, I didn't even leave a scuff on his dark red armor.

"The hell you calling me the *Thunder Falcon* for?"

"Oh, I just happened to overhear some people calling you and Teoritta by those nicknames. It seems you're both very popular with the children around here."

"Listen, you—"

"Relax, Xylo. What is the issue? The Shining Goddess of Swords and the Thunder Falcon. Heh-heh. What fitting names for two great champions—"

Though I hated to admit it, it looked like Rhyno had managed to convince the civilians, and the door to the warehouse creaked open before Teoritta could finish her sentence.

"...Is what he says true?" someone asked.

A few skeptical faces peeked out from the open door. You couldn't blame them for being cautious. Seeing Tatsuya fight would scare anybody... At any rate, their reluctance certainly wasn't because I did a bad job of persuading them or anything...

"Did you really come to rescue us?" asked another civilian. "Are goddess Teoritta and the Thunder Falcon really here?"

"Yes, the two champions who protected Mureed Fortress are here, and I swear that they will protect each and every one of you from harm as well."

*Who the hell is he to decide that?* I thought, but I was in no position to complain, and this was no time to have it out with him.

"Now please!" Rhyno entreated. "We must hurry and strengthen our defense before the faeries return!"

The door swung open, revealing a large number of people inside. I estimated around a hundred, and each of them was armed with either a lightning staff or some sort of spear. They were all genuine military-grade weapons. It seemed this really was a Verkle warehouse.

"Perfect," I said with a firm nod. "Let's get everyone in position for battle. Rhyno, you teach them how to use the lightning staffs. The bare minimum should be enough."

"As you wish. I won't disappoint you, Comrade Xylo," he muttered. His voice held no trace of tension. Then, in a whisper, so only I could hear, he added, "I would like to discuss one thing with you first, though, Comrade. We need to decide the order in which the civilians will die."

"You can't be ser—!"

"I believe we should start with the elderly. They have already gotten a chance to enjoy life—far more than the children, so I believe it would only be fair if they died first. Does that sound reasonable to you?"

I probably would have kicked the shit out of him if he weren't wearing armor. He was always trying to work out what was logical or what was fair. *What's the use of getting pissed off at him?* I told myself.

"What am I supposed to say to that? 'Yes, that sounds great'? What kind of person do you think I am?"

"Oh, do you take issue with the morality of the question? That makes things difficult."

"...Someone once told me..."

Who was it? I knew. I *had* to know. Yes, it was Senerva. I hadn't forgotten. There was no way I could forget. *Dammit.*

"...You should always work toward the best outcome until the very end, and then you should work a little more. Only after all options are exhausted should you consider sacrificing civilians. The people trying to evacuate right now aren't soldiers. They aren't lives we can put a value on."

"I see. We can't put a value on their lives, huh..." Rhyno repeated the phrase, though I couldn't tell from his tone if he'd understood it. "In other words, their lives aren't worth considering this early on."

"That's not what I meant at all, but if it's easier for you to think about it that way, then be my guest. Just keep in mind the situation can change at any moment. For example..."

I looked up at the cloudy night sky and caught sight of a sparkling, vivid blue. It was a glowing sacred seal meant to alert your allies to your location. I could hear the flapping of wings. Then a roar. Some of the people in the warehouse looked up as well.

"You still haven't finished cleaning things up yet?" came Jayce's voice. The roaring was Neely. Her azure wings descended rapidly toward us. "You're so slow. How many did you kill? ...Wow, that's it? Looks like we beat you again."

A gust of wind blasted right over our heads as Jayce spoke. At the same time, I noticed a small ball of fire heading right for an alley to our north. A group of bogies rapidly approaching us with reinforcements was quickly swallowed in the flames. Neely seemed to have held back quite a bit, and none of the surrounding buildings caught fire.

"You see that? Perfect, huh?" said Jayce.

They circled around above our heads, showing off. Neely gave a fierce cry.

"Thank you, Comrade Jayce and Comrade Neely!" Rhyno said cheerfully, and waved at them. Once again, it sounded fake. "You are as skilled as ever, I see. Allow me to express my gratitude on behalf of the citizens in need of evacuation."

"Shut up, idiot," said Jayce. "...Dotta, where's my next target?"

*"Ah! A-about that...,"* Dotta said in a fluster. *"I see something! And it's bad!"*

"That doesn't help at all," I said, frowning. "Tell us exactly what you see, dammit. Why does your vocabulary always suffer whenever you're talking about something that you can't steal?"

"Actually, he often has a poor vocabulary even when he *is* talking about things he can steal. Comrade Dotta is always like this when he's flustered."

"Stop disrespecting Dotta like that," said Jayce. "...If nothing else, he has really good eyesight."

*"Guys, we don't have time for this! Listen! That red tower...! Like, I don't really know what's going on, but there's a guy wearing black armor like Rhyno's and—"*

A beam of light shot across the sky before exploding in a blinding flash. It was clearly aimed for Jayce and Neely. An anti-aerial attack. This was something we'd predicted as soon as we learned the enemy had an artilleryman on their side. Tui Jia had petal-like fortress walls at its base. If they were going to strike with someone like Rhyno, it would come from there.

"*Tsk.* Must be their artilleryman." Jayce clicked his tongue, and Neely began flapping her wings to gain altitude. "This is going to be a real pain in the ass…"

Attacks like these were extremely dangerous for dragons and dragon knights. As long as they were being targeted, they wouldn't be able to descend low enough to provide backup, and Jayce was going to have to constantly move around and dodge to avoid getting hit…which left us with only one option.

"Rhyno, we're sticking to the plan," I said. "You're in charge of giving Tatsuya orders. Protect the warehouse even if it kills you. The faeries will soon have bigger fish to fry…since we're going to attack Tui Jia directly."

"But of course. Let us combine our strengths and overcome this difficult situation together. You can count on me."

"Nothing you say ever sounds sincere."

"How can that be? My only wish is to win the favor of my comrades. Should you reject me, I would lose my place in this world. I'm simply desperate. That's all."

The things he said never made sense. All they did was give me the creeps. He looked back at me as I remained silent, and I was sure he was smiling—no, positive.

"Now is the time to show them our bravery and the strength of our bonds," he said. "Let us fight. For victory and peace for mankind!"

"…I missed?" muttered Iron Whale.

He was clad in jet-black armor, and Boojum was watching him fire at the azure dragon. White steam rose from the barrel on his right arm and from his shoulder.

"I'm impressed. That dragon knight must be pretty good to dodge my shot."

"Indeed."

Even Boojum had never encountered such a skilled dragon-rider pair. They moved unlike anything he'd seen before, easily dodging a swarm of guided bullets. Not only that, but they appeared to be getting ready to descend to the surface to support their allies.

"We cannot have that dragon moving freely. Iron Whale, maintain your fire and keep it busy."

"You better do something about the people on foot, then. Artillerymen are worthless in close-range combat. And that one guy... That's the goddess killer, right?"

"Yes, I know. A formidable foe."

Boojum had already encountered Xylo Forbartz once, and now he had that goddess of swords by his side.

"I will handle him," said Boojum. "Is that good enough for you?"

"Yeah, that's great, but...you're pretty weird, aren't you? I thought demon lords were supposed to be more ferocious, and that they all despised humans."

"There are many like that, but I'm different. I don't hate humans." Boojum slowly shook his head, caressing the book in his hand like a cherished possession. "Specifically, I like mankind's culture and civilization. I especially enjoy poems. They're wonderful."

"A demon lord that loves poetry? Now I've heard everything," said Iron Whale with a sneer as he fired his cannon into the sky, then quickly loaded up the next round. He needed to keep that dragon at bay with a continuous volley of guided artillery shells. "There must not be many like you."

"It is truly frustrating not being understood. I genuinely believe it is necessary to pay our respects to the enemy before we eliminate them, and yet..."

"Heh! Should you really be saying that in front of one of those you're gonna eliminate? I'm still human, you know?"

"It isn't good to lie. That's something I don't like about Spriggan. She lacks respect. My king is the only one who understands me." Boojum wearily closed his eyes. "And that is the very reason why I fight—for the sake of the only one who understands me. I am fighting for my king."

"Hold up. 'King'? Do even demon lords have lords?"

"Hmm... Perhaps I have said too much. Now that I think about it, I was told to keep my mouth shut, so I'm afraid we will have to end this conversation here."

"All right. I'd rather not know anyway," said Iron Whale, nodding disinterestedly. "Stuff like that's common in this business. If you know too much, you get erased, and it isn't pretty."

"A wise decision."

Boojum stood. His eyes were usually pointed down, his head in a book, but now he looked up, gazing into the night sky and listening to the wind as it gathered strength.

"The goddess killer is coming. I rather like humans of his type, but I must kill him for the sake of my king," he whispered coldly. "How truly unfortunate. I feel sorry for him."

Rhyno climbed on top of the warehouse and anchored his armored legs, using the spikes in his heels and in the balls of his feet to dig into the roof. After reloading his artillery with a shell and another luminescence cylinder, he neatly lined up boxes full of reserves. As one might expect, the Verkle Development Corporation's warehouse had more than enough supplies for one person.

"I'm in position, Comrade Xylo," he muttered. He crouched as low as he possibly could, extended his right arm, and looked up. The tower of Tui Jia stood tall under a thick blanket of clouds so dark that it looked like it might rain at any moment.

Rhyno watched as Xylo leaped through the air toward the tower, holding Goddess Teoritta in his arms and disposing of any faerie that got in his way. Meanwhile, Jayce and Neely danced across the sky, tirelessly dodging the rays of light shooting out from the tower and dipping toward the ground to torch some faeries whenever they got the chance. *What a majestic sight*, thought Rhyno.

"Impressive," he said. He meant it from the bottom of his heart. "You two look like real champions. It makes me so happy to be part of such a grand battle."

*"Will you shut up already? Asshole,"* replied Xylo through the sacred seal on his neck.

Jayce simply ignored him. But that was fine. While the others might not understand him, Rhyno was being genuine. That was how he really felt, and he truly looked forward to battles like this. The Demon Blight was their enemy, and the horde's leader, the demon lord, waited inside the looming crimson tower.

"How wonderful," he continued. "Our enemies must be terrified of you. How I would love to join you."

*"Then start working. The people in the warehouse are still okay, right? Don't let your guard down."*

"Yes, they're absolutely fine. No need to worry about them." Rhyno could see Tatsuya below, throwing himself like a wild beast at incoming faeries before they could reach the warehouse. "I have Comrade Tatsuya here to help me, after all."

Their objective was to protect the people of Ioff, and Tatsuya loyally followed those orders. He wasn't even giving the incoming bogies a chance to counter. He was literally pulverizing the enemy. And that wasn't all he was doing.

"He is truly incredible," said Rhyno.

*"Yeah, I know."*

"No, I don't think you do, Comrade Xylo. Shall I tell you…?"

*"What is it already?"*

"Comrade Tatsuya is using a lightning staff."

*"Seriously?"*

"Seriously."

Rhyno watched from above as Tatsuya flew through the air. A group of goblins had climbed on top of a roof, formed a line, and were getting ready to fire their lightning staffs, but the instant Tatsuya saw them, he kicked off the wall and joined them on the roof, charging them. That was already an astonishing display, but what happened after was even more shocking. After sweeping through the line of trolls, he grabbed one of their lightning staffs and began firing bolts from it.

"I was shocked. Maybe we should consider issuing Comrade Tatsuya a lightning staff of his own."

Rhyno had known Tatsuya for a long time, but he'd never seen the man use a sacred seal, let alone a lightning staff. This was probably the first time anyone had seen such a thing. He often stole an enemy's weapon or used their bodies as shields, and perhaps you could claim this was merely an extension of that behavior. But Rhyno found it a refreshing surprise.

*Of course, he doesn't have the precision of Comrade Tsav, but still.*

He'd hardly missed a single goblin or bogie on the street. Not only that, but when the lightning staff ran out of charge, he removed its luminescence cylinder and replaced it with one from another staff. One simply had to conclude that Tatsuya knew how to use the weapon. But how? It was a mystery to Rhyno.

"There is never a dull moment around Comrade Tatsuya," he said. "He is using the newest model with ease."

*"…What do you think is up with him anyway?"*

"I wish I knew. But there is one thing I can say with confidence." He looked down at Tatsuya as the man let out a strange battle cry. "We should be glad that he's fighting for mankind. We ought to show him more gratitude."

Those were genuine words from the bottom of Rhyno's heart… though people hardly ever believed him.

We headed toward the red tower of Tui Jia in a direct line from the warehouse. Holding Teoritta in my arms, I leaped forward, shutting out the world behind from my mind. Rhyno and Tatsuya would be able to protect the warehouse. Rhyno aside, I saw Tatsuya as the ideal infantryman. He felt no fear, didn't talk, and couldn't die. I was amazed to hear he was now using a lightning staff, too.

At any rate, there was no reason to worry about them. Someone above us sure was making a lot of noise, though.

*"Hurry up and do something, Xylo,"* complained Jayce, clearly not in a good mood. I could see Neely and him circling the sky, balls of light grazing right by them. The shells seemed to be following Neely's wings.

*"Tsk. That artilleryman's using guided shells. We won't be able to get close to the tower at this rate."*

Neely squawked, as if in agreement.

*"Yeah, I'm fine, Neely,"* Jayce said in reply. *"You don't need to worry about me. You're much faster than those shells, so there's no way he'll hit us."*

Jayce's attitude toward Neely was clearly different from the one he showed us. Sometimes I wondered if he really could understand what the dragons were saying.

"So… What you're trying to tell me, Jayce, is that you can't do it?"

*"Hmph. Neely's fire breath can't reach them from this far out, especially with those walls in the way. We could try diving toward the tower to fight at close range, but are you really gonna make us do something that reckless?"*

I knew what he meant. A diving attack would make them an easy target for an artilleryman. It was a gamble, and the odds wouldn't be in our favor. Dragon knights had low defense, just like cavalry soldiers. Although dragons had tough scales capable of blocking things like stones, they weren't strong enough to repel sacred seal–based attacks like a shot from a lightning staff.

*"Come on. Hurry up, Xylo. You're supposed to be handling things on the ground, right?"*

"Yeah, yeah… Dammit," I said. "Where the hell is Tsav, Venetim?! We need to do something about their artilleryman to shut Jayce up."

*"I'm trying my best, but it's going to take some time. It's chaos outside on the streets at the moment. I've had a report that faeries are invading the inland district now as well."*

"There, too?"

*"Yes, and King Norgalle is furious. The citizens' safety is—"*

*"What is the meaning of this?! Guards! Holy Knights!"* Norgalle's crackling, enraged screaming cut Venetim off. *"I have repeatedly called for backup and have gotten nothing! The people are the heart of my kingdom, and we must protect those trying to evacuate. Commander-in-Chief Xylo! This is your fault for slacking off!"*

"Hey, what did I do?"

*"Isn't it obvious? You're not exercising proper control over the military, and look where that has gotten us. This is the result of your vicious temper, inability to work as a team, and lack of dignity. Once this battle is over, I shall have you learn proper etiquette!"*

*"Sorry, Xylo,"* said Venetim. *"The king has been working tirelessly for a while now. He's probably just exhausted."*

"Yeah, I know how you and Dotta are allergic to hard work, so I get it."

I thought about the base we'd set up at the city wall. It must have been unbelievably busy, since they had to protect all the people evacuating. But I was sure things would be even more chaotic if it weren't for Norgalle's strange charisma.

"Forget it. I'll do something about the tower and the artilleryman myself. Jayce, Neely! Just hold out for a little bit longer!" I shouted, shutting Norgalle's and Venetim's voices out of my head.

Then I looked down at Teoritta in my arms.

"Teoritta, I'm about to take us to the tower. We'll be surrounded by faeries, and they'll probably be shooting at us. Are you ready?"

"I like your attitude, Xylo. You are being very prudent." She smiled, though I couldn't tell if she was more happy or relieved. "I would have been furious if you had left me behind again."

"I'm not sure this is the right decision. I might have to kill you for the sake of mankind—for someone we don't know and won't ever meet. Something terrible might happen to you. Both of us might die today."

"Is it not a little late for that?" Teoritta kept smiling, just as I thought she would. "The chances of any of that happening are very low. You have my blessing, after all. And that is exactly why you brought me with you, is it not? You need to recognize me as your goddess—the one who fights by your side!"

"You're out of your mind. Unlike me, you won't come back to life."

"But you might lose memories that will never return." Teoritta grabbed on to my arm, clinging to me. "That woman who calls herself your fiancée probably fears that the most."

"Pfft. Yeah, right. Nothing scares her."

"Yes, I am sure you truly believe that."

"What's that supposed to mean?"

"You will have to figure that out on your own. At any rate, I will protect your memories. That is worth risking my life for."

She looked up at me, fire burning in her eyes. It made me extremely uncomfortable. *What the hell is she talking about?* I thought. Why would someone like her—basically a child not even a year old—risk her life? It was absurd. She idealized being recognized as "one of us" and being praised, and because of that, she was driven to reckless behavior.

Nevertheless, I kind of understood how she felt. There were times when foolish actions seemed so glorious.

*I'm ending this tonight.*

Right then, I made a decision.

"We're finishing this by dawn, and after that, we're getting breakfast. Freshly baked bread with zeff butter."

"Onion soup, too! Oh, and with a side of crispy bacon!"

"Heh. You're making me hungry. Moving words fit for a goddess."

I held Teoritta tightly in my arms and kicked off the ground. The air was numbingly cold. The world passed us by in a flash as we rapidly approached the tower and its surrounding walls.

*Ugh. Asshole.*

I looked up and saw the enemy artilleryman fixed in place on the petal-like fortress walls, his sacred seal glowing. He was covered in jet-black armor. It looked even sturdier and larger than what Rhyno wore. The cannon on his right arm was pointing right at us. He fired seven— no, eight—balls of light.

*"Those are guided shells, Xylo,"* said Jayce. He was challenging me. *"Neely had no trouble dodging them, but what about you?"*

In other words, avoiding these without the help of a highly trained dragon was going to be difficult. I still had Teoritta on my side, though. I could manage.

"Teoritta, the usual." There was no reason to change our route. We didn't have time for detours.

"Knock those down."

"I could do it with my eyes shut," she replied.

I now had a good understanding of how her summoning powers worked. She had surprisingly good precision against airborne targets, and could hit flying faeries even as I leaped through the sky, carrying her in my arms. Her powers couldn't cover large areas like the storm-summoning fourth goddess or like the sixth goddess, who could summon power itself. But Teoritta made up for this with her precision. Her spatial awareness must have been extraordinary.

In other words, shooting down those incoming balls of light would be easy for her.

"I shall protect you," said Teoritta.

The swords she summoned collided with the homing shells and detonated every single one of them. The explosions lit up the sky as I sailed past.

"But, Xylo, it is your job to win."

"You got it."

I was probably smiling as I held Teoritta tightly in my arms.

We were rapidly approaching the tower. The artilleryman in black slowly stretched out his arm-cannon as its sacred seal glowed. He wouldn't be using homing shells anymore, now that we were this close. He would aim carefully and try to hit us with normal shells.

But just then, I noticed something. The iron gate at the front of the tower was wide open, as if they were inviting us inside. Numerous kelpies were waiting there, and at their center stood a woman and a man with a hunched back.

I thought I could make out the woman saying, "They're here." Or perhaps she was laughing. I'd seen her before. She was slender, with two black gauntlets covering her arms, and eyes that could only be described as emotionless. The man with the slouch, however, watched us with a sorrowful gaze.

The adventurers who Norgalle had captured—or should I say "made his followers"—had told us all about these two. The woman's name was Shiji Bau, and the man with the slouch was Boojum. The artilleryman up above was called Iron Whale. They were each powerful adventurers, skilled mercenaries, and at times, assassins. This job wasn't going to be easy. I was probably going to work myself to the bone...literally.

*But even then...*

What I had to do was clear. I would fulfill my duty as a Holy Knight accompanying a goddess. In other words, I had to win.

Meanwhile, Norgalle's line of defense was under attack. They would wind up fighting until dawn, holding back the enemy.

"Barghests incoming! Do not fire until I give the order!"

This battle was only possible because of Norgalle's leadership. He placed himself at the front line, all the while giving orders to adventurers and civilians alike. He gathered up those capable of fighting and positioned them behind a fence engraved with sacred seals. This was the only strategy possible with such a group.

Those who could use lightning staffs got them, and those who couldn't received bows. It was a very primitive way of fighting, but it was an effective defense. At any rate, they needed to land as many attacks as they could. In this situation, that was their only hope.

Norgalle, however, didn't even flinch. As a commander, he was a professional. It was almost eerie how skilled he was at this, and it was particularly effective with exhausted civilians looking for someone to turn to.

"Good." Norgalle lowered his hand, giving the order to attack. "Now fire!"

Bolts of lightning and arrows shot forward, piercing the elephant-sized barghests, tearing into their flesh and breaking their legs. It wasn't easy for such large creatures to get back up, and that made them an excellent target for everyone to focus their attacks on. Norgalle's forces did just that, finishing them off one by one.

"Your Majesty, the next wave is coming. It's a horde of fuathan. They're charging up the river!" shouted Dotta from the tower above.

He sounded like he wanted to cry. "There's too many! Maybe we should consider running away?"

"I will not allow it. You take one step down from that tower, and I will execute you myself."

"Ughhh…"

"Dotta, how about putting that great eyesight of yours to good use? You have a staff. Snipe them."

"I can't. This thing's too hard to use."

A weapon engraved with a sacred seal Norgalle had tuned was installed in the tower with Dotta. It was a lightning staff, even bigger than Dotta himself, with a lens for sniping.

"I tried shooting it, but I completely missed what I was aiming at."

"How can you miss with a weapon I modified to perfection? How inept can one man be?"

"Yeah, yeah. Say whatever you want. I still can't snipe."

"Then protect your post with your life. It's the least you can do. Tsav should be here any moment now. He'll be able to use that staff."

"I dunno… Is he really coming? I mean, if it were me, I'd probably pretend like I was coming and run away instead."

"He'll be here," assured Norgalle with absolute certainty. "He may be a scoundrel, but he isn't the kind of scoundrel to run away."

"Is it just me, or are you implying that I'm the no-good kind of scoundrel who would?"

"That isn't what I'm saying. In the past, I may have felt that way, and I may have discussed putting you to death with Venetim and Xylo, but—"

"Could you, like, not talk about stuff like that when I'm not around?"

"The commander-in-chief said that these foolish tendencies of yours sometimes bring about miracles."

Xylo should be getting close to the tower. All Norgalle had to do was fend off the enemy, and victory would surely be theirs. He had near absolute trust in his army's commander-in-chief, and he knew that Jayce would be able to fulfill his duty as well. After all, these were the guardians of his kingdom that he himself had appointed.

All that was left was to wait. Norgalle believed that once a king entrusted his subjects with full authority, it was his chief responsibility simply to stand by and trust that they would fulfill their duty.

Ioff's government office was located more or less right in the middle of the Road of Steel and Salt. The block had a large open plaza for festivals and gatherings, and by the time Patausche arrived on horse, lines of soldiers had already filled it.

In addition to the city guards stood armed priests from the Temple. These were members of the Temple's private army, carefully selected from its followers. What they lacked in skill, they made up for with morale. Moreover, the man leading them was someone Patausche knew very well: her uncle, Marlen Kivia. He appeared to be wearing chain mail underneath the simple, black-lined robe signifying his status as a high priest. He was currently acting as the city's defense adviser, so if he was taking command, that must mean...

"Uncle!"

Patausche got down from her horse and bowed reverently.

"Thank you for coming all this way, Patausche. That was quick," said her uncle cheerfully, nodding and prompting her to lift her head. "I apologize for how sudden this is, but I need the support of the Holy Knights. The citizens of Ioff are already under attack."

"As you wish." She looked at her uncle. His sharp, stony, dignified gaze was pointed not at her but off toward the city. "Uncle, is it true that faeries have appeared inside the commercial district?"

"According to the report I received from the guards, the faeries broke in through the remains of an underground structure beneath the outer walls. There are quite a lot of them. This is most likely their main force."

Ioff had existed long before the founding of the Federated Kingdom. Beneath the town were ruins from the era of the old kingdom, but they were nothing more than tourist attractions now.

*So that's how they got in,* thought Patausche. *In that case, will we still be able to send reinforcements to the port?*

"Wow, your uncle is a real strategist, huh?"

The jocular voice came from someone approaching Patausche from the side. It was Zofflec, commander of the cavalry. He had already entrusted his men to the high priest and was now on defense duty.

"He predicted the enemy's movements and did a beautiful job gathering all the soldiers here. It looks like we aren't needed."

"I simply had luck on my side," said the high priest. "I'd like to believe it's because of my faith."

As the two of them spoke, Patausche quietly thought to herself. The situation was urgent and getting worse by the second. But perhaps they could get things under control, now that they'd located the enemy's main force. The only problem was...

"Uncle Marlen, I would like a little more detail, if you don't mind. Who first discovered the enemy, and where are they now?"

"Ioff City Defense Force Unit 7110. The sole survivor was severely wounded in battle and cannot speak right now. Check with my aide if you want more information."

"Understood." Patausche bowed once more.

"We're counting on you and your people, Patausche."

Her uncle's dignified expression betrayed a faint grin.

"I am especially thankful for you," he continued. "This is no time for the military and the Temple to be feuding, so perhaps this is a blessing in disguise. I hope that we can overcome this together and strengthen our bond."

Marlen Kivia formed a sacred seal with his hands.

"Maybe the blessings of Saint Mahaeyzel be with you."

There was nothing strange about the gesture. Saint Mahaeyzel was a legendary figure and a leader during the First War of Subjugation. Almost everyone at the Temple used his name when praying for another's good fortune. Patausche had heard that her uncle admired the man as well.

And yet something about that name bothered her.

Mahaeyzel's family name, Zelkoff, was a pronunciation unique to her people in the north. People from the inner lands or anywhere else would pronounce his name "Zelkoof."

This was what planted the seed of doubt in her mind.

Tui Jia was right before our eyes.

I gripped Teoritta tightly and launched forward. But I didn't pass through the front gate, which the enemy had opened like some kind of invitation. I knew the range of the lightning staff in Shiji Bau's hands, so I got as close as I could to make it look like I was going to rush the gate, then I jumped to the side, dodging her attack and using the wall surrounding the tower as a shield.

"I need stairs," I called out.

"On it!" Teoritta replied.

I kicked off the ground, then began running up the outside of the tower. It was a piece of cake, because Teoritta had rubbed the air, causing swords to emerge like steps from the wall. Our point of entry had deviated significantly from the plan, but I had anticipated that. After leaping over the wall, I got a full view of the enemy forces within. There were faeries as far as the eye could see, and they immediately rushed over to where I was going to land.

"Look at us, waltzing into the demon lord's fortress alone," I joked. I had to keep things light, or I wouldn't be able do this. "We must be crazy. We'd be done for without the divine blessing of a goddess."

"Then you're in luck," she replied, forcing herself to smile back. "Since you have mine."

"When you're right, you're right."

I dropped to the ground and looked over at the approaching faeries.

The first horde was a group of kelpies—beasts covered in algae. They were about the size of humans, with sharp claws on each limb, and they would lunge at their prey, digging into their bodies while secreting a flesh-melting mucus. They were a real pain to fight at close-range, so dispatching them with a single shot would be ideal. But it was almost impossible to figure out where their vital organs were in their bodies, which made everything much more complicated. They'd probably been put here just to slow me down.

It wasn't only Iron Whale on the tower's fortress walls I had to worry about. There were goblins with lightning staffs as well. Their earsplitting cries were accompanied by a rain of lightning bolts. If I'd stopped moving, they would have taken us out for sure. So I swiftly threw a knife at a kelpie up ahead, blowing it to pieces and rushing through the resulting flames.

My destination was the fortress itself, now a little over a hundred paces away. I could make out Iron Whale straight ahead. Shiji Bau and Boojum were nowhere to be seen, but I suspected they would mix in with an incoming horde of faeries and try to take me by surprise.

*There's too many of them for me to handle alone. But I'm not alone.*

I had Teoritta with me, and they had no idea how precise her summoning was.

"Teoritta, it's time for the first batch, just like we planned."

"Very well," she replied, smiling.

I had already told her what we needed to do. The strategy wasn't anything complicated: She would use her summoning ability three times, and then we'd simply pray that everything went well.

"I need not hold back...if we are up against faeries!"

Her sparking golden locks danced in the air. Countless swords emerged from the void, pinpointing only the kelpies and skewering them to the ground. They had no way to dodge, and our strikes didn't need to be fatal. All we had to do was stop them in their tracks so that I could run freely without anything getting in my way.

As a result, Iron Whale's artillery shell completely missed us. It exploded in a massive firestorm to our rear, lightly warming my back and nothing more.

"*Tsk.*"

The click of a tongue—Shiji Bau.

I was heading in a straight line for Iron Whale's position on the fortress, forcing Shiji Bau to try to cut me off. The enemy couldn't let me get into close combat with their artilleryman, where he'd be a sitting duck. The kelpies had all been immobilized, and I vaulted through the air, passing over a desolate sea of corpses.

Goblins equipped with lightning staffs were showering rays of light down on us from the fortress, but their aim was pathetic. I hardly even had to dodge. A bolt or two may have grazed my cheek or burned the tips of my boots, but they were incapable of landing a direct hit.

"Teoritta! You're in range for the second batch, right?"

"There is no need for doubt. Simply have faith in my miracles."

Sparks flickered against the void as Teoritta's entire body grew hot. Countless swords appeared over the fortress, above the heads of the goblins. The distance hindered her aim slightly, but it was good enough. The legion of summoned blades terrified the goblins. Sometimes, all you needed to neutralize an enemy was fear, not some ultimate attack.

*How do you like that? Thought outnumbering us was enough to win?*

This was the power of a goddess and her Holy Knight. Together, we could crush thousands of enemies without breaking a sweat. Once we made the decision to fight, it was over for them. They simply hadn't understood that.

"Perfect, right? I even impress myself sometimes!" said Teoritta proudly.

The tables had turned, and the enemy was pressed. Iron Whale swiftly aimed the cannon in his right arm at me. As it began to glow, I hid myself behind a kelpie's corpse, using it as a shield and lowering my posture so the artilleryman wouldn't spot me. But no sooner had I done so than the corpse shredded into pieces, dark black blood spewing into the air as I caught sight of steel rope stretching out from a little ways ahead.

Someone had been trying to shred me into pieces along with the kelpie.

*She's here.*

Shiji Bau moved to stand between Iron Whale and us, then promptly closed the distance. We were now one-on-one. I'd been waiting for this moment. Shiji Bau assumed her unique fighting stance, her right hand held out. The outer layer of her gauntlets broke apart into steel ropes and spread out as if to wrap around Teoritta and me.

*She doesn't hold back with the violence, huh?*

I smiled wryly and faced the female assassin head-on.

"Don't shoot, Iron Whale!" she shouted. "You're too close. I'll take care of them."

The steel ropes on her right gauntlet began twisting into the shape of a fang—this was our only chance. I gave Teoritta the signal to attack.

"Teoritta, let's finish this!"

"All right, here comes the third batch!"

Her hair glowed with golden light as countless swords appeared in the air—but these weren't for attacking. They were meant to tangle Shiji Bau's steel ropes while they were in the middle of changing form.

"*Tsk...!*"

I could tell she was scowling. Metal clinked and cracked as the steel ropes coming from her right hand dropped to the ground, tangled and unable to function. She tried covering with her left hand, which she'd kept in reserve, but we were too close now. There were no other enemies around us that could move. The kelpies were skewered to the ground, and it would be a few moments until the other faeries could make their way to us. And besides, Teoritta could easily defend herself against non-humans. I was close enough now, so I patted Teoritta on the shoulder.

"This'll do. Watch my back."

"Understood." Teoritta let go of me and jumped out of my arms.

"Allow me to handle this! Behold the power of the great goddess Teoritta!"

She rubbed the air, summoning a sword that pierced a desperate goblin recklessly charging for her.

It was my turn now, and all I needed were the guts to pull this off. I stepped forward as Shiji Bau charged toward me. Right before we clashed, I grabbed her by the lapel and jerked her forward, pulling her off-balance.

"I envy you guys," I said.

I prepared for what was about to happen. I could tell her eyes were opened wide. She must have caught a glimpse of the sky as well.

"Seems like you have teammates that stop when you tell them to." We were different.

Flames rained down from above. A roar, azure wings, Neely's eyes, and Jayce. It all happened in the blink of an eye. Shiji Bau tried to activate her left gauntlet to protect herself from the incoming flames, but she was too late.

"Ah…!"

She screamed, trying to lean back out of the way, but I tightened my grip around her lapel and lowered myself into a crouch, using her body as a shield as her screams turned more desperate. I wanted to scream, too, but I somehow managed to hold it in.

"How do you like that, Xylo?" asked Jayce as his dragon scorched me along with the enemy. "We saved your ass, so you better thank Neely and me."

I decided to save my complaints for later and kicked Shiji Bau's body as far as I could to the side, making sure to use my flight seal to its full potential. I could see Iron Whale in his jet-black armor, but he was still too far away to attack, around eighty or so paces away. I would need to push my way through the horde of kelpies, dodge the goblins' lightning staffs, and stay out of the way of Iron Whale's artillery to get there, and that would be difficult even with my flight seal—under normal circumstances, at least.

*There's no way I can close the distance with all these obstacles in my path. I bet that's exactly what you're thinking—that I'm too far away to do anything.*

Iron Whale already had his arm-cannon aimed at me, its sacred seal glowing. He was going to fire any moment now. But it was already too late.

"Rhyno," I said through the sacred seal at my neck. "You're ready to go, right? Surely you've had enough time to aim."

*"But of course."*

A ray of light appeared over my head—nearly blinding me as it exploded. Iron Whale must have looked up at it.

*"I have finished calculating all the necessary factors, and the target has been distracted,"* Rhyno said, his tone aggravatingly pleasant. *"It's time to destroy."*

The next blasts came back-to-back: two—three—four—on and on. Over ten artillery shells went soaring through the sky. Iron Whale easily shot down the first with his cannon. It was clear he was an unbelievably skilled artilleryman.

But that's as far as he got.

"What the…? Who the hell is firing? What kind of person can manage so many shots…and with such accuracy…?!"

Those words from Iron Whale signaled the end. Each and every one of Rhyno's remaining artillery shells struck Tui Jia. Explosion after explosion rocked the tower. I could tell that the foundation had started to crumble as the structure leaned to one side. The tower was going to fall. The fortress where Iron Whale was standing came crumbling down in a thick cloud of dust. Just before it swallowed him, I saw his jet-black armor bend and crack as he was crushed.

The rain of debris pelted the faeries below. We watched them from a safe distance, far enough not to get caught up in the collapsing foundation, and with plenty of room to dodge any falling rubble.

*"It appears I hit the target,"* noted Rhyno calmly.

It was amazing how he could act so composed after what he'd just done. His long-range attack had defied sense, but Rhyno had the skills to pull it off. I'd had no doubt he could make the shot from the warehouse rooftop.

If you asked Rhyno, he would say it all came down to math. As long as you could calculate the appropriate variables, you could tell if a shot was possible. And he'd told me this was possible, so I'd asked him to do it.

*"Wh-what did you do, Xylo?!"* I could hear Venetim's voice through a layer of noise and static. *"The tower's collapsing!"*

"Yeah, I had Rhyno destroy it."

*"What would you do that for?! How am I going to explain this to our superiors?!"*

"Just blame it on the Demon Blight. You'll figure something out."

*"I'll 'figure something out'? Xylo! Help me think of an excuse, so—"*

"I'm busy right now. Talk to you later."

Venetim sounded upset, but I didn't have time for it, so I blocked out his voice.

My strategy for this mission was mind-numbingly simple: Create a distraction on the ground that the enemy couldn't ignore, then have others attack from the sky, locking up all their forces. Rhyno's ability to shoot at long range with incredible accuracy was the key to winning. The building itself was at risk of becoming a faerie, so whatever use it might have was moot—destroying it was our best option.

But the fight wasn't over yet. There was still one enemy left: the source. I saw something wavering in the dust. Something wriggled. And then, a flash of light.

"Teoritta!"

A crimson sickle—or maybe a claw—sliced through the dust cloud, headed right for us. I unsheathed a dagger with each hand and blocked the incoming attack with my left at the very last second. The steel cried in agony on impact, and it didn't end there. A second, then a third attack followed, all of which I swiftly blocked with my knives.

…Maybe that was a bit of an exaggeration. To be honest, the attacks were faster and far more powerful than I had expected. I was barely managing to deflect them, and my arms and shoulder were being shredded. But the wounds were shallow, and the pain still dull.

"Dammit!"

I held my knives with a reverse grip and launched a counterattack, but it failed to connect. The reason was soon apparent.

"Your reflexes are quick. Very impressive," said a familiar voice. Its gloomy tone belonged to none other than Boojum. "You have exceeded my expectations, and are worthy of respect."

I could see a colossal crimson shadow inside the cloud of dust—a giant suited in ominous red armor. At first, I thought it was the remains of the tower, somehow still standing, but I was wrong. Rhyno would never leave so much intact. It was a giant suit of armor towering over me, perhaps twice the size of Neely—a heavily armored infantryman the size of a fortress. The surface of his armor was a blackish red, and it bubbled, expanding before my eyes.

The reason was right under my nose. It appeared the armor was absorbing the blood from the dead faerie's carcasses. *Interesting. So that massive body of his is made out of blood?*

"Xylo Forbartz, if possible, I do not wish to fight you," said Boojum, his voice muffled behind the armor. "I recognize that you are an incredibly strong opponent. Would it be possible for you to leave the goddess and withdraw from battle?"

"Now that's a new way to negotiate."

I could tell Teoritta's body had tensed behind me. Her hair was sparking intermittently. She was reaching her limit.

"Do you guys really want to kill Teoritta that badly?" I asked.

"Yes, very much so," Boojum replied. "She and she alone must be killed at all costs, and I feel no pity for her."

"Interesting."

*At all costs? Why were they so obsessed with killing her?* Thinking back, Teoritta was at the center of everything that had happened in Ioff. At any rate, there were forces that wanted her dead, and they were desperate. It seemed every demon lord and their followers were out to get her.

*That must mean there's something special about her.*

Could it be the Holy Sword? The special ability only the goddess of swords possessed?

*Looks like I don't have much of a choice.*

When I glanced back, Teoritta was already gazing up at me. She seemed confident. Flames flickered in her eyes, and her golden locks were sparking. This close, it was obvious to me that she had only one desire.

"I have no doubt," she began. "We shall win. We shall not be hurt. And we shall end this before dawn, yes?"

"Exactly. I'll kill the demon lord. That's my job as a penal hero, after all. In other words…" I gave the knife in my hand a half spin, adjusting my grip as I pointed the tip of the blade at Boojum. "Piss off, asshole."

"How unfortunate. It won't be easy, but I'm afraid I must kill you." He lifted his colossal arm into the air and sighed heavily. "If there is even a chance I can kill the goddess, then I must try."

Blood shot out of his fingertip, almost casually, creating an arch like a scythe as it soared toward us.

Dodging was the only option. Activating my flight seal, I grabbed Teoritta and lunged into the air. Blades shot out from Boojum's fingertips in quick succession, giving me no choice but to keep jumping. I couldn't block this many hits. I'd reached my limit a moment ago at two or three. I was lucky this Boojum guy was a complete amateur and stopped to politely ask me to surrender. *What an idiot.* But if I had to keep dodging like this, I'd never get anywhere near him.

*He knows about Teoritta's Holy Sword.*

The Holy Sword was a unique weapon that could destroy anything it touched. Allowing me to get close would mean certain death. Even the immortal demon lord Iblis had been erased from existence, so it was only natural that Boojum would try to keep me as far away as possible.

"Jayce!" I shouted, touching the sacred seal on the nape of my neck. "I need backup! You can hit him from the sky!"

*"How do you expect me to do that, idiot?! Those attacks are flying all the way up here! And that dust cloud is making it really hard to see, too. Or would it be okay if I reduced the entire area to ash and took out all of you?"*

SENTENCED TO BE A HERO, VOLUME II

"Obviously not! But…"

The situation was urgent—it seemed the incoming blades of blood were targeting Jayce and Neely as well. This demon lord had some extremely powerful moves.

"Rhyno! What are you doing?! Shoot!"

*"Unfortunately, I can't see very well, either. I calculated the variables multiple times, but I'm not confident I can hit the target."*

"Who cares? Just fire. You might get lucky!"

*"I believe the chance of that is almost zero—"*

"I told you to shoot! Just do it!"

My yelling seemed to have worked, and I heard the sound of his cannon firing. But in all honesty, I didn't expect any of the shots to hit Boojum, either. My goal was to create a distraction, even if only for a second. I fixed my eyes on Boojum's colossal body, visible in patches through the dust. He was at least fifty paces away, aggravatingly far. But I was going to do this.

*Bring it on.*

Three—four bloody blades were headed our way. Glaring at them, I threw a knife and activated Zatte Finde, blowing them apart. I then used the opening to rush toward the demon lord as quickly as I could. But Teoritta stopped me.

"Xylo! Behind you!"

She rubbed the air. Sparks. A sword emerged from the void and pierced the ground, followed by a hard, metallic clink echoing through the air. It was the sound of something bouncing off the blade. Teoritta shared her senses with me, letting me know what was happening. An arrow made from blood had been shot at us from the ground.

*Asshole.*

That was when I realized that the ground was practically submerged in a pool of blood. Each time Boojum fired a blood-blade at us and I dodged, it left more blood on the ground that would bubble and wriggle, gathering together like some kind of slime mold with a will of its own. From there, it would transform into yet another of Boojum's weapons and attack me.

At times, the blood would take the form of an arrow, and at other times, the shape of a spear. Once, it even took the form of a large, fanged serpent that moved with incredible speed. The serpent chased me relentlessly. I couldn't completely evade it, and eventually it chomped down on my leg. I could feel a dull pain in my thigh.

"Agh! You little...!"

The blood serpent attacked the sword Teoritta had just summoned and almost immediately snapped it in two. It was quick—too quick. I barely managed to stop myself from toppling over. For some reason, my feet seemed to stick to the ground.

*I can't jump. Seriously?*

The gathering blood had turned the entire area into a swamp, and now it had latched on to my feet.

"You've stopped moving," noted Boojum, stating the obvious. "I suppose it's time for me to kill you, Teoritta."

Something rippled through the blood swamp. It bubbled and shook. The tip of a crimson spear began to emerge from the liquid as Boojum raised both of his arms into the air. It looked like he was about to unleash his ultimate attack.

"I must finish you off, even if it is the last thing I do."

I could feel his unmitigated bloodlust. It overwhelmed everything else.

"Ugh!" Teoritta grunted in breathless suspense. "Xylo, I..."

"Stop making that face. Don't be stupid." I smiled in an unconscious attempt to encourage her. "You're a goddess, so all you need to do is believe in your knight and look important. No one can defeat me. Just make sure you believe that. Besides, this Boojum guy is a total amateur."

The reason I'd almost lost my balance a moment ago wasn't just because of the pool of blood. The ground had begun to slant as well. I'd been hoping for this. All the pieces were now in place.

"Time's up, Boojum."

I could hear the sound of water—seawater, to be precise. It began flooding the area. This made perfect sense. Not only had Tui Jia already fallen, but Rhyno was still firing randomly in our direction. The pillars supporting the land under the tower were slanting, and once those supports were gone, there would be no way to prevent the place from flooding. It wasn't long before my feet were submerged in water, washing away the blood. The pool of it holding my feet to the ground, too, was helplessly swept away.

"I see," muttered Boojum. I couldn't detect a hint of concern in his voice. "Time is up, you say? ...But I am not finished yet!"

He swung his arms, using more blood to create even larger blades than before. These splashed rapidly through the water, with enough force to slice anything that got in their way. I swiftly dodged the giant, crimson scythes, but there was one I knew I wouldn't be able to avoid. I quickly infused a knife with Zatte Finde's power and threw it at the remaining blade.

Hurling myself through the light and roar of the explosion, I formed an arc through the air and bore down on Boojum.

"Piercing Blood."

Boojum pointed at me and shot a bolt of red lightning from the tip of his finger, or at least, that was what it looked like. In reality, it was probably closer to an arrow. Either way, it was fast. I was far too focused for something like that to hit me, though. It grazed me, but I paid it no mind and barreled on. I knew I could win if I just got close enough. I had Teoritta with me, after all.

"Xylo! You're wounded—"

"Don't worry about it."

Through Teoritta, I could tell that blood was gathering from within the seawater to create some sort of weapon right where I intended to land, so I threw a knife and blew it to bits before it could finish.

*I just gotta keep this up.*

I had fought a battle like this once before, and I felt like something I'd lost was returning to me. In the past, I'd taken on the Demon Blight like a true knight, and I'd never lost. All I had to do now was replicate that. I could do this.

"I am truly impressed, Xylo Forbartz." Boojum opened his arms wide, as if to welcome me. "You will be written about in poems one day as a great warrior, and I'd rather like to read them."

He swung his crimson arm high in the air, creating a whirlpool of blood and pulling in some seawater as well.

He muttered the words, "Spiraling Blood," as a cyclone of red ooze swept through the area like a tornado. I didn't have to get near it to know that touching it would be fatal.

*I'd have a hard time fighting him one-on-one.*

But he was no threat to me now, because I had the goddess of swords, Teoritta, by my side.

"Go forth," she whispered, as sparks violently scattered in the void. "Let us end this."

"I just have to land the final blow," I said. "Can you manage?"

"Of course. I shall succeed, just as you will. No matter the cost!"

"Heh." I smirked and took another leap, diving into the cyclone Boojum had created.

"There is nothing my Holy Sword cannot destroy," cried Teoritta.

A one-handed, double-edged sword emerged from the void. Its silver blade shone with its own light. The rest of the sword was plain—it looked like the sort you might find anywhere.

I grabbed the hilt and slashed straight down in front of me, slicing the cyclone of blood in half. I saw what looked like particles of light burst before my eyes.

The timing was perfect. That had been my only concern, since Teoritta couldn't summon this sword for any longer than a few seconds. It was enough, in the end. The Holy Blade erased Boojum's cyclone of blood from existence. This sword really could destroy anything—even things without form. After all, the Holy Sword wouldn't allow something it could not destroy to exist.

"That's…!" Boojum cried out as I rapidly closed in on him. "That's the Holy Sword that will end this world!"

He transformed his left hand into a colossal blade, but all I needed to do was counter. It only took a single swipe. I swung the sword into the air, touching his weapon with the tip of my blade.

That was all it took.

A glittering light burned my eyes—light so powerful that I started to feel dizzy. It scorched the night air, erasing my enemy in the blink of an eye. Boojum didn't even scream. The wind howled as bolts of light shot into the sky, briefly forming a whirl of dust. That was it. I blinked a few times, and my legs began to wobble as if I was intoxicated. Then the sword in my palm faded into nothingness, leaving only pale white sparks in my hand.

The giant suit of blood armor had left no trace, and the only noise was the sound of water flooding in from the sea.

"Teoritta."

I somehow managed to keep myself standing. I couldn't drop to my knees just yet. It was time to share this victory with the great goddess at my side and shower her with praise.

"We did it."

"...Of course we did," she replied, a cheeky grin on her wan face.

Somehow, we'd managed to finish the job before dawn.

The faeries occupying the tower began to withdraw after Boojum's fall.

My only concern now was Teoritta. She could hardly move after summoning the Holy Sword. I lent her my shoulder and helped walk her to Tui Jia's gate as the tower slowly sank into the sea. Her face was pale, her body sparking uncontrollably. The electric discharge was so bad that her hair looked like it was glowing.

"...I am impressed, Xylo," said Teoritta. She maintained her arrogant attitude, despite barely being able to stand. She even tried to smile. "Surely, I must have impressed you as well."

It was obvious what she wanted. It was the whole reason she fought.

"...I give you permission to rub my head and shower me with praise. Worship me to your heart's content. You may tell me what a great goddess I am. How I met all your expectations..." She seemed to grow uneasy as she spoke, and looked up to gauge my reaction. "Right?"

"Yeah." I rubbed her head, maybe a little too hard. I could feel the sparks burning my palm. "You did great, Teoritta. That must have taken a lot of courage."

"Did I help?"

"You helped a lot. You're an amazing goddess."

Her reaction might be on the extreme side, but I bet just about anyone would enjoy being complimented after a hard day's work. Who wouldn't be happy if their teammates told them they were a huge help. Some might even believe stuff like that was worth risking your life for.

"...Oh." Teoritta suddenly raised her voice and pointed over my shoulder at something. "Xylo, look..."

When I followed her gaze, I saw the cloud of dust kicked up when Tui Jia fell, and hidden inside, a person. A very small person. A child? It must have been a little girl. She looked even younger than Teoritta did. She staggered toward us, dragging something large behind her.

"Help...!" she shouted. She looked about to cry. In fact, she was probably crying already. Her clothes were stained with blood. Was she hurt?

No, that wasn't it.

I could finally see what she was dragging. It was a person. An adult male, bleeding from a hole in his chest. Her clothes were probably stained with his blood. She continued toward us, unsteady, but the man didn't even twitch. It looked like she was using every bit of strength she had to drag his body.

*Just great*, I thought. Teoritta was almost drained, and now I had even more people to protect. I counted how many knives I had left. Three. I was going to have to use them wisely.

"Help! My father...," cried the girl. She sounded almost nauseated. "My father s-stopped moving... A monster... A monster came out of nowhere and..."

"Do not fear." It was Teoritta who replied first, recklessly breaking free from my support. "You have nothing to worry about." Her voice no longer sounded weak.

"I, Goddess Teoritta, and my knight, Xylo Forbartz, are at your service. I promise you will be safe." Teoritta took a step toward the blood-covered girl. "We must hurry and get your father some help. Did you lose your way during the evacuation? What is your name?"

"My name..."

The girl staggered—or rather, appeared to stagger. That was when I noticed it. All emotion had disappeared from her face.

*Shit.*

But it was already too late. I was an idiot for letting Teoritta get too close. The little girl hadn't staggered at all, she'd *sped up*. I'd let my guard down. Was it because I was tired? But exhaustion was no excuse.

*What is wrong with you, Xylo Forbartz?*

I prayed that I would make it in time. It was only later that I realized who I was praying to. Senerva—a goddess who was nothing but a faraway memory now.

Nevertheless, reality was cruel. There was no way I could get to Teoritta in time. I was too slow to act. The girl raised her arm swiftly into the air. She was holding a knife, its blade sharp and thick. Teoritta's eyes opened wide. She didn't even scream.

*Pop.* I heard the sound of something slicing through the air.

*"Oops,"* said someone, sounding almost embarrassed. It was Tsav. *"Oh crap. Did I just shoot a kid? Uh…"*

*"What is wrong with you, Tsav?!"* shouted Venetim. *"Did you just shoot a civilian? Are you out of your mind?!"*

A white bolt of lightning soared through the air, hitting the blood-covered girl. Her expression twisted in astonishment—and that was no wonder. A bolt of lightning shot from an unbelievable distance had just blown off the left side of her body from her shoulder to her chest.

I heard later that this was Tsav's first shot after getting into position. "Bro, it looked like she was going to attack you and Teoritta," he later claimed. I had no idea how he came to that conclusion, but he was right.

"This…," groaned the little girl. "This can't…"

She could barely stand, and yet she was still trying to attack Teoritta. There was no way a human could move after losing so much of their upper body. The girl staggered forward, growling as she thrust her knife as far as she could with her remaining strength. But the tip of her blade was met with a heavy clink just before reaching Teoritta's body.

Immediately, I charged forward, kicking the little girl as hard as I could. What was left of her upper body tore off at the waist and flew through the air. It was over. Teoritta's legs gave out, but I somehow managed to catch her right before she hit the ground.

"Teoritta! Look at me! Are you hurt?"

"Xylo…"

Her lips were twitching, but she managed to smile. She was holding a small knife that looked very familiar. It was the one we'd bought at that street stall, with a blade barely sharp enough to cut fruit.

"It appears…I will need to learn how to use this properly," she said.

"You blocked the attack with that knife?"

It was basically a toy. After a deep sigh, I took a good look at the blade.

"We need to get you something a little better than this… And I'll teach you how to use it."

The enemy had approached alone in order to take Teoritta by surprise, ready to sacrifice their life. It seemed they'd do anything to kill her. Teoritta must be a real threat to the Demon Blight. But why? Because she could summon the Holy Sword? Or was there another reason?

At any rate, I felt that I—that we, the penal hero unit—was being forced into a key position in all this.

*I have to protect Teoritta.*

I could feel how important that was, now more than ever.

*Goddesses can be so demanding, but I'm sure you know that, Senerva.*

Now I was complaining to someone who was no longer here. I crouched, lending Teoritta an arm, and pulled her up.

"Come on. Let's get outta here. The others are probably waiting for us."

"Yes, let us return to the place where we belong." Still trembling, Teoritta stuck out her head. "Though I believe you are forgetting something."

"…Yeah, yeah. I know."

"Then go on! Praise me with every fiber of your being!"

And so, our mission at Tui Jia came to an end. All that was left was a little cleanup work.

Once he finished firing his artillery at the warehouse, Rhyno, along with Tatsuya, took the evacuating citizens back to the base. Rhyno, however, disappeared for a few hours after that, leaving his armor behind. This was later reported as a violation of orders, and he was sent back to solitary confinement.

Around a hundred and thirty civilians arrived at the base. No lives were lost.

Despite being attacked by frenzied faeries, there were few injuries. Nine people lost limbs or some other part of their body. They were all men, and ranged from fit and brawny to slightly chubby. Some claimed they were intentionally used as decoys, but there was no way to prove it.

Incidentally, the volume of these men's bodies, no longer whole, was about that of a woman of the same age, or perhaps that of a slender man.

The Thirteenth Order fought bravely in the commercial district alongside the city guards and armed priests.

Patausche's unit quickly responded to the crisis and eliminated the faeries. She had the snipers hold the enemy back while the cavalry scattered them. Then the infantry had overwhelmed the enemy's scattered troops and defeated them. Though the strategy was simple, Patausche's ability to deploy her troops and lead them to victory was evidence of her skill.

The city guards and armed priests, too, had capably protected the people of Ioff. If the Thirteenth Order could be said to have led the offensive, then the guards and priests had done the same for defense.

High Priest Marlen Kivia had led these men, and not only had he accompanied them on the front line, but he hadn't acted as one would expect from a priest.

Up until now, the Temple had always been somewhat timid and passive when it came to battling the Demon Blight. Priests loaned to the military for battle would usually end up tuning sacred seals rather than fighting.

And yet despite being a high priest, Marlen Kivia had fought on the front line, instantly gaining popularity among the people of the city. He was apparently quite the leader from a strategic standpoint as well. His excellent troop placement had allowed his people to block all the faeries' schemes before they got started, thus limiting the extent of the damage.

There could be no doubt that their work had kept the city of Ioff safe.

The underground water channels of Ioff were as intricate as a maze.

These were modified relics of the old kingdom that had seen constant use and many repairs over the years. Although humans had military control over the key points leading out of the city, anyone would be basically invisible if they made it deep enough inside the labyrinth. Especially if that someone was Demon Lord Spriggan.

Her body was covered in wounds. She was gravely injured—and all because of that sniper. Deceiving the goddess had been a good idea. Teoritta had come close enough for Spriggan to kill her, and she'd almost managed to destroy her vessel, but that bolt of lightning had ruined everything.

It seemed her chosen host's body had been too fragile. Spriggan had continued to use the body of Lideo Sodrick's attendant, Iri.

Demon Lord Spriggan was able to steal the bodies of other living creatures. She was a parasite by nature, and her true body was no bigger than that of a rat. It wasn't uncommon for a demon lord to have the ability to parasitize, take over, or simulate another living creature, but Spriggan's vitality was particularly exceptional. Even if the host's body was destroyed and all vital activity ceased, Spriggan could separate from the host and survive. Plus, her body was quick to regenerate. That said, there was nothing she could do to make up for her low combat ability. She had made the right choice in pretending to be dead and running away instead of trying to fight that Holy Knight.

*I need to focus on repairing my injuries for now.*

That was the conclusion that Spriggan had reached. The lightning bolt from the sniper and the knight's powerful kick had damaged not only the host's body but Spriggan herself, and she would need to repair her flesh while gathering her remaining faerie forces. Even if the humans had somehow surpassed her expectations and killed every last faerie in the city, there was still a way she could create an army. The Demon Blight could corrupt nearby living beings and inorganic substances as well. While it would take time, she could simply rebuild her army. And the best way to do that was—

"Oh."

Spriggan's train of thought was unexpectedly broken by the sound of a human voice. Someone was approaching her.

"There you are, Spriggan. You're hurt. How sad."

Spriggan looked up at the individual. It was a large man who appeared to be human, but there was something strange about his expression. He seemed to be...smiling, though she had no idea why.

*Impossible. If this person is human, then how did they recognize me? How could they have sensed my presence in this host?*

"You seem confused. Didn't you know? When the Demon Blight starts devouring and corrupting its surroundings, its demon lord gives off a unique—... How should I put it? A unique wave," explained the man, guessing the source of Spriggan's confusion. "Other demon lords can detect this. And that is why I left my post and came to find you."

The man slowly approached Spriggan. She couldn't move. She had taken too much damage. The most she could do was crawl, and she could hardly manage that.

"...My crime is the simplest, least offensive crime of those in the hero unit...as far as I can tell. Guilt is a concept that's still hard for me to understand, but I'm sure I'm right."

Spriggan had no idea what the man was saying, but she was

overwhelmed with a strange anxiety as he slowly approached her, step by step.

"I discovered the thrill of killing my own kind, you see... Humans truly are amazing, aren't they? This trait is quite common among them, and they would even consider my motive 'boring.' No big deal... Isn't that incredible?" The man chuckled, making a rumbling noise in his throat. "I felt I must surrender unconditionally. 'I'll do whatever you say,' and all that. Every day that I am with my fellow heroes, I am reminded of how shallow I am."

"Stay back," said Spriggan. Or at least, that's what she wanted to say. She currently lacked the vocal cords needed to speak, and she had no idea if the man could understand her. What she did know, however, was that he wasn't going to stop.

"...That's why I'm trying to suck up to the humans... I'm desperate. I would do anything to make them happy. I would undergo any hardship if it meant they would accept me. The only place I belong is with them. I have nowhere else to go."

"Stay back," repeated Spriggan. There wasn't anything else she could do.

"I'm currently learning about ethics, and I now realize that from the Demon Blight's point of view, I am nothing more than a bloodthirsty killer. Murdering my own kind for fun. What a cliché, boring sin..."

"Stay back."

"But I can become a champion in the eyes of the humans. Nobody will judge me for my crimes. It's baffling, isn't it? I am still working out the reasoning behind this myself, so I can't explain it very well."

"Stay back!"

"I decline. Your screaming, though..." The man smiled as the sacred seal at his neck glowed ominously. "I'm quite enamored with it. Nothing would make me happier or excite me more right now than to hear you scream in even greater agony. I'm in the mood to take my time today."

He reached out and tightened his hands around Spriggan's ankles.

"Oh, I forgot to introduce myself. I am Demon Lord Puck Puca, but the humans call me by the name of this body's original owner: Rhyno."

◆

The mission had failed. The goddess of swords wasn't killed, and conquering the city was most likely no longer possible. Therefore, he had no choice but to run away as quickly as he could. He didn't even have the strength, let alone time, to worry about Spriggan. Surely, she would be able to take care of herself.

*The penal hero unit... The goddess of swords and her Holy Knight, the goddess killer... Hmph.*

He thought over it all as he walked, his steps unsteady. He didn't have enough blood; he'd used too much of it.

*I won't be able to carry out my orders.*

Boojum was making his way out of the city.

*Ioff is in turmoil. Now is my only chance to escape.*

Fortunately, his gamble had paid off, and he'd survived. The blade hadn't erased him. Boojum knew that the Holy Sword Teoritta had summoned denied the existence of anything it touched. That was why he'd created a giant blood-puppet to battle them in his place. As a result, the only one erased was the puppet. In return, however, he had exhausted a copious amount of blood.

*But what pains me the most is that I let my king down once again.*

Boojum would need a large supply of blood before he could be of any more use.

*Those two are a threat. They are worthy of respect. Someone will have to do something about them.*

The goddess of swords and her lightning-fast Holy Knight. The two of them could put an end to the Demon Blight.

*I need more blood in order to kill them.*

It would take some time before he was in any condition to fight. He'd had an ample supply of blood, but the quality had been far from ideal. If he could realize his full potential, the speed with which he manipulated his blood, its hardness, its flexibility, and even his own basic physical abilities would far exceed what he had displayed that day. In order to achieve this, however, he had to do something that he was very reluctant to do.

*It appears faerie blood isn't good enough.*

Boojum was staggering down a dark alleyway like a sickly man on the verge of death.

*I need the blood of humans…*

He closed his eyes and heaved a hoarse sigh. He had no other choice. He could not betray his king.

The battle to defend Ioff had come to an end, but the worst was yet to come.

That day would serve as a turning point. For while it may have seemed like a victory, the enemy was now closing in on humanity faster than ever before.

By the time we withdrew to Norgalle's base, everything was already under control.

The Holy Knights and city guards had done their job. They had rescued as many evacuees as possible and had begun exterminating the remaining faeries that had escaped into the waterways.

This marked the end of our job as penal heroes, as evidenced by Tatsuya, who was now sitting on the ground, hunched over and holding his knees. Tatsuya never completely stopped moving when ordered to stand by. He would usually pace, or trace his finger in the air, for some mysterious reason. So the fact that he was completely inactive right now meant he'd heard the mission was over.

"Oh, Xylo. Rhyno's not with you?" asked Jayce. He had already removed Neely's harness and was cleaning her. It was pretty clear that he wasn't going to send her back into the sky again, even if ordered.

"No, I thought he was here with you."

I shifted my gaze to a suit of armor at Neely's side. It was seemingly empty at the moment. Teoritta was peering at it curiously as well.

"You didn't see him, either, right, Teoritta?" I asked.

"I did not… Does that mean he is roaming around somewhere without his armor? Is that not dangerous?"

"Heh! Sounds like he's off on his own and violating orders again,"

Jayce said, smirking before turning to Venetim. "You should get a leash for that guy. I mean, do you really want someone like that off doing whatever he pleases?"

"Jayce, you of all people shouldn't be talking…"

Venetim seemed unwell as he responded. I could see the exhaustion on his face. The situation appeared to have put a lot of stress on his nerves.

"I don't know, guys," said Tsav. "I think Rhyno'll be fine." He was just coming down from the watchtower, a flippant grin on his face. His right arm was still wrapped in bandages, but he seemed to be in high spirits. That made sense, though—he'd barely done any work, compared to the rest of us. "He's probably out looting or torturing a faerie for fun. I once saw him carry a live faerie back from the battlefield. Remember that, Dotta?"

"Didn't he say he was going to mount it on his wall or something?" Dotta replied, sounding creeped out.

Incidentally, it seemed Dotta had decided to end work early that day, made clear by the tilted bottle of booze in his hand and the cheese and thick-cut bacon making their way to his mouth. Where had he grabbed such a luxurious dinner? When did he find the time? This ability of Dotta's was borderline supernatural.

"Anyway," he continued. "I think we're wasting our time worrying about Rhyno. I'd much rather go back to the barracks and sleep."

"Same," said Tsav. "Teoritta and my bro here are just too nice, worrying about that guy. Like, does he have some dirt on you two or something?"

"No, I am simply concerned that… Well…" Teoritta seemed to hesitate for a moment, but she eventually continued. "To be honest, I am curious what he is doing. Something about his behavior seems strange."

"Yeah, 'strange.' That describes him perfectly," I said. "I'm not worried about him one bit, though."

I swiped the bottle of booze out of Dotta's hand, along with a piece of cheese. It was wine from the south, and it didn't look cheap. He'd really outdone himself.

"Ah!" Tsav swiftly slipped behind me, as if he were joining a line. "Bro, let me have the next sip! I haven't had wine from the south in forever!"

"You fool! Do you really believe you deserve such a treat? You hardly lifted a finger!"

Norgalle made his way over, a large wooden stake on his shoulder. It had a sacred seal engraved in it and looked like some kind of detonator. It was definitely dangerous, and Norgalle was the only one I would trust carrying it around.

"Tsav, you arrived late," he said. "Rewards shall be presented in the following order: Dotta, Xylo, Tatsuya, Jayce, Venetim, and then you. You are last."

"What?! I'm even after Venetim?!"

"Of course. You and Rhyno have issues that need to be addressed. Rhyno in particular shall be lectured once he returns. This constitutes a threat to our national defense."

Norgalle glared fiercely at the empty suit of armor, as if he were having trouble swallowing his anger. Then, mumbling complaints under his breath, he set to work fixing it up.

"...Damn that Rhyno! The fool! Just when I thought all my elites were going to be here together for a change, he goes off on his own. This is unforgivable. I even prepared a speech of encouragement and everything..."

"Oh, phew!" cried Tsav. "Man, this might be the first time I feel grateful to Rhyno!"

"We're saved... I dunno if I would have been able to handle it," said Dotta. "Those speeches are literally torture in every sense of the word."

"Whenever the king gives a speech, he starts going into his vision for the nation," said Venetim. "I honestly cannot think of a more unproductive use of my time."

"...Anyway, can we go now?" Jayce let out a big yawn, completely ignoring Norgalle. "Neely wants to take a bath and go to bed, and if Norgalle's going to start rambling nonsense again, we're leaving."

But right as Jayce patted Neely on the neck—

"Xylo!"

—a familiar voice called my name.

It belonged to a woman on horseback, galloping toward us. Her hair was the color of iron, and she had brown skin—it was Frenci, and she had around fifty knights with her. But there was something odd about her expression. She seemed upset. She looked like she was about to stage a retreat. But how could that be? The battle was essentially over. The moment she saw me, her eyes softened with relief.

"You're a mess, Xylo, but I am glad to see you in good health... Now, care to explain what you are doing still loafing about here?"

"Sorry, but this shop's closed for the day." I waved a hand at her, then took another swig of booze, followed by a bite of cheese. "The Holy Knights should be able to handle the commercial district without us." I had no intention of working any more that day.

Jayce suddenly swiped the bottle out of my hand, as if to say it was now his turn. *Asshole.* Tsav stole what was left of the cheese and gave it to Tatsuya, who sluggishly began sinking his teeth into it. In what felt like the blink of an eye, my hands were empty. They remained raised in the air, however, as if I was surrendering.

"I'm tired," I said. "And I'm not in the mood to listen to more of your verbal abuse today."

"Pathetic. And you call yourself a man of the Mastibolt family? A hibernating lemur has more energy than you."

"The hell is a lemur? Whatever. I already finished my work, so just let me rest."

"Yes, the town is quiet again, and things are safe for now. However..." A hint of irritation seeped into her voice. "...I have just received word that the Second Capital has fallen."

"Wait... What did you just say?"

"The Second Capital has fallen. The attack on Ioff was nothing more than a diversion."

Everyone fell silent at that. Dotta, Venetim, Tsav, Jayce—everyone. Tatsuya, of course, was already silent. The first to speak up was Norgalle.

"...Faeries attacked my capital?"

"According to the report," said Frenci, "Demon Lord Abaddon defeated the Ninth Order of the Holy Knights, slipped past the line of defense, and seized the Second Capital." It seemed she'd chosen to ignore the fact that Norgalle had called it *his* capital.

"Galtuile Fortress essentially has a knife to its throat. All that's left is for the enemy to take the First Capital." Frenci glanced at me. "Ioff is all on its own now."

By the time Patausche returned to the control room, High Priest Marlen had already removed his heavy chain mail and ceremonial sword. He was sitting in his chair in his usual attire, smiling faintly at Patausche and the leader of the infantry behind her.

"Welcome back." There was an unusual ring of satisfaction in his voice. "I heard about your hard work and contributions in battle."

"Thank you for your praise." Patausche bowed, followed by Rajit, who had been told to remain silent in such situations. "I heard your leadership was extraordinary, Uncle Marlen," she continued.

"I was lucky. I must have been blessed by the saints of old who fought against the Demon Blight before me. However, we lost far too many civilians today, and there is no time for rest. We must start preparing for the next battle."

Marlen's smile vanished, and he assumed his usual serious expression. Patausche watched with a cold gaze as he formed the sign of the Great Sacred Seal with his right hand.

"...Yes, you're right," she said. "I am sure the Temple will put you at the head of all the high priests after your accomplishments today."

"The Temple as an organization is rigid—calcified. But in the face of this unprecedented trial, we must band together if we wish to survive." Marlen nodded to himself. "If I were to receive such an honor, I would bring in some new blood. That would also mean improving your situation, Patausche."

He exhaled heavily, almost sighing.

"'Bring in new blood'? Does that mean…?" Patausche took a step toward her uncle. "…That you plan on switching out the current Temple leaders with coexisters?"

Marlen didn't respond. His solemn expression never faltered. Patausche felt like she spent minutes waiting for an answer. But in reality, only seconds had passed.

"…Did you interrogate Lideo Sodrick?" he asked.

"He was the start of it. He told me the name of a messenger for the coexisters: Mahaeyzel Zelkoff, using the northern lands' pronunciation for the family name. Then I remembered how you, Uncle Marlen, would often use that alias in the past."

Patausche thought back to how her uncle would occasionally sneak her out of the house when she was a child. Back then, she had still been under the control of her strict parents and had known nothing of the outside world. She had seen so many new things in the city, but what left the biggest impression on her were horseback riding, swords, and sacred seals.

The more obsessed she became, the more her parents frowned and reprimanded her. Sometimes, the scolding got out of hand and became violent, and when that happened, her uncle was her only ally. When he learned of her wishes, he immediately persuaded her parents to find a tutor, and took her to learn how to wield a sword and ride a horse. He brought her to the city to buy a practice sword, and they toured the street stalls together. The times she spent with her uncle were some of the only good memories she had of her childhood, and each one was precious to her. That was why she remembered it so clearly. There was no way she could forget. Whenever her uncle would bring her into the city, he would always go by the alias "Zelkoff."

"So you still remembered that," said Marlen, a wry smile on his lips. "What an incredible talent."

"I could never forget… And that's why I knew—it had to be you."

The culprit had to be someone with enough financial power to control the Adventurers Guild, someone born and raised in the north, and someone from the Temple visiting Ioff during the right time frame. Once Patausche had narrowed it down that far, few candidates remained.

"And that's not all. The records of your absences matched the times and dates when Lideo Sodrick met with the messenger. That would also explain why information was leaking to the enemy, and how they knew our strategy and our positions. And then, in this most recent battle..." Patausche's hand was already on the hilt of the sword at her waist. Rajit did the same by her side. "...I looked into the unit that first reported seeing the faeries in the city and its surviving soldier. According to your records, it was Ioff City Defense Force Unit 7110. But no such unit exists."

"I am impressed. How did you do it, though? I can't imagine you had enough time to investigate all that during the battle."

"I am not at liberty to answer."

It was Frenci and her men who helped, but Patausche made sure to withhold any information on the Southern Night-Gaunts from her uncle. That was what they wanted as well. For some reason, Patausche found the iron-haired woman extremely irritating, but she respected how quickly she and her men worked. This wouldn't have been possible without them.

"Uncle Marlen, why have you joined the coexisters? If mankind is defeated, then all will be lost. Am I wrong?"

"...Very wrong."

Marlen slowly stood, causing Patausche to tighten her grip around her sword. Rajit nervously circled around to the high priest's side.

"Do not move, Uncle Marlen."

"I am doing this for the sake of those important to me, Patausche. This is for me, my family, and the devout, loyal people of the Temple." The high priest did not heed her warning, instead walking slowly over until he stopped right in front of her. "I want to save you all. Mankind will surely lose, but I want to protect those with righteous hearts, and my family, whom I love. That is why I joined the coexisters."

"Then...what happens to those whose hearts are not righteous and those you do not love?"

"That, I do not know. I am in no position to worry about anyone else... Under the current circumstances, that is." His serious expression never faltered, making it clear to her he was telling the truth. "Surely everyone feels this way. Or are you telling me you wish to become a champion of mankind that saves strangers over the lives of your own family?"

"Uncle Marlen, I—"

"There is still a part of you that hasn't grown up yet, but it is time for you to change. Love your family and cherish those close to you." Marlen's smile was calm and gentle. "If possible, I want you to be a part of the new world as a coexister yourself."

"I—"

"Mankind will lose to the Demon Blight, but many will be spared, and we must act as shepherds to watch over and guide those who are left behind."

"That is enough." Patausche had already unsheathed her sword. The tip of her blade was at Marlen's neck. "I am disappointed. I deeply respected you, Uncle Marlen...from the bottom of my heart."

"Are you crying, Patausche?"

"I...don't believe we should abandon anyone...including strangers. I cannot allow myself to believe...that the happiness of my family and those I love...is all that matters."

"That isn't normal, Patausche. Your bloated ego is driving you to become some sort of savior and clouding your judgment. But, well, perhaps it was I who raised you that way... What a pity."

"Silence," demanded Patausche sharply. She then signaled to the infantry leader at her side. "Rajit, arrest my uncle."

"Yes, Captain!"

Rajit stepped forward to arrest the high priest, but all of a sudden, Marlen moved. From somewhere on his person, he pulled out a lightning staff and pointed the tip toward Patausche's chest. The sacred seal glowed, and sparks began to fly.

"Captain—"

Rajit must have moved on instinct. He pushed—rammed— Patausche out of the way. He probably didn't have time to consider the consequences. The bolt of lightning bore a hole through his chest. Flesh and bone exploded, spraying blood into the air. Patausche saw both their faces at once—Rajit's shock, and her uncle's sorrow.

*Rajit made the wrong call. Instead of protecting me, he should have attacked.*

Then he would've lived.

*…Which means I cannot make the same mistake.*

Biting her lip, Patausche swung her sword, slicing off the arm Marlen was using to hold the staff. Still, he didn't stop.

"What a shame, Patausche," he said, now holding a knife.

The weapon had appeared from nowhere, and she could tell it was engraved with a sacred seal of some kind—a powerful one meant for offense. She couldn't allow him to activate it.

"You were like a daughter to me."

Before Patausche realized it, she was shouting. She wanted to tell him to shut his mouth, but she couldn't get out the words. The sound that came out was likely closer to a scream as her body swiftly reacted, swinging her sword exactly as she had practiced so many times before.

In a flash, it was over—she'd run the tip of her sword right through Marlen Kivia's throat.

It was the seventh day of the first month of winter.

The Second Capital had fallen to Demon Lord Abaddon, and Patausche Kivia of the Thirteenth Order of the Holy Knights was imprisoned for the murder of her uncle, High Priest Marlen Kivia, and her subordinate, Rajit Heathrow.

TRIAL RECORD: PATAUSCHE KIVIA

A few days had passed since Patausche was thrown into prison. She had no way of knowing exactly how many. She was locked up underground, and the windowless, dark cage had dulled her sense of time almost immediately.

She didn't know what had happened to her knights, either. There was no way to find out. She tried to speculate on what was going on outside to keep her mind sharp and her spirits up, but her imagination almost always led her down a dark path.

No one had come to her aid, which probably meant that her family had abandoned her. That was no surprise. She had essentially run away from home. Her uncle was the only one who understood her, and she'd killed him. Her knights probably had no way to help her, either. She couldn't think of any other prospects. The faces of the penal heroes briefly crossed her mind before immediately vanishing once again.

*Why would I think of them now?*

And yet she couldn't help but wonder what Xylo was doing. The goddess killer. One of the most notorious criminals in history.

*I wonder how he views my crimes.*

She'd killed a high priest—her own uncle. Was he surprised by what she'd done? Did he think she'd lost her mind? That much she could handle, but if he now looked down on her because of it…

There would be no feeling worse than that.

Everyone probably thought *she* was a coexister now, a traitor to mankind. It was hard to explain why, but she got the feeling that would be the most difficult part to bear.

At the very least, she wanted the chance to talk. If those around her had misunderstood, she wanted to tell them the truth. To her knights, her friends, the penal heroes, and Xylo Forbartz...

*I've been backed into a corner...*, Patausche thought, trying her best to persuade herself. *That's why I'm thinking like this.*

It was the only explanation.

Patausche had originally pinned her hopes on the trial, but she realized that was pointless after the investigator stopped by her cell a few times. It was always the same person, and he always asked the same thing:

"Why did you kill Marlen Kivia?"

That was it.

Patausche was able to accurately explain what had happened, but each time she did so, the investigator would conclude that she was lying and demand she fix her story.

"You feared High Priest Marlen's personal magnetism and his ability to unite the Temple's forces," the investigator would say, over and over. "That's why you killed him and your subordinate and betrayed mankind."

The investigator seemed young, but he had an uncanny luster in his eyes.

"I can release you once you accurately testify to that fact."

He was trying to create a new story, and he was waiting for Patausche to start speaking that story with her own lips. If he kept wearing her down mentally and repeating the answer he wanted, it could easily become fact in her head.

*He's almost like a teacher.*

Patausche recalled her years at school as a child. Back then, her teachers would often wait for their students to tell them the "truth" in the form of an apology, even if, for the child, it was only a means of escaping the situation. How long would she be able to fight this? She hadn't been sleeping much, and the brain fog was starting to cloud her judgment. The investigator probably meant to keep up his questions as long as he needed to.

Patausche was afraid of dying as a despised member of the coexisters, and the fact that she was slowly growing numb to that fear scared her as well.

Then, one night, two people appeared before her cell in place of the investigator who had visited her so many times.

One of them—a man—seemed cheerful, but with a sadistic glint to his smile. The other was a tall woman dressed in a simple white priest's robe. She looked ready to doze off at any moment.

"Patausche Kivia, former captain of the Thirteenth Order of the Holy Knights, you have my apologies," said the man. "It took us a little longer than expected."

Patausche thought he was being sarcastic at first. That he was a new investigator, simply trying to come at her from a different angle. She glared at him coldly, bracing herself.

"We finished your investigation almost immediately," he continued, "but we needed time to discuss how to handle your case." The man barely seemed to notice her gaze. "After all, we only have room for one more hero at most, so it took a lot of consideration and debate... It was a difficult decision for us all, and honestly, I was against making you a hero."

Patausche showed a faint reaction to the word "hero," then instantly regretted it. The man's smile deepened—she found his way of smiling truly off-putting.

"Yes, I suppose you're close to the heroes, aren't you? ...We mainly look for two qualities when choosing new candidates." Still grinning, the man held up one finger and then another as he spoke. "First, we look at skills. Next, we look at mentality. Skill-wise, you are an exceptional leader and soldier. We have some need for your leadership abilities right now. On the other hand, that's really all you're good at. However..."

He was being very rude. Patausche really didn't like this man, and the way he smiled irritated her.

"Your mental state surprised me a little. I never expected that you'd be capable of killing a relative to whom you owed such a debt. Your actions had nothing to do with personal gain. You did what you did for the sake of total strangers…or perhaps for a delusion one might call conviction."

The man flipped through what appeared to be a booklet in his hand and nodded.

"How should I put this? There's a certain someone who pays a lot of attention to things like that—to abnormal workings of the heart and mind. The question is: How many people would be able to do what you did? The answer to that will guide your choice."

"How…?" Only then did Patausche finally speak. It felt like it had been forever since she last uttered a word. Her voice was hoarse and didn't sound like she remembered. "How do you know all that?"

No human could have known what happened then, let alone understand how she was feeling and what she was thinking.

"Oh, you're curious? Unfortunately, I can't go into detail, but let's just say that I have been blessed." The man closed his booklet, then passed it to the woman behind him. "I guess you could say that my goddess can summon books—information."

After taking the booklet, the woman in priest's garb silently sat down where she was, looking up at the man with half-closed eyes.

"Yes, I know… Thank you, Enfié," said the man. "I don't know what I would do without you."

The woman called Enfié quietly took the man's hand and placed it on her head, almost forcing him to rub it.

"…Your 'goddess'? Are you a Holy Knight?" asked Patausche.

"Yes, I am the twelfth, which would make me your former colleague, I suppose. My name… Well, I could give you a fake one, but that would be pointless, wouldn't it?" The man rubbed Enfié's head, all the while watching Patausche's expression. "Now it is time for me to present you with your options. You have two paths to choose from."

He once again raised two fingers into the air, putting them down one by one as he cheerfully listed off each option.

"Your first choice: Receive the death penalty as a former Holy Knight who joined the coexisters... If you choose this path, you should hurry up and admit to that investigator's version of the 'facts.' I don't know what happens after death, but at least your current suffering would come to an end."

Patausche stayed silent and tried to keep her face blank. She didn't know why, but her gut was telling her not to show this unpleasant Knight any emotion.

"Your second choice is to become a penal hero and continue fighting the Demon Blight." His tone was cruelly soft as he said this. "You will be resurrected whenever you die, and each time, your personality and memories will be worn down until there is nothing left. You will have neither freedom nor honor. And you will give everything you have for strangers you have never met and whose names you do not know."

The man's expression clouded over for the first time, though his smile remained.

"If it were me, I would probably choose death, and I will not recommend the path of a hero to you, because I do not believe you have the aptitude for it."

"...What does it mean to become a hero?" Patausche tried to speak up, though her voice was weak and hoarse. "What do you mean you only have room for a certain number? ...I don't really understand the concept of being resurrected after death, either... Though I have heard about heroes losing their memories in the process."

"You ask a lot of questions. There are some things you're better off not knowing, but I suppose I will answer to the extent I can. Not a word of this to anyone else, though, okay?" The man nodded to himself. "I suppose you're much like us, with relatively normal sensibilities... So I get why you're curious. It's probably hard to make a decision as you are now."

Patausche felt like she was being mocked. Every little thing this man did aggravated her.

"I'm sure you've heard rumors about the first goddess's ability to summon brave warriors, correct? Long ago at the beginning of the first war, she summoned champions from other worlds... But it was very inefficient."

Patausche got the feeling this was big. A very important, key secret. Knowledge about the goddesses was classified information of the highest level, even within the military.

"Some weren't able to communicate with us, and still others possessed a mental makeup we couldn't even comprehend. In the worst cases, those we summoned turned on us and became enemies to mankind."

Even Patausche had heard of the first goddess's ability to summon champions from other worlds... And indeed, if that were true, there must be some reason she didn't simply summon infinite numbers of them. Otherwise, you would think the military would have formed an entire army of otherworldly champions.

"That's why people back then decided to alter the policy. They would summon humans from our own world instead. That way, there would be no communication issues... And that was when they learned that the goddess's powers allowed her to summon even the dead."

"So that's..." Patausche had finally realized what was going on. "That's what...heroes are?"

"Yes, they are champions resurrected from the dead. At least, that was who they were in the beginning... Now we use the penal hero system due to, well, various reasons."

Were heroes in the past honored? Patausche imagined the group of heroes she knew, but none of them seemed worthy of honor.

*...What am I thinking? Of course they don't.*

Patausche cleared the thought from her mind.

"But the goddess's summoning isn't perfect. Humans apparently have something akin to a soul, and that something is gradually worn away each time they are brought back to life. Reproducing the person gets harder with each resurrection. And that's why..." The man pointed at his head. "...the first goddess needs memories of the heroes, and the ability to accurately recall—or, how should I put this? She has to compensate with something like her imagination. It's surprisingly primitive, right? But it's all we have."

The man's expression took on a note of pity. It was as if he was looking at someone with a fatal injury, having arrived too late to save them. And yet there was still something mocking in it. Perhaps that was simply how his face naturally rested.

"Of course, Enfié here can prepare records to supplement the first goddess's ability, but the quality of the summons itself depends solely on the first goddess's memory and imagination."

The goddess by his side, whose eyes were almost completely closed, lifted her head up slightly. Maybe it was because the man had said her name. Either way, her reactions were dulled. She seemed like a very different sort of goddess from Teoritta.

"And she only has enough storage—enough space in her memory, if you will, for one more person, at most. The first goddess uses most of her time repeating information about the heroes and remembering them… Why do you think that is?"

"Because…" Patausche groaned. "The heroes are a kind of trump card for humanity?"

"That's what I'm hoping for, at least, because it seems most people of sound mind are naturally drawn toward the coexisters." The man lowered his voice, as if sharing a secret. "A hero must be someone who can relentlessly kill their family, friends, and those they respect for the sake of justice and for a world made up of strangers they will never know."

Patausche couldn't argue. He was right. He was explaining exactly what she'd done.

"These are all the secrets I can share with you today. Perhaps some other time, I can tell you about the sacred seal collar and the place heroes go for repairs… So what will you do, Patausche Kivia?"

"If I tell you I'll become a hero, will you get me out of here?"

"I wish I could, but breaking out is impossible. I need you to die once, first."

He said this as if it were nothing. Patausche had a vague feeling that was where this was leading.

"I need to kill you, take you apart, and carry you out of here… There's really no other way." The man began to rub his goddess's head once more. "Enfié will be able to summon all your information in the form of a book. As for reproducing your personality and memories, however—well, you'll just have to believe in the first goddess."

Patausche could sense a cynicism in his voice.

She was born into a family of priests and had run away from home only to become a Holy Knight. And in the end, what she needed was faith—to believe in a goddess.

*I can believe in her and die, or not believe in her and die.*

Those were the only two choices left to Patausche. The man, still grinning, had finished talking and was waiting with his arms spread out, as if to say there was nothing more to discuss.

"So what will it be? I was right, wasn't I? You aren't—"

"I accept."

If nothing else, she wanted to surprise this man with the unpleasant smirk.

Patausche made her decision immediately, then declared in a clear voice:

"I will become a hero. And if I am allowed to fight again—one last time—then I vow to fight for mankind, for all the people I will never meet or know."

"All right." The man's smile disappeared, and a look of gloom covered his face. "There is no going back, and I don't think you should do this. I am still very much against you becoming a hero… But I must show respect for the oath you've made."

The man unsheathed a thick-bladed sword, similar to a machete. Light reflected off its surface as Patausche welcomed it into the flesh of her throat.

"Patausche Kivia, I sentence you to be a hero."

Hello, there. Rocket Shokai here.

I love antagonists whose sole purpose is to have their asses handed to them by the protagonist in under three seconds. I call them *kehyarists* for how they yell in battle before attacking (*keh-hyaaa!*). Today, I would like to discuss speed-type *kehyarists* and power-type *kehyarists*.

Speed-type *kehyarists* usually overestimate their speed. They like to approach their opponents from behind at a blinding pace to show off how fast they are. Their weapon of choice is usually a sharp knife or a whip of some sort. In fact, you almost never see any with blunt weapons or massive axes. That would put the character into the territory of a power-type and might devalue his position as a speed-type.

The antagonists of this type I love the most are the ones that rush around their opponent at top speed. If they add a few comments like "Too slow" or "Try to keep up with this," I'm just in awe. I might even start clapping. To these villains, speed is a symbol of power. Even if they end up tripping, they'll be shining brighter than the stars as they soar into the dirt.

Power-type *kehyarists*, on the other hand, overestimate their strength and tend to enjoy showing off by destroying nearby objects or making reckless remarks and disregarding strategy. Their weapon of choice is usually something like a giant hammer or a big stick covered with sharp points. There are hardly any power-types who use sharp knives or wires in battle, since they wouldn't be able to show off the power they are so proud of.

Now, this is just my personal opinion, but it's hard not to be a fan of a character once they say something like, "Do you really think you can beat me with puny muscles like that?" What really makes power-type antagonists shine for me is their ability to underestimate their opponent, based on appearance alone. And then, when they start wildly swinging their weapons, destroying random objects around them—well, nothing beats that. If even one swing were to land, surely the puny-looking protagonist would be reduced to dust. Yes, if their attack were to land... And if the protagonist was actually weak...

Anyway, that sums up my feelings about these two types of *kehyarists*. I hope this knowledge comes in handy if you ever decide to become a third-rate villain.

And it was all thanks to your support, dear readers, that I was able to introduce my favorite types of *kehyarists* again. Your thoughts and opinions really help me when I write. I don't know how to begin thanking you all. But for now, I send my gratitude to everyone who read this far. Until we meet again.